THE **Fantastic**

PHANTASMIC

Detective Agency

And the Woebegone Oddity
of the Underworld

D.L. DUGGER

Dedicated to my husband, Kevin

With special thanks to my biggest fans: my sister Terry, her husband Mike, and my friends Karen, Jyoti, and Laszlo

Chapter 1

"Are you guys up there?" I call up to the treehouse in Billy's back-yard, the official headquarters of the Fantastic Phantasmic Detective Agency, our blossoming business for ghostly clients.

"Yeah, come on up. We have another case," comes Billy's muffled response. So I climb up the boards nailed in the side of the tree that serve as a ladder and crawl inside the small wooden room.

Billy and Toby are sitting at the table we built last summer, watching the ticker tape feed out of the spirit communication machine Zeaflin gave us after we completed our first case with him. Zeaflin is an UnderWorld realm walker, a sort of undead bounty hunter who can traverse the realms of the living and the dead. He provided this telegraph-like machine so our ghost representatives, Mary, and her husband, John, can communicate with us in the living realm.

Mary and John reside in the OtherWorld StopOver, a place much like a living town except that it has shops and restaurants designed specifically for the newly departed. They set up a branch of our detective agency there, and this is how we acquire our spiritual clients in need of living assistance. Mary and John gather the facts, then forward the details to us through the spirit communication device and we answer via crystal ball. Of course, being only thirteen years old (almost fourteen, in Billy's case), our clientele is a bit limited to cases near home. Or to those that we can solve using our medium, Mr. Monsento.

Billy tears the ticker tape message from the machine and looks it over. "What's it say?" I ask, crossing over to join the boys at the table.

Billy lets out a disgusted snort. "Some lady wants us to retrieve her cat from the pet cemetery in Morrisville," he replies, handing the tape to Toby. Toby sets down his root beer bottle to accept the tape, his lips move faintly as he reads it over.

"Is the cat dead or alive?" I ask, hoping it's alive and took up residence in the cemetery after its owner died. It should be easy to catch, if that's the case.

"Dead," Toby responds without further elaboration.

My heart sinks. This probably isn't going to be an easy case then. Our last experience in a people graveyard ended up with us being chased by a bunch of shimmery ghosts who were desperate to escape the cemetery. Turns out that graveyards are a kind of limbo for ghosts. They can't leave it if they enter it as a ghost unless they latch onto a realm walker and he carries them out. In our last visit to a cemetery, we had to hide Zeaflin in an urn, covered in the ashes of a spirit named Walter in order to sneak him past a crazed mob of ghosts. If Walter hadn't helped, I doubt we'd have gotten out of the cemetery without a major battle. Of course, Zeaflin returned the favor by arranging for Walter to be summoned out of the cemetery and into his old house, where he now happily haunts a family of three small children and their parents.

"Guys, what if the pet cemetery is like a people cemetery and the cat can't leave? How would we get it out? It's not like we have a cat realm walker for it to possess," I say.

"Easy," Billy responds. "We summon it out with Mr. Monsento."

"But how? We don't have the required personal item," I point out before I realize what their answer will be--what it always is with these two!

Billy grins. "We'll have to dig it up and get the collar."

Toby leans forward. "Or take one of its bones if it doesn't have a collar," he chirps, with a gleam in his eye.

What is it with these boys and digging up graves? Toby suggested digging up a people grave to obtain a personal item in a previous case. Fortunately, we didn't need to do that since the person had donated his skeleton to the local college and all we had to do was sneak into the school lab and steal a toe bone for the summoning.

"But what if the animal ghosts are all milling around the cemetery, just like the people ghosts were doing in our last case with Zeaflin?" I fret. "Worse yet, what if the cat sees us digging him up and attacks us or something?"

Billy rolls his eyes. "Don't be such a *girl*, Abs," he responds with an annoyed sigh.

I give him a hard look. "I hate to be the one to break it to you, Billy, but I *am* a girl."

"That doesn't mean you have to act like one," Billy retorts. Tired of this line of conversation, I stand up abruptly to leave.

Toby jumps up to intervene. "Hey, cool it, you guys! Let's just visit the cemetery first, scope it out and see if there even *are* any animal ghosts. Maybe animals don't haunt graveyards like people do."

"Then why does this client say she wants us to retrieve her dead cat from there?" I respond. "I doubt she means for us to bring her a cat skeleton." At least I hope that's not what she means!

Toby looks thoughtful. "You're probably right," he concedes.

"I wish we had a spirit binding box. Then we could just suck the ghost cat up and carry it out," Billy says.

"Well, we don't. Besides, we don't even know if spirit binding boxes work on animal ghosts," I respond. Billy gives me a half-shrug in reply.

"If we retrieve the cat, does Mary give any details regarding how we would transfer it to our client in the StopOver?" I ask. Toby shakes his head.

"It just says to let them know when we have the cat and arrangements for pick up will be made at that time," he replies, looking over the ticker tape again.

"I certainly can't keep a ghost cat at my house and I doubt that you guys can either. Sure, maybe our parents won't be able to see it, but maybe they will. It's too risky," I point out. "Mr. Monsento would have to take it in until Mary arranges the transfer, and I doubt he'd be happy about that."

"Like Toby said, let's just go to Morrisville and check out the pet cemetery first, before worrying about how to catch the cat or what to do with it afterward," Billy replies. "Maybe we can get Mr. Monsento to drive us over there. It's kind of expensive to take the train and I'm not sure how often it runs in the afternoon. Probably not that often."

I glance at my watch. It reads 1 pm. If Monsento agrees to drive us to Morrisville, we should have plenty of time to check out the cemetery and still be back by 4 pm, if not sooner. And if there *are* dog and cat ghosts milling around the cemetery, I'd prefer to have Monsento around to stop the boys from doing anything rash.

"Okay, Billy. If you can convince Monsento to drive us to the pet cemetery, I'm in," I say. We all head down the tree house ladder to climb onto our bikes and ride over to Monsento's house.

───────◆───────

The workmen are just finishing up installing my new front door when I see Abby, Toby, and Billy riding up the sidewalk. The young detectives are definitely a study in contrasts. Abby, with her red ponytail, green eyes, and freckles, looks like she could be cast on the *Andy Griffith Show* as Opie's older sister. Billy sports blonde curls and dashing baby blues, while the other boy, Toby, is the polar opposite of Billy, with his dark brown hair and eyes. Come to think of it, I fit right in as the medium for this motley crew, with my salt and pepper hair and gray eyes. Yeah, we're definitely a band of misfits, all right.

"Hey Mr. Monsento!" Billy calls out, propping his bike up against the side of my porch, next to the stairs. "Getting a new door?" he asks. Abby and Toby add their bikes to Billy's and follow him up the steps.

"Had no choice, kid," I reply, watching the workers pack up their tools. "That is, unless I want Zeaflin's symbols scratched in my door forever. They won't sand off and I doubt my landlord will be amused if he stops by and sees his door all marred up." One of the workers glances up at me.

"Did you try 80-grit?" he asks.

I give him a look. "Yes, I did."

The worker shrugs. "It should have come off easily with 80-grit." I give him another look and he shrugs again.

The other worker rises from the toolbox, his packing up complete. "What do you want us to do with the old door?" he asks.

"Put it in the shed out back," I reply, figuring it's probably best not to have those symbols wind up on someone else's doorstep. I can chop the door up for firewood in my spare time. That's if these kids ever give me any spare time. The four of us wait on the porch while the two workers cart my old front door to the back shed. They return shortly with the work order for me to sign and then pile into their pickup truck and drive away.

"Come on, kids. I'll get you a glass of lemonade," I offer, grabbing hold of the doorknob of my new door to open it for the detectives.

Billy shakes his head. "No time for that, Mr. Monsento. We were hoping you could give us a ride out to Morrisville," he responds.

"Is that so? And why do you need to go to Morrisville?" I ask.

"Mary sent us another case," Toby says, handing me a ticker tape from their spirit communication machine. I read it over.

"A ghost cat named Fluffy, huh? Are you sure you kids are game to go back into a cemetery?"

"As long as Zeaflin doesn't come with us," Abby replies. "Or an animal realm walker, if they exist." I nod in agreement. It was bad enough trying to smuggle Zeaflin past a bunch of angry people ghosts in the cemetery; I'd prefer not to repeat that with animal ghosts.

"And just how do you think you are going to catch this ghost cat? It's a cat. Or rather, it was a cat, so it's not likely to follow you home; cats don't do that sort of thing. And if cat ghosts are anything like people ghosts, the cat may not be able to leave the cemetery," I inform the kids, wondering if they are planning to dig this cat up for a "personal item" and then ask me to summon it out. Not sure I want a piece of that action.

"We just want to check it out first and see what we need to do. We aren't even sure ghost cats haunt cemeteries," Billy responds. I hold up the ticker tape.

"This implies they do. But I suppose the cat's owner may not know for sure. Do you know how much she's willing to pay?" I ask.

"Not yet, Mr. Monsento," Billy replies.

"I thought you kids agreed you should get some money up front, at least to cover any expenses while you work a case. It's going to cost me a few dollars in gas to run you over to Morrisville for your little exploratory expedition," I grumble.

Abby rolls her eyes and motions to Billy, who pulls a fiver from his jeans pocket and holds it out toward me. At the price of fuel nowadays and with the gas mileage my old clunker gets, that might cover half the expense of the drive out to Morrisville. I decide to float the kids the rest of the cost. I can always get it back later, after the client pays us. That's *if* we can find this ghost cat, that is. Or at least its grave. "All right, let's hit the road then," I say, tucking the bill into my pants pocket. I pull out my keys to lock the front door and we all hop into my car for our visit to the Morrisville pet graveyard.

———— ◆ ————

I stop at a gas station on the outskirts of Morrisville to ask directions to the pet cemetery. The clerk behind the counter points at a two-buck, crudely-drawn map of the Morrisville area that looks like the product of a kindergarten art project. Well, that or a finger painting drawn by monkeys; I'm not sure which. I scowl at the clerk and dig out the two bills, pushing them forward with a disgusted shake of my head. Now the kids owe me seven bucks I may never see. I grab one of the "maps" and jump back into the car. Since Billy is riding shotgun, I hand him the map so he can guide me to the kitty cemetery.

Billy unfolds the map and looks it over, then he points to a small square on the map with tiny tombstones sketched out in the shape of dog bones and cat paws at the far left corner of the page. "If the map is drawn to scale," Billy says, drawing a line with his finger from the tiny gas pump, representing our current location, to the tiny tombstones, "it looks like the pet cemetery is about two miles from here." I raise my eyebrows. Small odds *that* map is drawn to scale, but I put the car into gear anyway and head down Plantation Road and on toward Pet Cemetery Drive, as the map outlines.

———————◆———————

I stop just shy of Pet Cemetery Drive and gaze down the road. It's not paved and it's overgrown with weeds, not to mention there are some deep ruts filled with water from our recent spring rains. My car isn't four-wheel drive so no way will it make it very far down this quaint, rustic country lane. I kill the engine. "Sorry kids, we'd better walk from here. If the car gets stuck in the mud on that road, we'll be stranded," I say. We all pile out of the car and begin the walk up Pet Cemetery Drive, veering off onto the grassy edge when necessary to avoid the mud puddles. After about a half-mile, our destination comes into view.

This pet cemetery obviously isn't visited very often. The black wrought-iron fence around it is as overgrown with weeds as the road was, and it's badly in need of a paint job. The small tombstones in this graveyard are all stained green with moss or some sort of mold and some of them have even started to crumble, peppering the ground with bits of marble rubble. A few grave markers near the front of the graveyard are tilting to one side, as if the earth had settled around them and the stone had sunk partially into the ground. Or maybe the occupants of those graves, in a final act of denial, tried to shove their tombstones away and didn't get the job done properly. Pushing down *that* unsettling thought, I look around in all directions. There's not a single building in sight, only fields of wildflowers and tall grass. We are completely alone other than maybe a few animal ghosts, not yet seen. I feel a small shiver run down my spine. Geez, I really hate graveyards!

We stop in front of the entry gate to the cemetery. It is waist high to the kids so it probably wasn't much of a deterrent in its prime and it is even less so now. It was once two gates that opened inward but now one of the gates is missing and the other is dangling precariously by a single rusty hinge. I put up a cautionary hand.

"See any ghost shimmers?" I ask. Spirits tend to be faint when they haunt graveyards (or rather, they are "more ethereal," as Zeaflin would put it) and the kids have sharper eyes than I do. All three kids shake their head so, with a deep breath, I step through the gate and enter the pet cemetery. It's not going to be easy to find Fluffy's grave since most of the tombstones are covered with weeds or moss. We'll have to clear off each one to read it, and that's going to take some time. It looks like there might be a few hundred pet graves here. I have to give it to them: Morrisville residents sure are animal lovers!

"All right, kids, we should split up and start looking for Fluffy's grave. I hope there isn't more than one Fluffy or we might wind up bringing your client the wrong cat," I say. The kids split up and head deep into the back of the cemetery. I decide to start my search near the front in case ghost dogs and cats do haunt cemeteries and I need to make a quick getaway. After all, the kids can run faster than I can.

———————— ◆ ————————

I glance back toward the cemetery gate and see Monsento has opted to search the front of the graveyard. Being such a slow runner, he probably doesn't want to wander very far from the exit. Billy is to the left of me and Toby is to my right, so I decide to head up the middle, deep into the graveyard, and start from the very back. It's more methodical and no tombstones will be missed that way. I wish we knew when Fluffy died because it looks like these back tombstones are all animals that died in the past few years. They must have started the burials at the front of the cemetery and worked their way back.

"Beloved Bruno, you will always be my best friend" reads the first stone. "Sweet Agatha, you now run in the giant hamster wheel in heaven" reads another. This could take a while. With a sigh, I wander over to the mausoleum, the only one in this pet cemetery. It's unlikely to be Fluffy's grave because it seems a bit elaborate for a cat, but obviously somebody decided their pet was worth the expense.

This particular mausoleum is a small, free-standing concrete building around five feet tall and is very plain. It has a rusty iron gate spanning its threshold, with a jagged-shaped keyhole that's probably a lock to keep out grave robbers and mischievous local children. As I get closer, I notice there is a bronze or copper medallion, now green with age, affixed to the gate just above the keyhole. The medallion has the image of a girl climbing a mountainside wearing what looks like a heavy fur coat--a bit strange for a pet grave but maybe the girl was this pet's owner. I step forward to peer between the bars of the gate.

Something is inside!

I jump back, startled, snapping a twig under my foot as I stumble backward. The noise alerts the occupant of the tomb and it steps out of the shadows to look at me. It's a dog--a big, fluffy black dog with a pale brown muzzle. I stand frozen in place as it steps forward and passes through the metal gate to stand before me. I've found a ghost dog!

"You see me," it states in a female voice, tilting its head to one side. It talks! I didn't know spirit dogs could talk.

"And they do too," the ghost dog adds, gazing somewhere behind me. It must mean Billy and Toby. I turn slowly to look behind me and see they have both stopped looking at tombstones and are staring in my direction. Then I look back at the dog.

"You can talk," I finally am able to rasp out through my closed throat.

The ghost dog furrows its brow in irritation. "Of course I can talk. Who are you, girl who can see *and* hear me?"

In the distance, I hear a muffled, "I think I found it, kids!" from Mr. Monsento, somewhere near the front of the cemetery. That draws the attention of the ghost dog.

"And what do you seek here?" the dog asks, with a touch of a frown. I didn't know dogs could frown. But as of a minute ago, I didn't know that ghost dogs could talk either. Behind me, the cemetery weeds are rustling. Toby and Billy must be heading our way. I hope they don't spook the ghost dog. But it doesn't look rattled. Instead it is eyeing me closely, waiting for my answer. I clear my throat nervously.

"I'm Abby," I say, fighting to keep the tremor out of my voice. "And Toby and Billy are the two boys who are probably heading our way."

"And the man who has found what you seek?" the dog asks.

"That's Mr. Monsento. Um, Arthur Monsento. He's our medium," I reply, just as Billy and Toby pull up beside me. The ghost dog turns its gaze to Billy, who is stepping forward with his hand outstretched.

"Hi, puppy–"

"I am not a puppy, boy. I am nearly full-grown; I was fourteen when I died," the ghost dog retorts, obviously insulted.

Billy's jaw drops. "You can talk? Awesome!" he exclaims.

The ghost dog snorts in disgust. "Of course I can talk. Now why are you here? What do you seek?" it asks again. Before Billy can answer, Monsento comes crashing through the weeds to join us, puffing out loud gasps from his jog through the cemetery.

The ghost dog narrows its eyes. "What do you seek here, Medium?" it asks Monsento, who is too shocked to answer. He just stands there, slack-jawed, staring in disbelief at the talking dog.

"We're looking for Fluffy the cat," Toby answers for all of us. "His owner wants us to bring him to the OtherWorld StopOver so they can be together."

The ghost dog widens its eyes in surprise, then recovers and nods. "I have heard of the OtherWorld but I am unfamiliar with the term StopOver," it says.

"The StopOver is a place where people spirits go right after they pass on. It's sort of like the living realm but it's in the OtherWorld. Spirits use it as a temporary residence on their way to Halcyon, their final resting place," Toby explains.

The ghost dog nods again. "Well, you will not find Fluffy here. Fluffy is in the animal spirit menagerie, where all of the pet spirits in this graveyard reside."

"Can you take us there?" Billy requests. "It would help us out a lot."

The ghost dog shakes its head. "The living cannot enter the menagerie. I could bring Fluffy out here for you, but he cannot go with you because animal spirits in a graveyard cannot enter the realm of the living. But if you help me leave the cemetery, because I am a ghost, I can carry Fluffy to this StopOver place for you," it offers.

"Would you? That sounds great!" Billy gushes.

"Hold on a second," Monsento says to Billy before turning to the talking dog. "How exactly do you expect to carry Fluffy out?" he asks. "After all, you're a dog and cats don't like dogs, so I doubt the cat will be too happy about you coming after him. And even if the cat agreed to let you pick him up, I'm not sure they'll let dogs into the OtherWorld unescorted by a person, especially one carrying a cat." The dog glares at Monsento and lets out a low growl.

"I am both a dog *and* a human. When I died and they buried me here, in that mausoleum--" the ghost dog sweeps its paw to indicate the tomb behind it. "—I was a dog. But I do not always have to be a dog; I can be a human too."

Chapter 2

The four of us stand in mute shock over the dog's comment that it is both a human and a dog. I've seen and heard a lot of strange things since I started working with these kids but this is a new one. Of course, it would explain why this particular dog ghost can talk. Unless they all can after they die, this being the first ghost animal I've met so far.

"She's a shape shifter!" Billy exclaims, recovering quickly from his surprise. "Right?" he asks the ghost dog, who nods.

"I am. My name is Kayla. Before I died I was a fourteen-year-old girl who liked to dabble in witchcraft. I created an amulet that could transform me into any animal I chose to be," the ghost-dog-girl says proudly. "I could scamper through the treetops as a squirrel, soar through the air as a bird, and run through the forest as a fleet-footed deer. It was great fun!"

"Could I try it?" Billy asks excitedly. "Your amulet, I mean. I'd like to turn into a bird and fly around!"

Abby rolls her eyes. "Are you crazy, Billy? What if you got stuck as a bird? How would we ever explain that to your parents?" she admonishes.

Kayla shakes her head, causing her long, droopy ears to flap against her skull. "He wouldn't get stuck as a bird," she retorts haughtily. "*My* amulet is a good amulet. But it only works on me and anyway, even if it would work on him, I don't have it for him to borrow. My father took it from me when I was still alive. I was a dog when he tore the amulet off my neck and pushed me out of the attic window to my death, and this is why I am a dog ghost now. But if you can find my amulet and bring it to me, I can change back into a human again and carry Fluffy to the OtherWorld for you. As a human ghost, I can leave the pet cemetery but as a dog ghost I cannot."

"Why did your father take your amulet?" Abby asks.

"*And* push you out the attic window?" I add, thinking that's a little more important thing to know. After all, if we do agree to retrieve her amulet, we might have to deal with her murderous father.

Kayla sighs. "My father is a very religious and superstitious man. He caught me changing into a dog in the attic and was furious that I'd been dabbling in witchcraft. It was then that he ripped the amulet from my neck. I was only trying to get it back when I leapt toward him. I knew the only way I could get my amulet back would be to use my mouth; dog paws are quite useless for grabbing things, you see. But my bared teeth scared Father. He panicked and shoved me away, hard, against the window. As you can see, I'm a large dog and the window had wood rot. When I slammed against the window, the whole frame tore away and I plummeted to the ground."

"But why didn't he give you the amulet back then? You know, so you could change back into a girl before you died. Did he *want* you to stay as a dog?" Billy asks.

Kayla sighs again, puffing out the cheeks of her muzzle. "I don't think so. He might have tried to give the amulet back to me but I died the moment I hit the ground. Father must have arranged for my burial in this mausoleum because I woke up here. I think he felt guilty and did the best he could for me. Since I was a dog…" she trails off wistfully.

"Think your dad will give us the amulet if we tell him about you?" Toby asks.

I shake my head. "He'd never believe us, kid."

"Yes, he would, because he already knows," Kayla says. "Father died soon after I fell from the attic and is a ghost himself now, so he can see and hear me just fine. In fact, he visits me every day but refuses to give me the amulet. He knows I'll leave the pet cemetery and go to the OtherWorld if he allows me to turn human again. And Father believes we both must stay here in the living realm as punishment for our sins: mine, for practicing witchcraft; his, for raising a daughter who practices witchcraft. As I mentioned, he is quite superstitious."

"So what you're saying is that he won't give up the amulet voluntarily," I conclude, "and you are asking us to steal it from him."

Abby huffs. "It's not stealing if it's Kayla's amulet and we're returning it to her."

"Yeah. And she'll help us with Fluffy too," Billy chimes in.

Speaking of Fluffy, I have a few questions I need answered before I'll allow the kids to commit to stealing a necklace from a ghost dad. "Just how exactly are you going to carry Fluffy out of the cemetery?" I ask, turning to Kayla. "People ghosts can't leave their graveyards without a realm walker. I imagine it's the same for animal ghosts, right? And you're obviously not a realm walker or you'd already be out of here."

"I am not sure what a realm walker is, Medium, but I am a ghost and a witch. I can gather Fluffy into my ectoplasm and carry him out that way," Kayla replies.

"And you're *sure* you can do that?" I prod.

Abby lets out another huff. "Even if she can't, I think we should help Kayla escape the pet cemetery. She doesn't belong here," she asserts.

"It's worth trying, Mr. Monsento," Toby urges.

"Yeah," Billy chips in.

"Let's say we do agree to retrieve this magic amulet--just how do you suggest we get it from ghost dad?" I ask, feeling a bit defensive. "We don't even know where he is."

"He told me that he is haunting our old house. The bank put it up for sale after he died and missed the mortgage payments, but he has been scaring away all the buyers so the house is still vacant. He has hidden the amulet somewhere inside the house so its 'wicked dark magic', as he calls it, can't cause anymore grief," Kayla responds.

"I say we take Kayla's case and find her amulet," Billy declares, as if someone had called for a vote. He looks at Abby and Toby, who both nod their assent. "And as payment for our services, Kayla will bring Fluffy to the OtherWorld. We can have Mary meet her at the lake house to show her the way and arrange the transfer of Fluffy to our client in the StopOver. All agreed?" Abby and Toby nod again. Billy looks at me. I'm tempted to remind the kids that I'm the medium and this doesn't appear to require my services but then I remember that I won't get a cut of the money from Fluffy's owner (other than what the kids owe me for the car ride and map) if I drop out of this now. Besides, I suppose I should be there if Kayla's ghost dad raises a ruckus over a bunch of living kids wandering around his house. So I give Billy a reluctant nod of agreement.

Kayla lets out a little yip of excitement. "Wonderful! My old house is in Rupert Town, about twenty miles from here," she says.

Swell. I'm going to have to start keeping an expense report before this is all over. "All right," I respond, trying not to think about the gas expense. "What's the address then?"

"One-oh-one Cherry Lane," Kayla replies. "But don't go there today; go tomorrow morning. Father visits me every morning around an hour after sunrise and he usually stays until lunch hour, so he will be out of the house until at least high noon."

Oh happy day! I think. *We get to drive out here again tomorrow. Not just one trip to the boonies, but two!*

"What does the amulet look like?" Abby asks.

Kayla smiles proudly, her white canines glinting in the weak afternoon sunlight. "I fashioned it from a dead shrew I found in the meadow next to our house. I cut off its head and scrambled the brains so I could pull them out the shrew's nose. Once all the brains were removed, I boiled the skull to soften the flesh and pulled off the skin and muscle from the skull carefully using a small paring knife and tweezers. After all the flesh was removed, I soaked the skull in hydrogen peroxide to give it a lovely snow white finish. It was very beautiful," she declares. Billy and Toby look completely fascinated…I wonder if they are planning to try this one at home.

"Er, okay. We'll look for a shrew skull then," Abby responds, giving me a sideways glance of disbelief. Yeah, this Kayla was a real girly-girl when she was alive, all right.

A question enters my head. "If it's just some mouse skull—"

"Shrew skull," Toby corrects. "Shrews aren't mice; they're a whole other species, Mr. Monsento."

"Got it. Appreciate the biology lesson, kid," I say to Toby before turning back to the ghost dog to finish my question. "If this talisman is just a *shrew* skull, why doesn't your father destroy it? It has to be pretty easy to crush into dust, right?"

Kayla's eyes widen in shock. "Oh, he'd never do that!" she exclaims. "He knows if he did that, I would leave this mausoleum and reside in the menagerie with the other animal spirits and he would never see me again. He holds the amulet to give me hope that he will one day bring it to me so I can change back."

Nice dad, I think before clapping my hands together to signal to the kids that it's time to go. "All right then, it's getting late. Let's call it a day, shall we?" I suggest. "It's bound to be a busy day tomorrow, what with visiting haunted houses and ferreting out shrew skulls. And we should probably contact Mary, give her an update and ask her to meet Kayla and Fluffy at the lake house." Not that I'm anxious to conjure Mary in the crystal ball today, but it is the only way to arrange the lake house meeting since that spirit communication device the kids have only transmits one-way.

"If my father is still here when you return to the cemetery with my amulet, pretend you don't see us," Kayla advises. "You can visit Fluffy's grave until he leaves. Father is very reclusive so he'll probably leave right after you arrive."

The four of us make our way back to the car for the long ride home. I dial in the news on the radio, turning up the volume to drown out the boy's protests over my program choice and to distract myself from the weird talking dog encounter at the pet cemetery. Abby sits quietly in the back seat, staring out the window at the passing fields and farmhouses.

———————◆———————

I stare out the side window at the passing scenery, trying to focus on a little bit of normalness after a very strange afternoon. It's odd enough being able to see and talk to ghosts without adding in witches and magic amulets too. Before today, I didn't even believe in magic. Well, certainly not the kind of magic that can change girls into dogs and squirrels. And it's hard to believe that Kayla's father won't help his own daughter turn back into her original form so she can leave the pet cemetery and ascend to the OtherWorld. What kind of dad could be so harsh?

I look away from the passing farmland and take a glance around the car at my companions. They don't seem to be disturbed by any of this, at least not that I can tell. Except maybe Monsento. He's blaring some news talk show on the radio so loud that it makes it hard to think of anything outside of the screeching of some woman who called in to complain about a proposed increase in parking ticket violation fees. I fail to see how that could be even remotely interesting so maybe he's using it to distract himself. It's starting to work on me, that's for sure!

———— ◆ ————

When we pull up to Monsento's house, he snaps off the radio and turns to look at Billy and me in the back seat. "I want to keep this crystal conjuring short, all right? I have a bit of a headache (*small wonder after the blasting radio!*) and need to lie down soon, so keep it short and tell Mary to meet us at the lake cabin around 4 pm tomorrow afternoon, *capisce?*" he instructs. We both nod. Monsento kills the car engine and we head inside the house.

"Billy, you lead the conjuring this time," Monsento says as he lights the candle next to the Table of Practice and takes his seat behind the crystal ball. The rest of us grab chairs at the séance table and join hands to form a circle. Since Monsento has to clear his mind, he closes his eyes and we all sit in silence while he focuses on conjuring Mary. After several minutes, Monsento finally calls out for Mary to join us and the crystal ball immediately fills with white puffy clouds. They soon part and Mary's face appears before us, hovering inside the glass ball.

"Hello children, have you found Fluffy?" she asks in Monsento's gruff voice, their lips moving in sync as she talks through him.

"We found him. Well, sort of found him," Billy replies.

"Sort of found him?" Mary asks with a shake of her head, causing the white clouds framing her face to swirl around her nose.

"We found someone to get him for us. She's a ghost dog who is really a girl and if we help her become a girl again--a ghost girl, that is--she said she will bring Fluffy to you," Billy explains.

Mary thinks on this a moment. "I'm not sure I understand," she responds. Both her and Monsento's brows furrow with confusion.

"She's a witch...or rather she was a witch," I clarify. "Her name is Kayla."

"I don't think there are such things as witches, children," Mary replies with a deep frown that also crosses Monsento's face.

"Before today, we didn't think so either," Billy says. "But she said she can help us get Fluffy, so can you meet us at the lake cabin around four tomorrow afternoon to take Kayla and Fluffy to the StopOver?"

Mary looks hesitant. "I will need to talk with the Department of OtherWorld Immigration about this first. Fluffy was cleared for entry into the StopOver but not this Kayla. I'll get back to you as soon as possible with an answer." The clouds swirl over her face and Mary vanishes from the crystal ball.

The connection now broken, Monsento snaps his eyes open and stands up abruptly from the table, yanking his hands from Billy and Toby's grip. "Okay, kids. We set for tomorrow afternoon?" he asks.

Billy shakes his head. "Sorry, Mr. Monsento. Mary needs to confirm that it's okay to bring Kayla to the StopOver. She said she'll get back to us soon."

Monsento lets out an annoyed sigh. "*Fine.* You can let me know what the ticker tape says when you come by tomorrow morning. Now scoot and let an old man get some rest, all right?" he says grumpily. Obviously no longer welcome, we give Monsento a quick wave goodbye that he doesn't acknowledge, and the three of us make our way to the front door to head for home.

———— ◆ ————

"If we're going to be spending most of the day in Morrisville and Rupert Town tomorrow, I need to get started on my math homework," I tell the boys. "Ms. Grady wants us to solve all of the problems in the back of chapter sixteen by Monday and there are twelve of them."

Toby gives me a sympathetic look. "Our class with Mr. Johansson is still on chapter thirteen and we always solve the chapter problems during class hours. But we still need to read chapter fifteen in our American History book, don't we, Billy?"

Billy nods. "Why don't you come over to my house, Toby, and we can read the chapter together?" he suggests.

Those two are so lucky to be in the same math and history classes this year, our first year in middle school. And to get Mr. Johansson for their math teacher! Everyone knows he's the easiest math teacher in school. I swear Ms. Grady feels like she needs to make up for him by being one of the most difficult.

The boys veer off toward Billy's house, tossing me a hasty "see you tomorrow!" I watch them ride away enviously before kicking into high gear and biking home to my math homework.

———— ◆ ————

"Hey, Pumpkin. How was your day?" Dad asks when I walk through the front door. He's sitting in his favorite armchair in the living room, a big, velvety maroon recliner he likes to relax in after a hard day working in the garden.

"Swell, Dad. Billy, Toby and I rode our bikes out to the lake for the day, hoping to catch a frog or two, but we didn't find any frogs. Maybe they've moved to a shallower lake or somebody's pond because the lake is really deep now after all of the spring rain we've had. That makes it good for fishing, though, so we thought maybe we'd go fishing there tomorrow…if that's all right with you and Mom," I add, figuring it's best to get permission to be away all day tomorrow, having no idea how long it will take to find the amulet

Dad frowns while he thinks it over. "What about homework? Did you get it all done?" he asks. I shake my head.

"I still have some math problems to do but I'm going to go do that now," I reply, making my way toward the stairs to head for my bedroom and the mound of math. Just as I reach the bottom stair, Mom walks into the living room from the spare bathroom off our downstairs guestroom. She is drying her hair with a towel, apparently fresh out of the shower.

"Dinner will be at seven tonight, Abby, so that should give you a few hours to finish up your homework. Then perhaps we can watch that nature documentary on the African savanna together as a family?" Mom suggests. Dad and I exchange a look of dismay.

"I thought maybe we could catch the last episode of *Bayou Bounty Hunter* instead," Dad responds. "He's supposed to finally catch that crocodile poacher he's been chasing." Mom purses her lips in disapproval and looks to me for the final decision.

"Sorry, Mom. I'm sure they'll rerun the documentary sometime this summer," I assert to reassure her. Mom rolls her eyes and heads back into the bathroom with a sigh. Dad gives me a thumbs-up and a grin. I grin back and head upstairs to tackle my math.

———◆———

I toss the math book and a pad of paper onto my corner desk, sharpen a few pencils, and sit down to begin. But the numbers and symbols just blur into nonsense. Now that it's quiet and I can think about Kayla, I'm a little disturbed by it all. I've read so many fantasy books where witches truly are magic and can fly on brooms and make magic potions. But that's all it ever was--just fantasy. Now

Kayla tells me that it's all real, that she actually created a magic amulet that could turn her into animals. That's scary.

And what's with her dad trapping her as a dog ghost in the pet cemetery as punishment? I understand he's probably afraid of the magic too, but it sounds like he's had a few years to adjust to the idea and *still* he refuses to allow Kayla to become human again. It seems heartless to hold the amulet over her, giving her false hope that he might change his mind and let her turn back into a girl. I only hope we can find the amulet quickly tomorrow and help Kayla move on to the OtherWorld before her father finds out we helped her.

I shake my head to clear it. I need to get serious about this math! I pull the calculator closer and force myself to concentrate on finding the value for X in the equation $7X-4X=12$. After a stab at solving that, I dive into the rest of the problems at the back of chapter sixteen. I finish the last one by 6:30 pm, leaving me plenty of time to run downstairs and help Mom make dinner. I love chopping the vegetables for the salad so hopefully she hasn't done that yet!

————— ◆ —————

After we eat dinner (and I did get to chop the salad vegetables), Dad and I settle down to watch *Bayou Bounty Hunter*. Mom just shakes her head and wanders upstairs to "do something constructive and read a book." I feel bad but I think my aching math brain deserves the indulgence of at least a few hours of mindless entertainment.

Since it's the final episode of the season, *Bayou Bounty Hunter* is on for two hours. It's an exciting episode, with a hair-raising hydroplane chase of the poacher (who I gently point out to Dad is an alligator poacher, not a crocodile poacher, by the way). Happy for the distraction that leads straight to bedtime, I give Dad a goodnight peck on the cheek and head upstairs to crawl under the covers and slip into sleep.

Chapter 3

I snap awake abruptly, the sweat pouring down my face and my heart pounding. It's been months since I've had a nightmare about "work".

This one started off with Monsento, Billy, Toby, and me in Monsento's car, pulling up the driveway of an old deserted house. In my dream, I assumed the house was Kayla's and that we were on our mission to find her amulet. It was a dreary day, with dark, low-hanging clouds, and a strong chill wind blew hard against the trees. The air smelled of wet dirt and earthworms, threatening that it could begin to pour rain at any moment. *We should hurry up and get inside the house*, I thought, *before those clouds let loose and we all get soaked.*

Kayla's house looked like one of those old Victorian mansions you see on postcards of San Francisco, except this one had been seriously neglected. Its windows were all cracked and dirty and much of the pale blue paint that once covered the house had worn away, leaving vast areas of the wood bare. The hedges were completely unruly and you could barely see the path to the house under all the weeds growing wild in the front yard.

The four of us got out of the car and pushed through the weeds to mount the sagging porch steps. "Is the door open?" Billy asked anxiously. Monsento tried the doorknob. It turned easily and the door opened with a loud screech of rusty hinges. After a furtive look around to be sure no one was watching, we all stepped inside the house.

"All right, kids, we have to get this done fast so we need to split up. I'll search the upstairs bedrooms. Toby, you take the downstairs bedrooms. Billy, you're on the living room. Abby, you search the basement," Monsento outlined.

I began to object but the three of them were already heading to their assigned areas so I walked through the dining room and into the kitchen to search for the basement door. Next to an incredibly filthy stove was an open door with a down staircase. I hesitantly made my way over to the door and found a light switch at the top of the stairwell. *At least I won't have to search in the dark*, I thought as I snapped on the switch. But no light came on. *Of course, no electricity. Why didn't we bring a flashlight, especially if I had to search a basement?* Sucking in a nervous breath, I slowly descended the stairs to allow my eyes time to adjust to the gloom. Thank goodness, the basement had a window or I'd have been groping around in complete darkness.

When I reached the bottom of the stairs, I paused to take a look around. The basement was empty, except for a few boxes in the corner next to a rusty old furnace. My heart jumped with joy. Since there weren't many boxes to dig through, that meant I wouldn't have to spend much time in the bowels of the house.

I hurried over to examine the boxes, anxious to finish my search so I could head back upstairs. Each box was labeled with a different woman's name in thick black ink, and they were all sealed tight with packing tape. The top box was labeled "Kayla" so I pulled at the tape on that box first. The tape was very sticky but I kept at it until I managed to strip away a section. As I tugged back the tape and prepared to rummage through the box, a high-pitched voice called out from behind the furnace.

"Little girls are always so curious. They never seem to remember that curiosity killed the cat."

I jumped back, startled, as the owner of the voice scurried out from behind the furnace and stopped next to the box I was opening. It was a large gray rat--a *VERY* large gray rat. When it stood on its hind legs, it was almost as tall as I was! The monster rat's incisors curled sharply downward like yellow-stained sickles and thick, stringy mucous dripped down them to the basement floor. The claws on the ends of its paws were as long and sharp as kitchen knives.

"You want to see what's inside the box?" the rat asked with a screech. I backed away and shook my head but the rat turned toward the box I was opening and stabbed it with one of its claws. With a hard downward thrust, the claw tore a deep gash down the side of the cardboard and a young girl's penny loafer popped out of the opening.

There was a severed dog paw inside the shoe!

The shoe hit the basement floor with a dull thud, dislodging the paw from its leather abode. I stared at the cracked anklebone pushing up through the muscle of the dog paw and fought hard against the rising bile so I could scream for help. But no scream would come out of my closed throat. All I could manage was a faint whimper of terror.

The rat darted forward and grabbed my shirt, dragging my head toward its mouth and those awful drool-caked teeth. Its breath smelled like rotting meat and decaying leaves. I started to gag.

"Let me tell you a secret, girlie. Curiosity kills more than just cats. Sometimes it kills dogs and little girls too," the rat hissed in my ear. I let out a loud scream and shoved it away.

And that's when I woke up in this horrible sweat.

———— ◆ ————

I look over at my bedside clock. 6:30 am is a bit early but I'm awake and I definitely don't want to go back to sleep. I roll out of bed and stumble into the shower so I can head over to Monsento's house. I could use some company after such a horrible nightmare.

It's Sunday morning so Mom and Dad are still sleeping when I go downstairs. I grab a yogurt and some apple juice from the refrigerator, making sure to close the door quietly. I eat quickly, put my dirty juice glass and spoon into the dishwasher, then walk over to the telephone niche to grab a pen and notepad to scrawl a quick note to my parents. I write that Billy wants to get an early start fishing this morning and, since my parents rarely get up before 9 am on Sunday, that should buy me almost two hours before they even know I'm gone. I add to the note that I'll be home by 6 pm but they can call me on my cell if they need to reach me before then.

Billy bought both Toby and me a cell phone using the company funds he made from selling one of the silver coins Zeaflin gave us after we solved the Belial case for him. Billy originally bought the phones so we could keep in touch with each other about agency business without our parents knowing, but I've found it's more useful in keeping my parents calm on those days when I'm gone most of the day. They can call me anytime they need to, avoiding any meltdowns if I'm late coming home.

It's still a bit cold in the morning even though it's the end of May, so I grab my jacket from a peg by the door, tuck the cell phone safely into the front pocket, and slip quietly out the back door to head to Monsento's house.

———————◆———————

I'm just setting up for my second cup of coffee when the front doorbell announces that I have a visitor. I look at the clock by the sink: 7:30 am. If it's the kids, they're early. I put the instant coffee jar down on the counter and go to open the front door. It's Abby, sans the boys.

"You're a little early," I tell her.

"I thought maybe we could talk before Billy and Toby get here," she replies.

I raise an eyebrow in curiosity and step back. "By all means, come on in then."

Abby hesitates a moment on the front porch before finally stepping inside. Obviously something is troubling her. I wonder if it's the same thing that's troubling me--like what might happen if we get caught by ghost dad while we're rifling through his house?

"Look, why don't you come into the kitchen? I was just getting ready for a cup of coffee. You can talk to me there," I say, pointing to the panel that separates the kitchen from the salon. We both head into the kitchen, where Abby sits down at the table and waits for me to settle in with my coffee.

"Do you think we'll be able to find Kayla's amulet today?" she begins. "Her dad could have hidden it anywhere. He might have even buried it in the backyard."

I take a sip of coffee and give the girl a short nod of agreement. "It's a long shot that we'll find the amulet but I agree that we should at least give it a try. I'd hate to leave that kid stuck as a dog in a pet cemetery with no way for her to switch back into a human so she can ascend to the OtherWorld."

Abby stares at my coffee cup sitting on the table, watching the steam rise. I decide to wait her out and find out what else might be troubling her. After a minute, Abby draws her eyes up to meet mine. "Do you think Kayla's magic is black magic?" she asks. I puff out a sigh. This kid tends to see things as good versus evil, with very little gray area in between.

"I don't know. Her father seems to think so. Makes me wonder if he thinks Kayla will be sent to the UnderWorld if she turns human. That makes it all the more important that the OtherWorld agree to take Kayla in *before* we turn her back into a girl. If they won't take her, she might prefer being a dog ghost in the pet cemetery over being a girl ghost in the UnderWorld.

"I didn't think of that. Hopefully Billy has heard back from Mary and can let us know if the OtherWorld will take Kayla in before we head out there today," Abby replies. I see movement in the backyard through my kitchen window. Speak of the devil; it's Billy, with Toby close behind. I motion for the boys to come inside.

"What's the news, Billy? Did you hear from Mary about whether the OtherWorld will take Kayla in if we turn her back into a girl ghost?" I ask.

Billy nods. "She said the OtherWorld Department of Spirit Immigration has no record of a missing spirit named Kayla, but they see no problem with admitting her into the OtherWorld because sometimes records get misplaced," he replies, tossing his jacket over the back of one of my kitchen chairs and taking a seat at the table. He eyes my coffee cup expectantly until I offer him a cup. After I make the coffee for Billy, I pour a couple of glasses of milk and pass them to Toby and Abby, catching Toby's grimace of disgust that it's not soda.

"Drink it, kid," I tell him. "Didn't anyone ever tell you that soda rots your teeth?" Toby bites his lower lip, wisely opting not to object any further. I make a drinking motion to the kids.

"Hurry it up, okay? We have a long drive ahead and need to hit the road. And be sure to wash your own glasses, *capisce*? It's the maid's day off," I say as I head into the salon to grab my jacket and car keys.

After the kids finish washing and drying our cups, I hustle them out the front door and into my car parked on the street in front of the house. I glance at my watch just before I pull away from the curb. It reads 8:15 am, so we should be in Rupert Town by 9:30 am if we don't hit any "Sunday-morning-going-to-church" traffic. I snap on the radio to catch the morning edition of the news and start us off on our road trip to find a magic amulet and rescue a ghost girl in distress.

———— ◆ ————

I look out of the window at the passing scenery, which starts out first as rows of houses with neat manicured lawns and gradually changes to farmland and cows, trying to block out the arguing inside the car that's been going on since we pulled away from Monsento's house on our way to Rupert Town. Billy and Toby have been fighting with Monsento for control of the radio for most of the ride out so far. The boys want music while Monsento wants to listen to the news. Monsento finally puts his foot down, insisting that it's his car and he's doing the driving so he gets to listen to what he wants. I choose to ignore the radio, which is now moving from news to sports. Billy perks up when they start discussing whether the Yankees can beat the Orioles in today's big game, suddenly not so bent on listening to a music channel. Toby just stares out the passenger side window, looking very bored.

The farmland slowly merges into a small town that a roadside sign identifies as Rupert Town, population 85--our destination. Rupert Town is pretty much just a bunch of small houses dotting both sides of the road. Almost all of the houses are painted white and they all have the American flag mounted in a small holder on the porch wall next to their screen doors. It appears to be a very patriotic little town.

Monsento stops the car and pulls out a small piece of paper on which he has written down the address of Kayla's old house and reads it over (*like it's a difficult address to remember? One-oh-one Cherry Lane?*). "OK, kids, based on the addresses, the house we're looking for is at the end of this block. What I'm going to do is park the car around that corner—" we all follow the direction of his pointed finger "—so we don't raise any unwanted attention. Then we're going to go around to the back of the house, keeping an eye out for nosy neighbors. It looks like this house is fairly secluded, being at the end of the town here, so I think we should be all right," Monsento says. His plan outlined, he puts the car into gear and pulls away from the curb.

We pass by our assigned house slowly, taking the time to get a good look at it. It's different from the rest of the houses on the block in that it's brick instead of wood. It also has two stories and an expansive front yard. For a vacant house, the yard is surprisingly well maintained, other than the front hedges being a little overgrown.

"Are you sure it's vacant? The front yard looks like it's been mowed recently," I point out, worried the house might have sold and Kayla doesn't know about it yet. If the house has new owners, I don't want them catching us breaking into their house.

"The bank probably arranges for the lawns to be mowed, right, Mr. Monsento?" Billy says. Monsento just shrugs and turns the car around the corner to park it on the side street next to the house.

"This is good. It has a gate in the back fence so maybe we won't have to climb the fence to get in through the back," Monsento notes. I close my eyes, trying to envision Monsento scaling the fence, but I just can't see how he would be able to do it. Sure, he's a tall man but he's a little overweight and he has to be at least fifty.

Monsento catches my doubtful expression and scowls at me in the rearview mirror. "What? I can climb it," he says defensively.

"Good. Because you might have to if the gate is locked," I tell him.

"Nah, I can climb it and let you in if it's locked," Billy volunteers.

"If it's a latch, sure; if it's a key lock, no," I respond.

We all get out of the car and head over to the back gate, Monsento taking the lead. He presses down on the gate handle and gives the gate a push with his shoulder. It opens easily with a creak of squeaky hinges. Grateful that we won't have to scale the fence after all, we all slip inside and Monsento closes the gate behind us.

While the lawn in front of the house is well kept, the backyard has been ignored. The grass back here is tall and has gone to seed. There are also dandelions and crabgrass, as well as lots of those horrible weeds with stickers on their leaves, causing me to regret my choice of flip-flops for shoes today.

Monsento forges on toward the house, casting a worried glance at the upper windows of the neighboring home but luckily, no one is looking. Billy and Toby follow close behind Monsento but I decide to take my time, gingerly stepping between the sticker weeds. Going slow doesn't work. One of the weeds brushes my big toe and embeds a sticker in the tender flesh. I let out a small cry of pain and, in what would be comedic under other circumstances, all three of my companions turn as one to shush me.

Monsento reaches the back door of the house first and tries the knob. Not surprisingly, it doesn't turn. "Should we try the front door?" Billy asks.

"That's visible from the street. We'd have to worry about the neighbors across the street *and* cars passing by," Monsento replies.

We all stand around trying to think of a plan when Toby points up to a small window about eight feet off the ground. "If you can boost me up, I can see if it's locked," he suggests.

Monsento shakes his head. "It's probably locked."

"Should I break it then?" Toby asks. Monsento purses his lips and looks toward the neighbor's house.

"If they hear, we'll be done for," he replies and turns back to the door to push on it harder.

"I think it'll be louder if you try to break down the door," I tell Monsento.

"You think so?" he retorts sarcastically before he turns back to Toby. "All right, Toby. I'll boost you up to the window but take a rock with you in case you have to break it. I don't want to have to boost you up twice; my back won't handle it."

Billy suddenly tugs off his T-shirt and hands it to Toby. I quickly look away, my face burning at seeing Billy's bare chest. I haven't seen him without his shirt on since we went swimming at the lake a few years back. It looks like he might be developing a small patch of hair on his chest now, although his hair is pale blonde so it's difficult to tell. I sense eyes on me and look up to catch Monsento eyeing me curiously. I give him a defiant glare in return.

"Here Toby, you should wrap the rock in my shirt so you don't cut yourself if you have to break the window. Just peck at the glass and it should crack rather than shatter," Billy is telling Toby, neither of them noticing Monsento's and my silent exchange.

"Sounds like you're an expert on breaking and entering, kid," Monsento observes, turning away from my angry glare.

Billy shrugs. "I read a lot of detective novels," he replies nonchalantly.

Toby wanders over to the stone flowerbed that lines the back of the house and grabs a fist-sized rock for his window-breaking tool. Under the rock is something shiny and gold that sparkles in the sunlight. Toby picks up the shiny object and heads back to us wearing a big grin. It's a key!

Monsento lets out a sigh of relief and takes the key from Toby to try it in the door lock. It turns the tumblers easily so we file into the house and Monsento quietly closes the door behind us. Once inside, Toby hands Billy his shirt while I stare up the back stairs until Billy pulls his shirt over his head and settles back into it.

"All right, I don't want to stay here any longer than necessary, so we should all split up," Monsento says. My heart skips a beat.

"I am *not* searching the basement!" I declare sharply, remembering my nightmare from last night.

Monsento gives me a bemused look. "We can search the basement last, okay? Let's start with the upper floors first," he responds. "Toby, you take the downstairs bedrooms and bathrooms; Billy, you're on the living room and dining room; Abby, you search the kitchen."

"I'm going with Toby," I demand. The basement door might be off the kitchen, just like it was in my dream, and there's no way I'm going anywhere *near* the basement door. Monsento tries to stare me down.

"I'm going with Toby," I repeat firmly. With a sigh of frustration, Monsento gives in.

"All right, *fine*. I'll take the upstairs rooms *and* the kitchen," he concedes testily and heads up the back stairs that lead into the kitchen. The three of us keep a close pace behind him, with Toby leading and Billy taking up the rear.

When I step off the last stair and into the kitchen, I pause to take a look around. There is a closed door in the left-hand corner of the kitchen that looks suspiciously like a basement door. I'm so glad I refused to be assigned to the kitchen!

Monsento starts his search of the kitchen cabinets while we head for the dining room that leads to the rest of the house. From there, Toby and I leave Billy and head down a narrow hall leading away from the living room. From what I've seen so far, the house is empty. There are no packed boxes, no furniture, no drapes--nothing at all but an empty house.

Toby goes straight for the closet in the first bedroom off the hall and runs his hands across the top shelf, stirring up a layer of dust. He backs away with a sneeze. "Nothing up there," he wheezes, so I head for the attached bathroom. There is a medicine cabinet on the wall over the sink--a good place to start my search.

The mirrored cabinet door creaks open and I peek inside. It is completely bare except for a small slot in the back labeled "used razors". The slot is too narrow to fit a shrew skull (I think, even though I'm not sure how big a shrew skull is), so I decide to move on to the bathtub. Maybe the amulet is hiding inside the spigot or the drain.

Toby walks past me to look inside the water tank of the toilet. I pause in my search when he lifts the lid off the tank and peers inside, but he just shakes his head and puts the lid back on the tank. I turn my attention back to the bathtub.

A cursory search reveals nothing in the tub but a few rust stains around the drain. I stand up and look at the window over the tub, thinking, *What a strange thing to do, placing a window over a tub… wouldn't the neighbor see you taking a bath?* Then I peer through the dingy glass of the window. It's an older style, with an inner glass in front of an outer storm pane. There is something in the gap between the two windows so I raise the inner sash to take a closer look. The something is a small white object jammed into the left-hand corner of the storm pane. I try to dig it out with my fingernail but it holds fast.

"What is it?" Toby asks from behind, startling me into banging my head on the window frame.

I lean out of the window gap and take a deep breath to calm my racing heart before answering. "I don't know, Toby. Could be a shrew skull but it's stuck fast."

"Hold on a sec! Billy has a pocket knife," Toby says and races out of the room. I sit on the edge of the tub to wait for Toby to come back with the knife. Instead he brings Billy.

"What's up, Abs? What'd you find?" Billy asks, handing me the knife.

"I'm not sure. It looks like a bone or maybe a tiny skull," I reply and stand up to step into the bathtub for better access to the object.

Billy leans in to take a quick look before I start digging with the knife. On my second dig, a little skull pops out and falls into the tub, skittering around with a rattle.

"Don't lose it!" Billy cries out in a panic as the bone bounces dangerously close to the bathtub drain. I slap my flip-flop over the drain in the nick of time to trap the bone with the edge of my sandal, and Billy leans over to pick it up. He holds the tiny skull aloft so we can examine it.

"What? What is it?" Toby asks from near the bathroom door.

"It's a shrew skull! Abby has found the amulet!" Billy exclaims, giving me a congratulatory slap on the back. "Let's go find Mr. Monsento!"

We look in the kitchen first but Monsento isn't there so he must have moved on to the upstairs already (*I hope he's not in the basement!*). Billy clambers up the stairs like an elephant, anxious to show off our prize. The noise draws Monsento to the top of the stairs.

"What are you kids doing? You're making way too much noise!" he admonishes harshly.

"Abby found the shrew skull, Mr. Monsento!" Billy calls up the stairwell. Monsento grimaces in disgust and heads down to meet Billy halfway.

"All right, give it here," he says, reluctantly putting out his hand to accept the tiny skull. As Billy places the skull into Monsento's palm, a loud metallic clang suddenly erupts from the basement.

"What's that?" Toby asks, his face blanching.

"Probably just the hot water heater. The water heaters in these old houses can be pretty noisy sometimes," Monsento replies, although he doesn't look like he believes it's a water heater. The metallic noise reverberates again from below our feet.

"I don't think that's a water heater. If it is, I think it's going to explode," Billy says.

That spurs Monsento into action. He grabs Billy's arm and propels him down the stairs toward Toby and me. "Let's go, kids!" he urges. As if we needed encouragement to get out of the house! We run through the kitchen and out the back door, where the three of us wait anxiously while Monsento fumbles with the key to lock the door behind us.

"Look!" Toby cries out, pointing to the upper window he'd planned earlier to break with a rock. We all step back from the door and look up. There is a white, blurry face hovering behind the glass, looking down at us. I feel a chill run down my spine. This ghost can't be Kayla's father because it's a woman ghost. Could she be Kayla's mother?

Suddenly, the ghost slams both hands hard against the windowpane, causing it to rattle against the wooden frame, and a small crack appears at the top of the glass. We watch in horror as the crack slowly spiders its way down to the center of the window. Then the ghost hits the glass again with a bang and the window shatters into small crystal shards that rain down on our heads.

"We should go now," Monsento warns, getting no argument from the rest of us. We all turn and sprint across the yard, hurry out the back gate, and hop into the car.

Monsento hands Toby the amulet, clips on his seat belt and starts the car engine. As we pull away from the house and head off for the pet cemetery, we are all grimly silent, everyone wondering the same thing but nobody wanting to ask because none of us have the answer. *Who is that woman ghost inside Kayla's old house? Is it her mother? If so, does Kayla know her mother is a ghost too?*

I look across the back seat at Billy. "She was plenty mad, wasn't she?" he remarks. Nobody responds. We continue the rest of the drive back to the cemetery in silence.

Chapter 4

This time I opt to drive up Pet Cemetery Drive because, after running into that angry ghost that must be Kayla's mother, I'm too rattled to leave the car a half-mile away from the graveyard. If the car gets stuck in the mud, I'm sure Toby and Billy have enough muscle to push us out of it.

If that ghost knows where we are heading, there are some good odds that she might beat us to the pet cemetery; I've seen how fast they can move. Of course, I can't explain why the ghost lady didn't follow us down the road. Or maybe that's precisely what she is doing, flying overhead or underneath the car. You never know with ghosts. But we're committed to this now and our best bet is to get this amulet to Kayla as quickly as possible.

I clutch the steering wheel tightly and gun the motor to force my old jalopy through the thick mud of Pet Cemetery Drive. I know it's just a pet cemetery but you'd think the fine folks of Morrisville, being the pet lovers they seem to be, could pop for paving the road.

Then again, based on the condition of the cemetery itself, I suppose I should consider myself lucky they bothered to put up a street sign. I'd have driven right by this little mud-patch otherwise, assuming it was just some old tractor trail for a fallow field.

Toby's hands are pressed hard against the dashboard as he tries to keep himself from bouncing around in the seat beside me; the seat belts can only do so much to keep you in your seat, after all. I glance in the rear view mirror and see Abby has her eyes closed and her jaw clenched tightly as she clutches the back of my driver's seat to fight the bouncing of the car. Billy is just letting himself go up and down with the car. It doesn't look like the rough ride bothers him at all.

The car gets stuck in the mud once before we reach the gates of the pet cemetery. Fortunately, I am able to work it free by shifting into a lower gear and giving the gas pedal a light pump until the tires grab hold. After that, we continue our lurch to the cemetery without any further complications. I hope the ride back out fares as well.

———— ◆ ————

Kayla is standing by the cemetery fence, watching our car pull up to the gate, when we arrive. I don't see her father so he must have already headed for home. It's good he's not here but that means he's probably already getting the skinny about our taking the amulet out of the house and will soon be on his way back here, so we have to move fast. I turn to Toby.

"Pass me the amulet," I tell him, holding out my hand for him to place the tiny skull into my palm. "I'll give it to Kayla. You kids stay in the car. That lady ghost at the house may have followed us and it could get dangerous."

Abby unsnaps her seat belt. "No. We all go," she states firmly. "We all agreed we'd get the amulet for Kayla so we're all in this together." Before I can object further, she pushes the car door open and walks straight toward the cemetery gate. Both Toby and Billy snap off their seat belts to join her. Sometimes I wonder why I even try to tell these kids anything.

I jump out of the car and take a quick look around but I don't see any angry lady ghost anywhere nearby, so maybe she didn't follow us after all. Billy is waiting for me by the gate. "Hurry up, Mr. Monsento," he urges. With a sigh, I walk to the gate to join the kids and Kayla, standing just inside the cemetery fence.

"Abby tells me that you have the amulet. Please, may I have it?" Kayla requests, her tail wagging in slow lazy sweeps. I eye her suspiciously.

"Don't you need to get Fluffy first? Like as a ghost dog? Didn't you say only animal ghosts can enter the menagerie?" I ask, wondering if she's trying to pull a fast one on us and change back to a girl ghost before we get our cat.

"Of course!" Kayla quickly replies. "I wasn't going to change to human form before I did that. Anyway, even with the amulet, I will still require assistance in changing back. The amulet alone won't do the trick."

I raise an eyebrow. "Is that a fact? You missed sharing that golden nugget of information earlier. In fact, you also missed sharing that your dad's house has a lady ghost haunting it too."

Kayla frowns. "It does?" She looks over at Abby for corroboration.

"There was a lady ghost in the house. We saw her through the back window on our way out after we found the amulet," Abby replies, omitting the window-breaking tantrum scene. "Is she your mother?" Kayla furrows her doggie brow.

"My mother died before I did but I never saw her ghost at the house. I assumed she ascended to the OtherWorld; that's why I want to go there. But you say she's at our old house? If she is, I have to go there and get her!" Kayla cries, her voice rising an octave in distress. "Please, will you help me?" she begs with a soft, throaty whimper.

"Of course," Billy replies. "What do you need us to do?"

Kayla looks at Abby and her tail droops. "It is much to ask," she says slowly.

"Then I suggest you start asking it. Your mother will probably tell your father we took the amulet and he could be on his way over here right now," I warn.

Kayla shakes her head with a faint slap of her ears. "Don't worry, my mother would not tell my father about that. The first shape-shifting amulet I ever wore, my mother made for me when I was quite small. As I grew older, she taught me how to make my own. Shape-shifting amulets have a limited lifespan and the magic eventually wears off."

"Why was your mother so angry when we took the amulet then? She started banging the pipes and she even broke a window after we found it," Toby says, apparently having no compunctions over telling Kayla about her mother's fit of temper.

Kayla frowns thoughtfully. "I think maybe she didn't know you planned to bring it to me. In all of the years I have been interred here, Mother never visited me--only Father."

"Well, while I'm glad we may not need to worry about your father coming back here, why don't we get this show on the road, just in case?" I suggest. "It's getting late and we're supposed to meet Mary at the lake cabin by four o'clock."

Kayla nods. "All right, I will go get Fluffy now. There are many cats to sift through so I might be gone for a short while but I'll be back as quickly as I am able." Kayla turns and runs swiftly through the cemetery. With a bound, she leaps straight through the bars of her mausoleum and vanishes into the darkness of the tomb.

"Come on, kids. Let's go sit by Kayla's grave and wait for her to come back with Fluffy," I say, hoping it won't be too long. I'd like to hit the road soon, maybe pick up some sandwiches for a late lunch before we have to drive Kayla over to the lake to meet Mary.

The four of us walk to the back of the cemetery and sit on the grass in front of the mausoleum, soaking up the noonday sun. Fifteen boring minutes pass by and I'm starting to nod off when Toby suddenly nudges me in the ribs. "There's a ghost at the cemetery gate, Mr. Monsento," he whispers. I follow his gaze.

There is indeed a ghost standing at the cemetery gate, staring straight at us. It's a man ghost. He looks so much like a living man that you'd think he was alive if it wasn't for the fact that you can see my car behind him through his body. He is tall and thin and is wearing a red plaid shirt tucked into his blue jeans. In his hands is a hat that he is twisting nervously in front of his chest. The man ghost looks hesitantly at the cemetery gate then back at us before he comes to a decision. Stepping through the gate, he slaps his hat onto his head and strides purposefully toward us.

"We've got company, kids," I inform Billy and Abby in a low voice. They both turn to look at the ghost, rapidly making its way to where we sit. I decide it's time to stand up. It's too late to pretend we can't see him; it's obvious he knows we can. The three kids rise to stand next to me as the ghost man pulls up in front of us and stops.

"You can see me," he states with a faint Southern accent. "Means you can see Kayla too, I 'spect." No surprise that this ghost is Kayla's father. I guess Kayla was wrong about her mother not telling him about us. The ghost man looks me over with piercing brown eyes. "You helping her?" he asks. I don't know what to say.

Fortunately, Billy steps forward. "I'm Billy Miller. Are you Kayla's father?" he asks pleasantly, holding out his hand toward the ghost. The ghost man stares hard at Billy before materializing to a more solid form and reaching out to complete the handshake.

"Name is Caleb Holder and, yeah, I reckon Kayla is a Holder. But she's no kin of mine," the ghost responds. "Of course, she likes to call me Father, but she's my dog, not my child."

———•◆•———

All of us are completely stunned. Billy drops his hand, the handshake finished, and stares at the ghost in confusion. "Wait… *What?*" he says, his jaw agape. Caleb looks at Billy like he thinks he's a trifle slow.

"Kayla's my dog, a dog that wants to be a girl. Not that I can blame her. The wife put her up to it, grieving like she did when we lost our baby Katie," Caleb explains. Then he looks at the mausoleum behind us. "She in there?"

Monsento finds his voice. "No, she went to someplace she calls the menagerie to bring us a cat." Caleb grunts and turns his gaze back to the four of us.

"Reckon she wants one of those magic amulets as payment for doing that. You know it's got no power right now, don't you? Needs a living girl to juice it up," he tells us. My heart starts to pound. What does he mean "a living girl to juice it up"? Since I'm the only living girl in the immediate vicinity, I decide I'd better find out what he means, and quick!

"What do you mean by that?" I ask, my voice cracking.

Caleb tilts his head to one side. "Didn't tell you, huh? Needs some blood--girl blood because she's a girl dog--and a bit of that red hair of yours too. Once she's got that, the amulet will make her a pretty little red-haired girl, just like you."

I can't believe what I'm hearing. I look at Monsento for some adult help here but he's blanked out again, still processing this horrible new information. I step closer to Billy. Maybe he can protect me…or at least try, anyway.

Caleb spits out a blue glowing glob of spirit spit onto the ground near Monsento's feet, who snaps out of his stupor to stare down at it in disgust before stepping back from the glowing blob. The ghost wipes his mouth with the back of his hand and carries on. "My wife gave her the first amulet. Grief made her do it, I suppose, after we lost Katie and all."

"Yeah, you told us that already," Monsento mumbles.

Caleb spits toward Monsento's feet again. "Reckon I did," he drawls. "After we lost Katie to the fever, my wife was so grieved that she locked herself away with the baby's body. Had to break the door down and pry little Katie from her hands so the undertaker could bury her proper. That's when I think she made the first amulet-- when she was locked up in the baby's room. She must have cut some hair and pricked the baby's finger. Had me a new puppy at the time. Puppy vanished and—," Caleb pauses to spit again, "-a small child that looked a lot like Katie showed up. The wife insisted we keep her; wouldn't tell me where the girl came from. After about a year, the puppy showed back up at the house, looking a little older than before. Didn't stick around very long, though--disappeared when the next child showed up at our door. That one had blue eyes and blonde hair. And so it went; every year or so, our little girl would vanish and the dog would show up at the door. Then the dog would vanish and another little girl would show up, each one different looking from the previous one."

The four of us stare at Caleb in horror. Obviously all of those girls were the dog shape-shifting into a new little girl after the amulet magic wore off and a new amulet was created. And when Kayla comes back with Fluffy, she's going to expect her payment: the amulet. And my blood and hair to activate it! A terrifying thought pops into my head.

"If she uses my blood and hair to make the amulet magical again, will she become me? Will I die?" I ask Caleb.

"Don't rightly know what happens to the girls the wife and Kayla use to repower their amulets," he replies. "You'd have to ask the wife about that. Not sure if she'd tell you, though."

"Well, Abby isn't giving anything to Kayla," Monsento says sharply, reaching into his front pocket and pulling out the shrew skull. He holds it toward the ghost. "Take it back. Bury the cursed thing. Or better yet, instead of hiding it, destroy it."

Caleb shakes his head. "Ain't me that hides them. It's the wife that does it. She started hiding them for Kayla to find soon after she died. I couldn't see her ghost when I was living, but I sensed her presence. Kayla did too, and she'd spend hours searching the house for the amulets. I destroyed them whenever I found them but the wife would just make new ones. Of course, I never understood why she kept making them after Kayla died. It's not like the living could see Kayla to give her the amulet now that she's a ghost. 'Cept for you all, that is. Mighty strange." Caleb studies us, looking thoughtful. "You say you came here for a cat?" he asks.

Billy nods. "We're detectives for ghostly clients. We were hired by a lady ghost to bring Fluffy the cat to the OtherWorld. He was her pet and she wants him to live with her there instead of here," he explains.

Caleb furrows his brow. "Well, now that clears up a few things. Fluffy was the name of my wife's cat so I reckon she's your client then. She lives in the OtherWorld but they allow her to come to the house sometimes. Spousal visitation rights, they call it. But she never cared much about visiting with me, living or otherwise. Instead, she spends most of her time creating those magical amulets of hers and hiding them."

The four of us are dumbstruck by the revelation that Kayla's "mother" hired us not to bring her Fluffy but to help her change Kayla back into a girl. She knew we'd be able to see Kayla if she sent us here to find Fluffy. But if she hired us in the hope that we would see and help Kayla, why was she so angry when we found the amulet? Isn't that what she wanted us to do?

A low growl suddenly rises up behind us, followed by a loud yowl and an angry hiss. We spin around to catch a cat-shaped blur come flying out of the mausoleum. It darts behind Beloved Bruno's tombstone and vanishes out of sight, but you can still hear it spitting and hissing.

"Reckon that'd be Fluffy. Going to be tough to catch him now that Kayla's got him all riled up," Caleb remarks.

Kayla comes flying out of the mausoleum and leaps straight for Monsento, who is still holding out the shrew skull for Caleb to take.

She slams hard into Monsento's chest, knocking him over and the shrew skull rolls from his hand and onto the ground. Kayla quickly snatches the tiny skull up into her mouth and slips back through the bars of her tomb.

"Are you okay, Mr. Monsento?" Billy asks, leaning over to try to help Monsento to his feet.

"Knocked the wind out of me," Monsento gasps, just before Kayla steps back out of the mausoleum. Her mouth is empty so she must have left the amulet inside her tomb. Giving Monsento and Billy a warning snarl, Kayla starts to creep up on me, her hind legs tensed for pursuit should I try to run. I back away slowly, glancing at Caleb, wondering if he is going to help me or not. He is watching the ghost dog stalk toward me but is making no move to stop her. Instead he decides to state the obvious.

"Looks like Kayla's going to try to get that hair and blood from you, girl," he says to me.

"How about you do something to stop her?" I snap back, keeping my eyes on Kayla.

"Last time I tried to stop Kayla from getting what she wanted, she wound up dead," Caleb replies.

"Well, it's not like she can wind up any deader now, right?" Monsento says testily. "*Do* something." Caleb shrugs and steps between Kayla and me.

"All right, Kayla, this has gone far enough now," Caleb chides, holding his hands up in a stop gesture.

Kayla growls softly. "I got their cat, just as I promised. They said they'd help me change back. A deal is a deal," she retorts.

"I never agreed to give you my hair and blood," I hastily counter, popping my head around Caleb's shoulder to look at the dog. "All you asked for was the amulet."

Kayla lets out another soft growl. "The amulet is useless without your donations."

Billy steps over to stand next to me. "Look, all you want to do is leave this pet cemetery, right?" he asks. "Join your mom in the OtherWorld?" The dog nods.

"What if you changed into another animal, like a squirrel or a mouse?" Billy suggests. "Could you leave the cemetery then?"

"I don't know. Maybe. But I don't want to be another animal, I want to be a girl," Kayla whines.

"What happened to the girls who gave you their 'donations'?" I ask, just in case Billy does convince Kayla to change into another animal instead of a girl. While I feel sorry for her, I don't want some poor mouse or squirrel to be harmed. Kayla's tail begins to wag a little at the tip. She must think I'm considering "donating" to her cause. Not a chance!

"Nothing that I could tell. Momma said they lose a year of their life is all. Because I borrow it, you see," she replies. "Momma paid them well for their donations and sent them on their way. She can pay you too, Abby."

"Sorry, no. I can't help you," I declare, not wanting to give up a year of my life. Kayla bares her teeth and growls ominously.

"Kayla, if we can catch a mouse, would you try that instead?" Billy asks, trying again to convince Kayla to leave me alone and become some other animal.

I look toward the cemetery gate. It's too far away for me to make it out of the graveyard before Kayla could stop me. But mice don't live very long so if Billy catches a mouse for Kayla's amulet, that poor mouse might just die right away. I can't let a mouse--or any other animal, for that matter--take my place.

"No, Billy. Mice don't live long enough. Why don't we just summon Kayla out of the cemetery like Zeaflin did Walter? Then she can go with Caleb and her mother to the OtherWorld," I suggest, even though I'm not sure Monsento can summon a ghost out of a cemetery. Zeaflin said it's not an easy thing to do. But we could at least try.

"I'd still be a dog. I don't want to be a dog," Kayla objects.

"Kayla, you *are* a dog. And even if you become a girl now, sooner or later the magic in the amulet is going to wear off and you're going to turn back into a dog. So you may as well start off that way," I reply.

"Momma can come back here, just like Father said she's been doing, and re-power the amulet with a living girl," Kayla rebuts.

Caleb shakes his head. "No, Kayla, I won't stand for it. I'll go to the OtherWorld and tell them what you and the wife have been up to. Didn't go there before because I felt I needed to keep an eye on you here and I reckoned the OtherWorld wouldn't let me come back here if I ascended. But if you go to the OtherWorld, I'll head that way too and keep an eye on you and the wife there. It's time for you to accept what you are, Kayla. You're a dog, *my* dog, and I love you just as you are, not as the wife wants you to be."

Kayla's tail droops between her legs and she lets out a small whimper. Caleb walks over and gives her a pat on the head before turning to Monsento. "What do you need to summon her out?"

"A personal item. Is there something of hers inside the tomb that we could use?" Monsento asks. "*Outside* of her bones," he adds, looking pointedly at the boys.

Kayla growls at him. "You're not taking one of my bones," she snarls.

Monsento rolls his eyes. "I said *outside* of your bones," he reminds her. Kayla hesitates. She looks up at Caleb with troubled eyes.

"But will Momma still love me if I'm a dog? Will she even want me at all?" she whines. Caleb kneels down and takes Kayla's muzzle into his hands to give her a kiss on the top of her head.

"I'll want you, Kayla. And don't you worry none. The wife could have left you here and just stayed with Katie in the OtherWorld, but having you go up there with her meant so much to her that she kept coming back here to find a way to get you out. That's a fierce kind of love."

Kayla gives me a forlorn look and then turns back to her mausoleum, where she flops down on the stairs and huffs. "All right. I still have that squeaky ball you buried me with. I could give them that, if it will work," she says, looking at Monsento, who nods. "But you have to promise to give it back. It's my favorite toy and I don't want to go to the OtherWorld without it."

"We can give it back to you at the lake house," Toby responds. "We can summon her directly there, right, Mr. Monsento?"

"Sure thing, kid. It'll save time too, since that's where we're meeting Mary for the transfer," Monsento replies.

"What about Fluffy?" I ask Caleb. "Do you want us to summon Fluffy out too?"

Caleb shakes his head. "Fluffy and Kayla never did get along all that well when they was living. I doubt that would change much now that they're not. Kayla can take Fluffy back to the menagerie. He'll be happier there, I reckon."

Kayla rises from the mausoleum steps and vanishes through the iron bars of the gate. She quickly returns with her personal item: a worn, chewed-up, red rubber ball. She drops it on the ground near Toby's feet and noses it toward him like a dog ready to play fetch. The ball is coated with the same blue glowing goo that Caleb was spitting at Monsento's feet earlier. I'm not sure it's a good idea to touch that stuff.

"Here, Toby," I call out, digging a pack of tissue from my jeans pocket and tossing it to him. Toby pulls a couple of tissues from the pack and wraps them around the ball before he picks it up.

"All right, kids. Let's hit the road. It's going to take some time to get back home, depending on the traffic. Plus we need to stop by my shop to pick up the talisman for the summoning before heading to the lake house," Monsento says. With a wave goodbye to the dog and her "father", the three of us follow Monsento to the front gate of the cemetery to make our way back home to prepare for Kayla's summoning.

Chapter 5

Before I hop into the driver's seat, I take a quick look back at the talking dog and her "father". Looks like he's hit the sweet spot on her ears because the dog's tail is wagging. Maybe Kayla won't mind being a dog after all. But that's probably not going to be true for Momma. I doubt she's going to be happy that Kayla is still a dog when she sees her again, and that probably means we won't get paid for this case. Why don't these kids ever ask for money up front?

When I slip into the car, I notice Toby has placed that nasty blue goop tissue wad onto my dashboard. I lean over and slap it down onto the plastic car mat--that's easier to clean than the dashboard. But I'm too late. There is goop already smeared across the vinyl.

"I have some vinyl cleaner. When we get to my house, Toby, make sure you clean that spirit spit up before we head to the lake house. If it sits too long, it's going to stain my dashboard," I say.

Toby turns red and mumbles a feeble, "Okay, Mr. Monsento."

"Hey, Mr. Holder," Billy pipes up from behind me. "Are you coming with us?" With my heart pounding in alarm, I spin around in my seat. Sure enough, Caleb is sitting between Abby and Billy. Abby is snuggled up against the car door, pulling hard against her seat belt to avoid touching the ghost.

"Have to. Don't know where this lake house is, so I reckon I should go with you all," Caleb drawls before leaning over to wave goodbye to Kayla, who is now standing by the cemetery gate, her tail swishing in quick sweeps through the air. She lets out a soft bark in return to Caleb's wave. *Swell, just swell!*

"Don't spit in the car," I warn him up front. Caleb leans back in his seat and merely shrugs in response. That settled, I flip on the radio, deciding some music wouldn't hurt for the ride home. It'll keep the boys quiet anyway--maybe Caleb too.

———•◆•———

After a short, bone-jarring ride down Cemetery Lane that I hope will be my last, I make a right turn onto Plantation Road and head for the highway. Sadly, the music only keeps the boys quiet for a short while before Billy starts complaining that he's hungry. And as much as I hate to stop with a ghost in the car, I have to admit, I'm empty myself. So I pull into the parking lot of the first eatery I see, a greasy spoon café with a couple of cop cars in the lot. I look in the rearview mirror in time to catch Abby scrunching up her nose.

"I don't remember seeing many eateries out here in the boonies so this place will have to do," I tell her. "Besides, if the local police like it, the food is probably pretty good." Abby gives me a skeptical look but goes ahead and opens the car door. I turn to look at my ghost passenger. No way am I bringing a ghost into a restaurant. All we need is for one of the boys to start talking to Caleb and draw a bunch of unwanted attention from our fellow diners.

"You stay in the car," I command. "Not like you can eat, right?" Caleb frowns but nods his agreement.

The four of us head into the diner and order the blue plate special of hamburger patty and fries. Okay, so I was wrong about the food: the hamburger is drier than the Sahara and the fries are greasier than an oil slick. But the true cherry on top is when the waitress hands me the bill and the kids all just sit there looking at me instead of pulling out some money. I decide to take action.

"The bill comes to $6.50 apiece, kids," I inform my companions. They reluctantly reach into their jean pockets.

"Sorry, Mr. Monsento. I only had seven dollars and I gave you five of them yesterday," Billy says with false regret, as he passes me two bucks. Toby sheepishly pushes two quarters and a nickel across the table. I turn to Abby as my last hope of reining in some of my expenses. She digs into her pocket, pulls out $3.21 and hands it to me with a disapproving frown. I frown back. I can never fathom why kids always expect the adult to pay the restaurant bill. I push the penny back at Abby, then gather up the rest of the money and tuck it into my pocket before I head over to the cash register to pay the bill with my credit card.

Our waitress, a bleached-blonde thirty-something lady with an updo, sidles over to the register to process my bill. She watches the kids file out of the café, wearing that sickly sweet smile that women paste on for babies and other such things they find "cute".

"Adorable kids. Are they yours?" she asks, as she pushes the credit card receipt toward me to sign.

"Yeah, triplets. Different moms, though," I reply and push the signed receipt back to her.

The waitress looks a bit confused before giving me a nod of understanding. "Oh, I see. That's why they all look so different, right?" she responds. I stare at her in amazement. *Is this lady for real?*

"Precisely right," I say and head out to join the "triplets", already sitting in the car waiting for me.

Much to my dismay and Abby's delight, Caleb has moved to the front passenger seat. I look at the seat belt across his waist. "Seriously?" Caleb follows my gaze and his pale face actually flushes pink. I didn't know ghosts could blush. You learn something new every day, I guess.

"Force of habit," he mutters and snaps off the seat belt.

I cast a quick glance at the kids huddled together in the back seat before I fire up the engine and pull out of the eatery parking lot to continue our journey. After a quick stop at my house to grab the talisman, an OtherWorld summoning totem that Zeaflin obtained for my use after it was "lost" during a battle for OtherWorld rule, I drive us all out to the lake cabin to meet with Mary. It's almost 4 pm by the time we pull up to the lake so Mary should already be here to meet us.

———————— • ◆ • ————————

It's getting late and I promised my parents I'd be home by 6 pm so I hope this summoning doesn't take very long. We've never summoned a spirit out of a cemetery before and I'm worried that Monsento's OtherWorld talisman may not be strong enough. Zeaflin's UnderWorld talisman might be powerful enough; it pulled a spirit out of Halcyon once, and that's no easy feat. But we don't have an UnderWorld talisman so we have to work with what we have and hope for the best.

Mary is standing in front of her old lake cabin when we arrive. As we approach the path that leads to the cabin, I glance over at the willow tree where Zeaflin first hid the moonstone that enabled Billy, Toby, and me to see ghosts and started this whole detective agency for the dearly departed business. If I'd stayed on the path behind the boys instead of passing under that tree, I'd never have stumbled upon the stone and we'd still be just a bunch of kids whose biggest adventures would be hunting for frogs and snakes. And Monsento would still be running fake séances for gullible clients.

Mary gives Caleb a double-take. "Who is this?" she asks.

Caleb extends his hand for a handshake. "Name's Caleb. I'm here to accompany Kayla to the OtherWorld." Mary allows Caleb to pump her arm, then she looks over at Monsento in confusion.

"Where are Kayla and Fluffy then?" she asks.

————

"Change in plans," Monsento says brusquely, brushing past Mary to walk up the front steps of the cabin. Mary shakes her head and looks at Billy for clarification.

"Kayla isn't a people ghost--turns out she really is a dog ghost. *And* our client is Caleb's wife. She calls herself Kayla's mother but she's the witch, not Kayla. She hired us to find Fluffy so we'd run into Kayla, who's buried in the same pet cemetery as Fluffy. She knew we'd be able to see Kayla and she thought we might help Kayla turn back into a girl by finding her a magic amulet. But the amulet needed Abby's blood and hair to work and so we offered to summon Kayla out of the cemetery if she let Abby go and stayed a dog ghost." Billy runs out of breath and falls silent.

Mary stares at him, blinking slowly. Her hand flies to her neck and she twists her heart pendant nervously. "I don't understand," she says, looking over Billy's shoulder at me. "You said Kayla was a girl that the magic amulet turned into a dog. Now you say she's really a dog that the magic amulet turned into a girl?"

I puff out a sigh. "It's complicated but that's the summation of it, yes," I respond. "Will you bring Kayla to the OtherWorld, even though she's a dog ghost? Her dad here…er…owner, will accompany her. And, of course, her…er…mother, our client, will be there too." This is very awkward. I can feel my cheeks flushing under Mary's incredulous gaze.

"Of course, she's not there now. Our client, that is," Billy interjects. "We think she's haunting her old house right now."

Mary swings her gaze back to Billy. "Yes, she probably is in her old house. Your client, Belinda Holder, has special clearance to visit her husband every few weeks or so at their living residence. She left the OtherWorld for another visitation a few days ago. I think she's due back tomorrow," Mary replies, appearing to recover from her shock.

"The wife will likely go back to the OtherWorld tonight, if she hasn't returned already. She knows I went after these living people here to stop them from changing Kayla into a girl, so I doubt she'll have any interest in visiting with me now," Caleb says.

"How'd you find out we were helping Kayla, Mr. Holder?" Billy asks. "Did your wife tell you?"

Caleb shakes his head. "She didn't need to. Since Belinda was in the living realm and probably making amulets, I cut my pet cemetery visit short today so I could keep an eye on her. I could tell someone living had been snooping around the house the minute I walked through the front door. Belinda banged about and even broke the kitchen window trying to scare you folks off fast, but I caught sight of you all, scurrying across the backyard. The big fellow there can run pretty fast for an older gent."

So that's why Kayla's "mom" made all that noise and broke the window after we found the amulet...to make us hurry off before Caleb could stop us.

"Look, now that you have the whole story, can we get started on this summoning and arrange this little family reunion in the OtherWorld?" Monsento grumbles, giving Caleb a deep scowl, apparently none too happy with the big fellow/older gent moniker. "I'd like to be free of this case as soon as possible. Especially since we're probably not going to get paid for it. That is, unless Caleb here wants to pony up for the summoning."

Caleb shakes his head. "Wife took care of all the finances. I got no money to give you," he responds.

"Yeah, I figured that's what you'd say," Monsento says, with a roll of his eyes.

Mary pulls a parchment paper from the pocket of her flowered dress and walks up the porch steps to hand it to Monsento. "I don't have a permit to perform a summoning. If you summon a spirit, our agency will most likely be issued a citation," she warns. "Plus, I only have immigration papers for a girl named Kayla. I'm not sure if they will let a dog and her owner here past the waiting room without the proper papers."

Monsento opens up the parchment and looks it over while Billy darts up the steps to look over his shoulder. From what I can see of it, the paper is full of all sorts of official-looking stamps. The name "Kayla" is printed in large block letters at the very top with a blank space next to it, probably for Kayla to fill in her last name, if she has one.

Monsento folds the parchment and hands it back to Mary. "Kayla is waiting back at the cemetery so we don't have time to wait for the summoning permit. We'll have to take a chance on the citation. What is it? Some kind of a fine?" he asks.

Mary nods. "Yes. The last time you performed a summons without a permit–the Jenkins case–the agency was fined fifty silver phantasmils," she replies.

Monsento shrugs. "Billy can cash in one of his gold coins," he says.

Hold on a second here! "He did that for the Jenkins case," I object. "You can cash in one of *your* gold coins, Mr. Monsento." Monsento glares at me but I stand my ground. Finally, with a disgusted sigh, he agrees to pay the fine.

"*All right*, kid. I just want this case over with so I'll pay the bill. But next time, the agency covers these expenses; I don't have that many gold coins, you know." That settled, Monsento turns back to Mary. "I don't see anywhere on that document a statement that Kayla is a girl; it only lists sex as female, which is correct. So technically she's clear as far as I can tell, not being well-versed in the legalities of the OtherWorld."

Mary bites her lower lip with worry. "They aren't expecting a dog though." She looks at Caleb. "They'll probably let you in, being Belinda's husband. Maybe you can keep Kayla company in the waiting room until I can obtain an updated immigration order to admit a dog instead of a cat?"

Caleb nods. "Sure, I'll keep her company. You should put my name down as her owner on the new request in case the wife throws a conniption over Kayla still being a dog."

"Good idea," Monsento responds. "All right, kids. Let's get this show on the road, huh?" He vanishes into the gloom of the cabin.

The rest of us file in behind him to prepare to summon Kayla and finish out the case of Fluffy the Cat.

Chapter 6

A spooky lakeside cabin, complete with two ghosts--the ideal place to perform a summoning, I'd say. All we need is a thunderstorm to create the perfect ambiance, but the sinking sun is all we'll get today. I choose to sit in the center of the room, brushing aside the leaf litter and dust that's accumulated on the floor before sitting down. The kids join me on the cabin floor while Mary and Caleb opt to remain standing, each taking opposite sides of the entryway. I'm glad they didn't ask to participate. After all, an undead realm walker in a summoning circle is positively ghastly…or so says Zeaflin. It's difficult to imagine what might happen if we put a ghost in the circle.

Toby puts Kayla's slimy rubber ball in the center of our living circle before joining hands with Abby, who has already joined hands with Billy on her other side. It's my lucky day so I get to hold the hand that Toby used to place the "personal object". I give the hand a quick once-over before deciding it is clean enough to grasp.

"You can all close your eyes now. I don't have a paper copy but I'm pretty sure I've got Vila's spell memorized," I tell the kids. It's been a while since I've used the spell; probably the last time was the Jenkins case a few months back. I prefer to crystal ball conjure but outside of calling Mary, I haven't had a case that calls for it yet. Crystal conjuring draws the ghost into the ball while talisman summoning brings the ghost into the room with us. Given a choice, I'd prefer my ghosts under glass.

"You *should* have it memorized. It's only three words: *inquam, exspecto, adiuro*," Abby mumbles under her breath. I rebut with a scowl but her eyes are already closed so I motion to Billy and Toby to close their eyes too so we can get started on calling our ghost dog.

I have to repeat the three words of the spell three times before Kayla's ball begins to lift off the cabin floor. A few dead leaves, stuck to the underside of the ball, float silently to the floor as the red orb rotates in slow, lazy circles a few inches off the ground. It stirs up a miniature dust eddy and I wriggle my nose to keep from sneezing. Sure wish that Mary ghost would take a broom to her cabin.

Thinking of Mary, I take a quick glance at our two ghost sentinels guarding the cabin door. They are motionless, staring intently at the spinning ball in the middle of our circle, waiting for Kayla to appear. Not much is happening with them so I look back at the kids while I continue to recite the spell. Abby is peeking. I give her a stern frown and her eye snaps shut with a pink flush of her cheeks.

Suddenly there is a loud pop, like someone uncorking a champagne bottle, and Kayla appears behind Billy. She is smoky gray and misty at first but soon solidifies into the firmer, less ethereal form of dog we first encountered in the pet cemetery. She bounds into the center of the circle, startling the kids awake, and snatches the rubber ball from the floor where it fell after she appeared before us. She lets out a yip of joy and leaps back out of our circle to run to Caleb, who leans down to give her a pat on the head. Kayla drops the ball and nuzzles it toward Caleb's feet, giving him the expectant look of a dog ready to play fetch. I decide I'd rather not have a slimy ball flying around in the cabin so I struggle to my feet to put a stop to any "father/daughter" playtime.

"Great! You're here so now Mary can take you and Caleb to the OtherWorld. It's getting late. Time for us to go, kids," I urge, anxious to get out of here in case the Department of Living Affairs decides to send a bureaucrat to investigate the summoning instead of issuing another citation. With our luck, they'd send Vila.

Caleb leans over to pick up the rubber ball but instead of throwing it, he tucks it into his pocket. Kayla lets out a little whimper of disappointment and her tail droops. "Yep, I reckon it is time we move on too," Caleb declares, with a pat on the ghost dog's head. "Kayla, this lady here says we'll need to wait in the waiting room of the StopOver while she works on our paperwork for admission. We can play fetch there, if they let us."

Kayla looks over at Mary and gives her a slow tail wag. "Thanks for your help," she says. Then she looks over at the four of us standing behind her. "For all of your help," she adds.

"Sure thing," I reply.

"Have fun in the OtherWorld, Kayla," Billy says.

Abby and Toby murmur a goodbye as I steer them out the door, giving a nod of thanks to Mary for taking these two ghosts off our hands.

———— ◆ ————

Monsento practically pushes us out the door of the lake cabin, obviously anxious to get away from Kayla--not that I can blame him because I feel the same way. After all, it was only a short time ago that Kayla was considering taking my "donations" for her amulet by force. I'm glad Caleb was able to convince her to accept being a dog so this case could end happily for everyone. Well, except maybe for our client Belinda, that is. I hope she'll be okay with Kayla living with her as a dog so she can be happy too. Her husband seems to think so but I'm not sure; she went through an awful lot of trouble to create and hide those amulets.

Monsento offers to drive us all home, dropping me off first--a good thing too, because it's almost 6 pm by the time I walk in the door of my house. I can smell dinner cooking and it smells like Mom's patented chicken pot pie is on the menu tonight. I hurry to the kitchen to find Mom and Dad side by side, chopping vegetables for a salad.

"Hey, Pumpkin. No fish?" Dad asks, reminding me of my little white lie about what I was doing today.

I shake my head and put on a disappointed frown. "I didn't even get a nibble. Toby caught one but it was too small so he threw it back."

"It's a little early in the season," Dad says. "They probably only just stocked the lake with fish a few weeks ago."

"True. That would explain why Toby's fish was so small," I respond.

"Your mom and I are just finishing up the salad. Maybe you could set the table, Abby?" Dad requests. "The pot pie should be just about done, shouldn't it, Fran?"

"I'd give it about five more minutes," Mom replies. She looks down at my hands. "And be sure to wash your hands before you set the table, Abby. They're probably dirty if you've been fishing." I nod and wander out of the kitchen to the back bathroom to wash up for supper.

———————◆———————

After dinner, I leave Mom and Dad watching a documentary about bumblebees and head for my room. It's been a long, strange weekend...okay, since we started seeing ghosts, almost every day is strange. You'd think I'd be used to it by now.

Tomorrow is Monday, the start of another long week of school, so I decide to treat myself and crack open one of my *Nancy Drew* mystery books. I've read them all before but I find the mysteries relaxing after a hard day of working a ghost case. I like the fact that all of Nancy's ghouls and goblins are fake. If only ours were!

With a flop onto the bed, I open the book to page one and begin reading *The Secret of the Old Clock*–one of my favorites–until the sun sinks low and my eyelids droop. Before I fall asleep with the book in my lap, I decide to put it aside and get ready for bed. Ms. Grady has another math quiz planned tomorrow so it's best to get a good night's sleep.

———————— ◆ ————————

Three days have passed since I summoned Kayla, and there have been no visits from OtherWorld bureaucrats and no requests from Mary for money for a fine, so I guess I'm off the hook. Maybe the OtherWorld can't detect the summoning of an animal ghost or maybe they don't care unless it's a people ghost. All I know is I'm glad I've had no bureaucrat visitors toting paperwork and notepads and I get to keep my gold coin safe in my sock drawer.

It's Thursday and that means today's afternoon movie is *Shane*. I'm a sucker for a classic Western so I switch on the TV and plop down on the couch with a ham sandwich and cola at my elbow. They've just finished scrolling the opening credits when I hear a sharp scratching sound on my front door. I jump up quickly, almost knocking over the side table next to the couch. I catch it just in time as it teeters dangerously close to spilling my sandwich plate and soda can onto the floor. Once the table stops jiggling, I hurry to the front door to rescue it before too much damage is done. I just replaced that door after months of fruitless sanding, and it cost good money too! I fling open the door to catch Zeaflin, yet again, scratching symbols into the wood with his sharp fingernails that I swear must be made of steel.

"Cut it out, Zeaflin! I just replaced this door!" I snap.

Zeaflin drops his hand and gives me a bewildered look. "Of course, Mr. Monsento, I noticed it right away," he replies and flashes me a quick sharp-toothed grin.

I look over his handiwork and shake my head in disgust. "And why are you carving things into my door again?"

"I do apologize but it is necessary. I'm afraid that I am in need of your assistance again," Zeaflin explains.

"Is that a fact? Then you'd better come on in then," I say, stepping back to let him in. The neighbor across the street is peeking through his front curtains again so I give him a cheery wave.

Zeaflin follows my gaze. "Ah yes, your neighbor. He does seem to have quite a fascination with your activities, Mr. Monsento."

"More like a morbid curiosity about my visitors," I correct.

"Is that a fact?" Zeaflin asks, a playful smile on his pale face.

"Yeah, Zeaflin, I'd say it is."

We step into the house and I lead the way to the kitchen. It's been several months since I've seen my undead friend and I was beginning to wonder if he'd ever pop back up. I have to admit, I'm glad to see him. His cases tend to be complicated, dangerous even, but he pays well.

"I should warn you," I tell him up front. "The detective agency *and* their medium have sworn off battling any more demons so I hope this isn't one of those sorts of cases or you're out of luck."

Zeaflin laughs lightly and takes a seat at my kitchen table. "Not at all. I seek only assistance in locating a missing UnderWorld spirit who escaped from the UnderWorld detention center. I have been assigned to find him and bring him back," he responds. I pause in filling our coffee cups with water and turn to look at Zeaflin.

"Are you serious? Do you honestly think we'd help you hunt down an escaped criminal? It's bound to be dangerous," I say, surprised he'd ask the kids to do such a thing.

Zeaflin shakes his head. "No, not at all. Nathan is not a dangerous criminal, Mr. Monsento. Nathan is as safe and gentle as any other spirit you might encounter."

I give him a skeptical look. "I've encountered a few that don't quite fit that description, Zeaflin. Like in the cemetery, remember?"

Zeaflin waves his hand dismissively. "Not to worry, Mr. Monsento. This spirit is not in a graveyard, of this I am certain," he replies.

"If this ghost is so gentle, why was he put in prison then?" I ask. "I imagine he had to do something very bad to break the law in a place like the UnderWorld."

"Not really. What is considered an egregious offense in the UnderWorld is sometimes quite minor in the grand scheme of things," Zeaflin responds.

"Enlighten me on this *grand scheme of things*," I say, going back to filling our coffee cups.

"Nathan volunteered to live in the UnderWorld for reasons we need not go through here, but he didn't fit in our realm well. He was too quiet and reclusive, keeping mostly to himself. The other spirits found him to be aloof and anti-social, and they can be a cruel bunch of ghosts when they feel spurned."

"I can imagine," I mumble. Zeaflin looks surprised.

"You can?" he asks. Before I think up an answer, the microwave dings so I skip the answer and prep our coffee instead. I pass Zeaflin a cup and sit at the table across from him. Zeaflin decides to carry on.

"Therefore, Nathan spent much of his time alone, drinking in the Toothy Tavern, a place that draws a less than reputable crowd—"

"There are reputable establishments in the UnderWorld?" I interject. Zeaflin smiles but declines to comment.

"One evening, after a particularly trying day, Nathan took refuge in a dark corner of the Toothy Tavern. From that corner, he could drink and watch the other spirits without them noticing him. On this night a realm walker named Nerjul visited the tavern. It is highly discouraged for a realm walker to consort with UnderWorld spirits; however, Nerjul is a senior realm walker and he follows his own rules. It is also highly discouraged to drink heavily with the lesser spirits but Nerjul never had much willpower and he definitely did not temper his drinking that fated evening. Nathan must have watched

Nerjul from his corner in the tavern and devised a plan of escape from the UnderWorld." Zeaflin pauses to take a sip of his coffee.

"And that plan was?" I prompt.

"To possess Nerjul and force him to carry him into the living realm," he replies, putting the cup back onto the table.

"Did he succeed?" I ask.

"He did indeed, Mr. Monsento. But Nathan made the mistake of heading straight to his grave after departing Nerjul, one of the first places the UnderWorld would check for an escaped ghost in the living realm. Graves have such a strong allure for the lesser spirits; they almost always gravitate to them. Nathan was captured within days of his escape."

"And so he's done it again? Possessed a realm walker and forced him to carry him here?" I ask.

Zeaflin shakes his head. "No. This time a realm walker entered the detention center and voluntarily helped Nathan escape. Realm walkers are forbidden to enter UnderWorld prisons because, just like graveyard ghosts, the detained spirits see the realm walker as a means of escape. If they sense the presence of a realm walker, they become agitated and difficult to manage. On the night of Nathan's escape, there was a horrible riot in the prison that took the guards hours to contain. Once things calmed down and a prisoner census could be performed, the guards discovered that Nathan was missing. Obviously, a realm walker had entered the prison and helped him escape. We are all under suspicion now."

"But not *you*, right? I mean, the UnderWorld hired you to find Nathan so they must trust that you didn't do it," I tell him.

Zeaflin shakes his head. "All realm walkers are suspected, Mr. Monsento, but I have been selected to find Nathan because they think me the most likely culprit. If I fail to find him, they will deduce it is because I helped him escape."

"Swell. *Did* you do it?" I ask, eyeing him closely. Zeaflin shakes his head again.

"No, Mr. Monsento. I did not allow Nathan to possess me."

"But you know who did, don't you?"

"Yes, Mr. Monsento, I know who did and it is he I hope we can help. If Nathan is captured, he will be forced to tell who helped him escape the detention center. This I cannot allow. We realm walkers must stick together, after all."

"But you said that you'll be the one blamed for the escape if you don't bring Nathan in. What's your plan here, Zeaflin?" I ask, troubled by the catch-22.

Zeaflin smiles. "So glad you asked! We find a personal item of Nathan's, we summon him here without the proper permits, Vila shows up and Nathan pleads for asylum," he outlines, the smile turning into a sharp-toothed grin.

I frown. "FYI, the last two times I summoned a spirit without pre-approval, Vila didn't show up. One time, he issued a citation and fined the agency; the other time, he either couldn't detect it or ignored it. So what makes you think he'd show up if I summon this particular spirit of yours?" Zeaflin reaches into his coat pocket and pulls out a small box the size and shape of a pen box and pushes it toward me.

"This will draw Vila. Your totem talisman, being from the OtherWorld, is weak and thus of little interest to Vila, which is why he only issued a citation instead of paying you a personal visit. But an UnderWorld talisman has a unique pulse and will definitely draw Vila's attention," he replies. I reach over and pop open the top of the box. Just as I thought, it's my old pal, the shriveled finger.

"It's gotten old again," I say. "Or is this a different finger?"

"Oh, it is the same talisman as before, Mr. Monsento. Talismans age quickly if they are not used often enough, and it has been several months since our last summoning with this talisman."

"Should I throw some water on it?" I suggest, remembering how that perked the talisman up the last time.

"Oh, let's not be cruel, Mr. Monsento!" Zeaflin exclaims. He rises up from his chair. "I must be off now but I will return shortly with the information you will require to find Nathan's personal item." Zeaflin vanishes in a puff of gray smoke, leaving me alone to mull over this troubling request of his.

Chapter 7

"Abby? Are you up there? Telephone!" Mom calls up from downstairs.

"Yes, Mom. Be right there!" I call back.

I bounce up from my bed, grateful for the break from my math homework. It's Friday but I like to complete my homework right away so I can be free on the weekends. You never know when a case might pop up and the weekends are the only opportunity we have to work our cases. At least until next Friday, that is. That's when school finally breaks for the summer, and I can scarcely wait. Next year's math teacher can't be nearly as tough as Ms. Grady!

I run downstairs to the living room and grab the handset, sitting off to the side of the phone. "Yeah?" I say to my caller.

"Abby, it's Billy. I think your cell phone is off so I had to call you on your land line. Zeaflin is back and he has another case for us."

I take a quick look behind me to be sure Mom is not nearby to overhear. My silence worries Billy. "You still there, Abs?"

"Yeah. What's the case?" I ask, unsure if I want another case from Zeaflin after he drew us into a brutal OtherWorld battle against a demon usurper named Belial in his first case.

"Another missing ghost," Billy replies. My shoulders slump. That's how the Belial case started out.

"Are there demons involved in this one?" I ask, with another backward glance behind me. Nobody there, thank goodness!

"I don't think so. Mr. Monsento said the ghost is an escaped prisoner from the UnderWorld," Billy replies.

"I'm not helping with that!" I loudly object. Mom steps into the room.

"Is everything okay, dear?" she asks, wearing a troubled frown. I can hear Billy talking through the line but I can't focus on him now. I pull the receiver from my ear.

"Yeah, Mom. Billy was just asking me if I'd help him spread fertilizer on Mr. Monsento's garden next weekend. The last time we did it, the smell was just horrible. No way am I helping with that again!"

Mom smiles. "Okay, dear, but try to be a little less passionate. A simple 'no, thank you' would probably suffice," she advises, turning away to head back into the kitchen. I raise the telephone back to my ear and lower my voice.

"No *way* am I helping Zeaflin find some poor escaped spirit just so he can drag him to the UnderWorld and toss him back into prison!"

"Relax, Abby. Mr. Monsento says that Zeaflin intends to help the ghost seek asylum in the OtherWorld, so he'll be safe. Look, it's a long story over the phone. Why don't we stop by Mr. Monsento's house so he can explain?"

"Okay, Billy. I'll meet you there in ten minutes," I reply and hang up the phone. Then I pop my head into the kitchen to find Mom. She is repotting one of her houseplants.

"Mom, I need to run over to Billy's house for about an hour. He has some math problem he can't figure out and asked me if I could help." Mom looks up at the clock over the kitchen sink.

"Make it half an hour, Abby. Your dad should be home soon and I thought we'd go out for dinner tonight; maybe try that new Italian place on Hollis Street."

"Okay, Mom. I'll make it quick and be back in thirty minutes." Not much time so I rush out to my bike and ride hard to Monsento's house.

———•◆•———

I'm just sitting down to dig into my plate of spaghetti when the front doorbell rings. It is probably a solicitor and I'm half-tempted to just ignore the bell. But that choice is taken away by the signal tone that indicates whoever was at the door has now stepped into the main salon of my séance room. *I knew I should have locked the front door*, I think with a sigh. But it could be a client. If so, I guess I can always pop the spaghetti into the microwave. I rise from my chair to head for the salon, bumping head-on into Abby at the kitchen door. *What's she doing here on a weeknight?*

"What brings you out, pestering an old medium on a Friday night at dinner hour?" I ask gruffly. "Didn't we agree that my week-days are supposed to be kid-free during the school year?" Abby rolls her eyes and lets out a snort through her nose.

"Zeaflin's case brings me here. You *did* clarify no demons, right?"

"Yes, of course. No demons," I reply, with my own eye-roll.

There is another signal chime from my front door mat. *Swell, another visitor!* Billy and Toby soon come into view behind Abby. Abby glances behind her, probably to confirm it's Billy and Toby and not some other visitor, before turning back to me.

"I don't have much time," she says. "We need details about this case before we can accept it."

"Okay," I reply slowly, trying not to react to the "oh, brother" look crossing Billy's face behind the girl. I muster the fortitude to keep that same look off my face. "What do you need to know?"

"Billy said the missing ghost Zeaflin is looking for escaped from an UnderWorld prison. Why was he in an UnderWorld prison?" she asks.

"That's easy. They sent him there because he hitched a ride on a realm walker to the living realm and that's a big no-no," I reply.

"He hitched a ride on Zeaflin?" she asks, surprised.

"No, some other realm walker. I can't remember his name--maybe Zeaflin never told me. Anyway, they found this ghost,

Nathan, at his gravesite and took him back to the UnderWorld and locked him up," I respond.

"But how did he escape from prison?" Toby asks, stepping past Billy and Abby to join the conversation.

"Just like Elizabeth did with Zeaflin when she escaped the OtherWorld prison; he hitched a ride on a realm walker. But this time, the realm walker took him out voluntarily," I reply.

"Zeaflin?" Abby asks with another surprised look.

"No. Or at least Zeaflin denies it was him. He said he knows who did it, which could be a deliberate misdirection, or it could be the truth," I respond. Abby thinks this over, then nods.

"Okay. We'll come back tomorrow with our decision," she announces. By the look of irritation on the two boy's faces, I'm guessing there is going to be some serious discussion on their way home. Glad I don't have to be a part of it.

———————◆———————

"Let's walk home so we have more time to talk before we have to split up," I suggest, glancing at my watch. I have time.

"What do we need to discuss, Abby?" Billy asks, as we walk down Monsento's porch stairs and approach our bikes. "It's a simple case of finding a personal item and summoning the ghost so it can ask for asylum. No big deal."

"Do you really want to cross the UnderWorld, Billy? What if they find out we helped this ghost? What do you think they'll do? They just might send a demon our way to stop us or maybe even to punish us," I warn, grabbing the handlebars of my bike. We begin the trek home.

After a moment of silence, during which I hope the boys are considering the possibility of UnderWorld retribution, Billy puffs out an annoyed sigh. "Abby, I don't think we should let this ghost be sent back to prison for something as minor as trying to escape the UnderWorld. Do you?" he asks. I stop walking and turn to face him.

"No, Billy, I don't. But why can't Zeaflin just find this ghost himself? Or the realm walker who helped him escape--*if* it wasn't Zeaflin, that is?"

"I don't know, Abby. But what sort of friends would we be if we didn't help Mr. Zeaflin?" Billy responds. I stare at Billy, completely confounded.

"Friends? Are you serious, Billy? Zeaflin isn't alive--at least I don't think he is. I think he's somewhere in-between," I tell him. Toby jumps in.

"That doesn't mean we can't be friends with him," he says with a pout. I shake my head, knowing it's pointless to argue with Toby when it comes to Zeaflin. After all, it wasn't all that long ago that he was trying to fix Zeaflin up with his mother.

"We'll take a vote," Billy declares. I stare hard at Billy. Neither of these boys have seen a demon, but I have and I never want to see another one again. Knowing how this vote is going to end, I decide to request a compromise.

"All right, Billy and Toby. How about we hold off on a final decision until after we talk to Zeaflin? **If** he can assure no demons will
come our way--or any other UnderWorld retribution for that mat-
ter--I promise to consider helping. Otherwise, you're on your own."

"Fair enough, Abby," Billy responds. The three of us split up and
head our separate ways toward home.

———————— ◆ ————————

I have a nightmare that wakes me up in the middle of the night.
This one starts off with Monsento, Billy, Toby, and me in a tiny room
with black walls and black floors and a bunch of black folding chairs
arranged in tidy rows behind us. Sitting behind a desk on a raised
platform in the front of the room, there is a demon that looks exactly
like Belial the Ugly, except for the black robe draped over its shoulders and the gray, curly wig it is wearing on its head. Smoke leaks out
of its nostrils with every breath, emitting a horrible rotten egg stench.
I breathe through my mouth but that doesn't help much because I
can still taste the stench on my tongue. After giving the four of us
standing before him a sour look of disdain, the demon looks down
at the desk in front of it and holds up a parchment, charred along the
edges. Clearing its throat with a whiff of sulfur, the creature begins
to read from the paper.

"You have been found guilty of harboring a known criminal of
the UnderWorld, an act of treason against our realm. As punishment, you have been sentenced to reside in the UnderWorld in the
fourth circle of the ninth ring, designed specifically for traitors like

yourselves." The demon looks up from the parchment with a leer. "It is a bit cold there but I hear the lake is beautiful in an austere sort of way. And with any luck, you may even run into your old pal Belial, there. I am certain he would just *love* to see you again."

The door behind the demon slowly creaks open. Waiting just outside the threshold is an immense winged monster with large horns and huge bat-like ears. It lets out a horrible, screeching laugh and points to what looks like a freight elevator.

"Going down?" it jeers.

———————◦ ♦ ◦———————

I wake up with a start, my pillow damp with perspiration. It takes several hours of listening to the splattering raindrops on the window pane before I calm my racing heart and slip back into sleep.

———————◦ ♦ ◦———————

I wake up to the sound of rain pattering against my bedroom window, sounding a lot like tiny mouse feet scampering across the glass. That probably explains the dream I had with giant mice chasing me through a maze filled with cheese. Very weird.

I take a quick look at my bedside clock. It reads 9 am. Today is Saturday so I consider turning over and sleeping another hour or two; it is raining, after all. But a cup of coffee would be nice and it won't make itself, so I crawl out of bed, toss on my robe and head for the kitchen.

———

No sooner do I pop my cup of water into the microwave than my doorbell rings. With a tired sigh of self-pity for an old medium who never gets much private time, I press the two-minute-high button to start the water heating before I head for the front door. Rather than opening it right away, I decide to peek through the peephole to see who is visiting me so early on a Saturday morning. Via the tiny hole, I see Zeaflin standing on my front porch. He looks to be struggling to collapse an umbrella. There is someone behind Zeaflin but it's difficult to see who it is due to the wide-brimmed hat he is wearing that hides his face in shadow. I open the door just as Zeaflin succeeds in closing his umbrella. He looks up at me and smiles.

"Ah, Mr. Monsento, I'm glad to see you are up. We didn't wake you, did we?" he asks, furrowing his brow with concern. I shake my head and look past Zeaflin at the tall stranger behind. Zeaflin half-turns and motions toward his companion. "I have brought someone who has the information you require for obtaining the personal item of the ghost we seek," he explains cheerfully. "Are the young detectives here yet?"

"Not yet," I reply. Zeaflin's smile fades.

"But they did agree to accept my case?" he asks, his brow furrowing again.

"Billy did; Toby, probably; Abby, I'm not sure about," I respond and step back to let them in. Zeaflin looks relieved. I guess he figures the boys can convince Abby to take his case.

The stranger steps out from behind Zeaflin and pauses just inside the door of my home. He removes his hat, allowing his long silver hair to drop down to his shoulders in thick waves, while he surveys my salon with olive-colored eyes flecked with silver dots that match his hair. His gaze lingers on my séance table in the right-hand corner of the room.

"How *charming*," the stranger pronounces with a touch of derisiveness. He wipes his boots on my doormat and steps into the salon. Zeaflin sets his umbrella down on my entry mat by the front door and joins his companion.

"This is Nerjul, the realm walker I told you about," Zeaflin says. I give him a confused shake of my head, causing a look of frustration to briefly cross Zeaflin's pale face. "The realm walker who carried Nathan to the living realm," he elaborates.

"You never mentioned him by name, Zeaflin," I respond defensively. *Or did he?* I look at Nerjul, who gives me a bloodless smile and then crosses over to my séance table.

"You gave him your old crystal ball, Zeaflin? How sentimental of you," Nerjul says, picking up the ball from its stand and twirling it absently in one hand. The clear glass begins to cloud up with a deep purple mist.

"Don't play with that!" I tell him, darting forward to grab the ball from his hand. I put it back on the stand, where it immediately returns to clear glass again. I turn to face Nerjul, who smirks and gives me a shrug.

"As you wish, Mr. Monsento," he says. I detect a note of condescension in his tone.

"Shall we have a drink?" Zeaflin proposes.

Nerjul's eyes light up. "Bourbon, perhaps?" he suggests.

"Sorry, I only have lemonade," I reply.

Nerjul's eyes dull. "If that's all you have…" he says with a heavy sigh. With the beverage reluctantly agreed upon, both realm walkers decide to head off toward the kitchen. I pause to confirm my crystal ball is still clear glass before I join them.

By the time I reach the kitchen, Zeaflin has already poured out three glasses of lemonade and taken a seat at the kitchen table. Nerjul is still standing, staring at one of the empty chairs. "It's called a chair. You sit in them," I inform Nerjul, who blasts out a loud laugh that almost startles me out of my skin.

"He is every bit the character you describe him to be, Zeaflin," Nerjul declares as he pulls out the chair to sit down. I stand a moment to glare at them both, not sure which one is more irritating.

"Please sit down, Mr. Monsento, and Nerjul will explain every-thing. You'll find his version of Nathan's escape is similar to my own; however, it is a tale best told by the one who has experienced it," Zeaflin says.

I take a seat in the chair across from Nerjul and settle back for story time. Then I notice Nerjul's gaze is focused behind me so I turn to look and see Billy peeking through the window in my kitchen door, with Toby and Abby standing behind. They are all in yellow rain slickers with the hoods pulled tight to seal out the rain.

"The detectives, I presume," Nerjul states dryly. I get up to let the kids in.

"Mr. Zeaflin! You came back!" Billy gushes.

"Yeah, and he brought a friend with him," I say, motioning to Nerjul. Billy and Toby pull off their rain coats and boots to leave them on the back stoop before they head over and grab a seat at the table. Abby steps inside but hovers by the door, looking uncertain.

"Come in, Abigail. It is for you that I have come," Nerjul calls out to her.

The look of uncertainty changes to fear. "*What?*" she gasps, wide-eyed, looking at Zeaflin.

"He means he came here for all of you. He hopes to convince you to take the case," Zeaflin clarifies. "Nerjul is the realm walker who helped Nathan escape and can provide you with the details necessary to find him." Abby is still frowning but she takes a step toward the kitchen table. I look down at the puddles pooling around her on my kitchen floor.

"Hey! Take your coat and boots off. You're tracking water in!" I growl. Abby murmurs a soft "sorry" and pulls her coat and boots off. She puts them on the porch stoop alongside the boy's garments and then takes a seat at the table between Toby and Billy.

Chapter 8

"Please, go ahead, Nerjul," Zeaflin encourages. Nerjul looks around the table before resting his gaze on Abby, who shrinks back in her chair under his cool stare.

"Where to begin?" he asks himself.

"The beginning would be nice," I suggest helpfully, drawing Nerjul's attention away from the girl. He gives me a look of exasperation for the thought intrusion.

"Please, Mr. Monsento, don't interrupt," Zeaflin scolds. Properly chastised, I sit back in my chair to listen to Nerjul tell his tale.

"I first noticed Nathan a few months back, inhabiting a dark corner of the Toothy Tavern. He was such a curiosity to me. He was always alone, always sitting at the same table in the same corner, and he was always drinking the same mixed drink concoction that I'm surprised Drevu, the bartender, even knew how to make. Nathan was there every time I visited the Toothy Tavern so he was obviously a regular. But none of the other spirits ever spoke to him; in fact, they scarcely even noticed him. The night of my possession there was a particularly lively bunch of spirits visiting the tavern. I agreed to play a game of poker with them with the unspoken understanding that the winner would buy the house a round. Alastor was the winner that evening and he is a ghost who keeps his word, so drinks were ordered for all.

"Unfortunately, Drevu made Nathan's drink first and this drew unwanted attention to the odd little ghost sitting in the shadows. Some of the spirits in the tavern that night knew of Nathan's past. They knew he was assessed as OtherWorld worthy but chose the UnderWorld instead, even if they didn't know the circumstances behind the switch. One of these spirits was the piano player, Phenus. He ad-libbed a song about Nathan which he titled *The Woebegone Oddity of the UnderWorld.* I don't find such hijinks amusing so I decided it was time to leave and quickly made my exit." Nerjul pauses to take a sip of his drink, grimaces, and immediately places the glass back onto the table, giving it a small push away from him. Apparently, lemonade is not to his liking.

"And that was when Nathan possessed you?" I ask.

Nerjul nods. "He must have followed me out of the tavern. I didn't notice him behind me until he entered my mind. Ordinarily, I could fend off such a weak attacker as Nathan but—" Nerjul smiles sheepishly, "—I made a little more merry than I should have that evening. I did fight him at first, but I was not very successful in repelling him so I carried him to the living realm, as he requested. During our travel, I had time to get to know him and I began to pity this poor, pathetic ghost."

"But that didn't stop you from reporting your possession after he left you," Abby observes with an air of disapproval.

"Oh, but I had to report the possession. There are rules and they are there so order is kept. The UnderWorld would be much more chaotic than it already is if we allowed what few rules we have to be bent so easily. So of course, I reported his occupation immediately after he left me and, while I didn't tell the UnderWorld authorities exactly where I had left Nathan, they captured him rather quickly nonetheless. You see, I dropped him off at the cemetery gate and since spirits in the living realm tend to gravitate toward their burial site—"

"So we've heard," I mumble. Zeaflin gives me a warning look. Nerjul ignores me and continues.

"—it was the first place they looked. They sent in Eurynomos, the only creature of the UnderWorld that can enter a cemetery unharmed, to find and extract him. Nathan was returned to the UnderWorld and sent straight to prison."

"No trial?" Abby asks with a frown.

"None needed. I had no reason to lie," Nerjul replies.

"What made you decide to bust Nathan out of prison then? Aren't there rules about that too?" I ask snidely.

Nerjul nods. "Oh yes, most definitely. But after I heard of Nathan's capture and his subsequent eternal sentence to the UnderWorld detention center, I felt an injustice had been done. Eternal imprisonment for possessing a realm walker seemed a bit heavy-handed. After all, I was not harmed."

"But if you hadn't reported the possession, Nathan wouldn't have been imprisoned," Abby points out. Nerjul turns his steely gaze to Abby.

"Yes, he would have. There is no escape for spirits in the UnderWorld except through a realm walker, so he would automatically be charged with that offense," he replies.

"But without your testimony, they'd have no concrete proof," Abby counters, keeping the pressure on Nerjul.

"They would have found out it was Nerjul that was possessed, Abby--if not from Nerjul, then from Nathan. The UnderWorld authorities can be quite…persuasive," Zeaflin responds.

"Indeed. If I had failed to report my possession, all my silence would have bought would be my sharing a cell with Nathan after the authorities persuaded him to divulge who he possessed. The UnderWorld would not be amused with a realm walker who would allow such a travesty and not report it immediately," Nerjul says.

"But won't you be imprisoned anyway if they find out you helped Nathan escape a second time?" Toby asks timidly.

"There is that danger, yes," Nerjul agrees.

"So where do you fit in here, Zeaflin? How did you find out about all of this?" I ask.

Nerjul laughs heartily. "You didn't tell them, Zeaflin?" he asks with a wolfish grin. Zeaflin shakes his head. "Zeaflin helped me break Nathan out of prison," Nerjul divulges. "I asked him to assist because I required a diversion only another realm walker could provide. It is Zeaflin who entered the detention center first and it is he who incited a riot so that I might slip into Nathan's cell undetected and carry him out."

"Does that mean you could go to jail, Mr. Zeaflin?" Toby asks anxiously.

"Not if we acquire Nathan and send him to the OtherWorld, out of reach of the UnderWorld," Zeaflin reassures him.

"Why didn't Nerjul carry Nathan to the OtherWorld directly after he broke him out of prison? Why did he drop him off here?" Abby asks, a look of suspicion crossing her face. Nerjul shakes his head in irritation.

"I planned to do that but I lost him. I'm not sure how or why but he dropped out somewhere between the living realm and the OtherWorld," he responds. Abby doesn't look convinced but she doesn't argue any further.

"Okay, let's say we summon Nathan and he goes to the OtherWorld. Won't the UnderWorld just keep on probing into who helped him?" I ask.

Nerjul shrugs. "Investigations that involve multiple realms can only be performed by realm walkers, Mr. Monsento, and we are a tight-knit community. There is little danger that the UnderWorld will discover who helped Nathan escape unless they capture Nathan," he replies.

Abby leans forward in her chair. "If we help you relocate Nathan to the OtherWorld and the UnderWorld ruler finds out, what will he do? Will he send a demon to kill us?" she asks in a shaky voice, staring intently at Zeaflin. Zeaflin pastes on a confident smile, which might be reassuring if his teeth weren't so pointy. It's like watching a crocodile smile, for Pete's sake!

"Demons aren't allowed in the living realm, Abby. They haven't been allowed to visit this realm since—" Zeaflin looks at Nerjul. "—1409, wouldn't you say, Nerjul?"

Nerjul shakes his head. "Since 1412, the year of Ambrogio and Razuul's sixth treaty. Among other things, part of that pact was that angels and demons may no longer visit the living realm," he replies. Zeaflin taps his blood red lip with a long fingernail while he thinks this over. Then he nods his agreement.

"Of course, 1412. So you need not worry over any visits from demons, Abigail. They are forbidden to enter the realm of the living as part of the 1412 agreement between the OtherWorld and UnderWorld. That's one of the main reasons you never see demons or, for that matter, angels here anymore," Zeaflin explains.

Abby looks skeptical. "Will they send something else?" she asks.

"There is nothing else to send, other than a realm walker. And because I am a senior realm walker, the realm walker they would send would be me," Nerjul replies. "And I am bound by the treaty of 1508 to cause no harm to the living or their realm. If I did, the

UnderWorld would lose its permit to utilize realm walkers for living work. Besides, while our leader Razuul will be quite angry about Nathan escaping to the OtherWorld, the focus of his ire will be toward the OtherWorld, not the inconsequential living who helped him escape the living realm."

"There now, you have nothing to worry about," Zeaflin concludes. "Now, will you help us find Nathan? Nerjul knows where you may find a personal item, if you agree to retrieve it for us."

Abby narrows her eyes. "Why can't he retrieve it himself if he knows where it is?" she asks.

"Oh, for many reasons," Nerjul responds. "But primarily because Nathan's personal item is at his grave inside your local cemetery. And from what I've heard of your experience in that graveyard with Zeaflin, you are already well versed in what occurs when a realm walker enters a cemetery."

"Cool! Do you want us to dig up his bones, Mr. Nerjul?" Billy asks, suddenly perking up. Abby takes in a sharp breath but it's me that jumps in quickly.

"Not doing that," I grumble. "One, my back won't handle it. Two, it's illegal."

"Not to worry, Mr. Monsento!" Zeaflin pipes in, a gleam of mirth in his eyes. "Nathan's personal item is above ground."

"Not breaking into a mausoleum either," I declare, countering his mirth with my scowl.

"Nathan's personal item is a bronze baby shoe, embedded in his tombstone, Mr. Monsento," Nerjul clarifies, drumming his fingers on my kitchen table. "His mother had it placed there for her dear baby boy, taken too soon from this world." He scrunches his nose as if he'd just encountered a dead skunk.

"You want us to go to a cemetery and pry a baby shoe off a gravestone?" Abby asks, a look of shock on her face. I have to wonder why she's so surprised. Nothing surprises me after Zeaflin requested the kids snip a bone off a skeleton for the required personal item in his last case with us.

Nerjul clears his throat. "Certainly not you *personally*. As a girl, you'd never have the strength." He ignores Billy's snort of laughter. "Mr. Monsento should do the hard work."

"I'm pretty sure vandalizing a tombstone is also illegal," I rebut.

"That may well be," Nerjul responds. "And yet, there is no other personal item that I am aware of for Nathan's summoning."

"Why do we even need to summon him?" I ask. "Why not just conjure Nathan up in the crystal ball and tell him to fly on over here for asylum? I bet Vila would come down here and give it to him, if you asked him nicely." Zeaflin studies me a moment.

"Have you ever tried using the crystal to contact any spirits other than Mary?" he asks.

I shake my head. "Not yet. I can't truly contact any of my old clients' relatives or they'll get wise to me fooling them all these years with the fake séances. I'm waiting on some new clients to try it out for real."

Zeaflin nods knowingly. "You will find your crystal ball will only evoke Mary. It was tuned specifically to her frequency back when she still worked for me as an OtherWorld spy. In order to conjure Nathan, we require his spectral frequency, and we do not have it. As for prearranging anything with Vila, I think it more prudent we 'paint him into a corner', so to speak. Vila can be quite intractable, and he may refuse to grant asylum beforehand. It creates quite a lot of additional paperwork which, even though he is a bureaucrat, he tries to avoid whenever possible. But faced with Nathan's imminent capture, we can appeal to his conscience."

"Swell. Nothing is ever easy with your cases, is it?" I respond.

"We could go get the personal item after dark, Mr. Monsento. Nobody would see us then," Billy suggests. I glare at him. *Is he nuts?*

"No. No graveyard visits after dark," I tell him.

"Then I suggest you go today. It is gloomy outside and the cemetery will most likely be vacant of its usual visitors," Nerjul says.

"But the caretaker will definitely be there, rain or shine. It's too risky," I counter.

"The rain should keep the caretaker inside his hut," Nerjul replies impatiently, the finger drumming starting anew. Suddenly I think I've found the answer.

"What about that Eurynomos thing? Why not have it get your personal item for you if it can enter a graveyard safely?" I propose.

Nerjul looks like I just suggested he eat worms for dinner. "Eurynomos cannot read, Mr. Monsento. He would never find the right tombstone, and even if he did stumble upon it, he is in no condition to pry anything out of a stone," he replies.

"Why is that, Mr. Nerjul?" Billy asks.

"Eurynomos never rises beyond a crouch. That tends to minimize leverage when attempting to pry items out of tombstones," Nerjul responds.

"Not to mention it would slow him down a bit in the search for Nathan's gravestone, huh?" I remark, giving up on trying to find an easy solution to an UnderWorld problem. There never seems to be one. "But speaking of that thing, what if they send it in to look for Nathan while we're in the graveyard getting your personal item for you? Is it dangerous?"

Nerjul sighs in frustration. "Is your medium always so fretful?" he asks Zeaflin. Zeaflin gives him an apologetic smile before looking over at me.

"Eurynomos is mostly harmless. Besides, he has already searched for Nathan at his gravesite. Not finding him there, the UnderWorld has determined this time, Nathan must be hiding elsewhere," Zeaflin tells me.

"But what if they decide to send it in again?" I ask. "You know, to double-check."

"They will not send Eurynomos in again. He is a difficult creature to pull out of a cemetery once he is released in one, so they send him into graveyards sparingly. Eurynomos is known to be quite gluttonous," Nerjul responds. I shake my head in confusion.

"Eurynomos likes to feed on corpses," Zeaflin explains. I involuntarily grimace in disgust at the thought of some monster roaming around cemeteries, munching on rotting flesh.

Billy lets out a low whistle. "Cool," he murmurs. Okay. Obviously, Billy doesn't find it disgusting. Why am I not surprised?

"Are your fears adequately addressed?" Nerjul asks me. "Will you collect the personal item? It is a simple request."

I think this over. If the UnderWorld recaptures Nathan and forces him to tell them who helped him escape prison, both Nerjul *and* Zeaflin are probably going to be sharing his cell. Sure, Zeaflin is undead and a little weird, but I don't want him locked up. So if we are going to take this case, we need a personal item. And if we need this *particular* personal item, it is best to try to "collect" it with few people around to catch us in the act. I turn around in my chair to look out the kitchen window. It has stopped raining but the clouds are still ominous. Nerjul is right. The gloom should keep cemetery visitors to a minimum today.

"Perhaps an offering will help ease your troubled mind?" Zeaflin proposes, interrupting my thoughts. He reaches into his suit pocket and extracts the little red sack where he keeps his silver. Abby slaps her hand on the table, startling us all.

"Not everyone can be bought!" she declares loudly.

"I beg to differ. Everyone has a price; it just isn't always money," Nerjul says, drawing Abby's ire.

"*I* don't have a price," she retorts.

Nerjul eyes her closely, wearing the trace of a smile on his lips. "Of course you do. Your affection for Zeaflin displays your price as plain as the freckled nose on your face. The price for your service is Zeaflin's gratitude," he replies. Abby gasps in indignation.

I glance over at Zeaflin. He is staring at his hands, neatly folded together on the table. I believe if the undead could blush, he'd be as red as a beet right now.

"I think you're mistaking me for Toby. *He's* the one with the affection for Zeaflin, not me," Abby says, pointing a finger at Toby's chest. Suddenly, I feel a sharp pain in my ankle.

"Ouch!" I cry out. Somebody kicked me. I duck my head under the table and see that somebody must be Toby. "Why'd you kick me, kid?" I ask him. Toby blushes and mumbles down toward his shoes.

"Sorry, Mr. Monsento. I thought you were Abby." *Seriously?*

"Abby is sitting next to you. How do you figure a kick across the table is going to land on her leg?" I ask testily. Billy's laugh is cut short by Toby's indignant glare.

Nerjul rubs his temple. "Are you *sure* there are no other suitable living for our case?" he asks Zeaflin. Zeaflin gives Nerjul an encouraging smile.

"Mr. Monsento and the detectives are the best the living have to offer," he replies. I try to figure out if he's being sarcastic or if, heaven help them, we really are the best living help on hand. Nerjul looks us all over, a doubtful expression on his face.

"If you say so," he responds, slowly rising from his chair. "I'll leave you to hash out the details then." Nerjul exits the kitchen and heads into my salon. He returns a moment later, wearing his hat. With a brief nod to the rest of us still seated at the table, he vanishes in a puff of bright yellow smoke.

Zeaflin pulls two silver coins from his red sack and places them on the table. "One for you and one for the detectives, to cover any expenses you may incur," he states, pushing the coins toward me. I gather them up and tuck them into the pocket of my robe.

"I'm sure your 'gratitude' is payment enough for the kids," I say, with a smirk toward Abby, who gives me a look to kill. Billy and Toby begin to object so I decide to provide a little reminder. "Besides, the detectives are into me for about thirty bucks from our last case, if I recall correctly," I say, giving the boys a stern look. "Not to mention I had to perform a summoning without reimbursement of any sort, and those can take quite a toll on an old medium."

Zeaflin laughs. "Yes, I imagine they can indeed. All right, is it settled then? You will acquire Nathan's personal item?" he asks. I hesitate, not sure that agreeing to do this is in my best interest. But maybe if we're very careful, we can get the shoe without being seen. I nod my consent.

"And we'll help him. Right, Toby?" Billy pipes up. "Abby?"

"Yeah, I'll help," Toby replies.

Abby sighs. "Someone needs to look out for these guys so, yes, I'll help," she says, drawing a pleased smile from Zeaflin.

"Excellent! Nerjul and I will return tomorrow for the summoning. Seven sharp?" he suggests. I see a look of distress cross Abby's face. That's right; the girl has an early curfew.

"Make it five," I say. Zeaflin nods.

"Five it is!" he replies enthusiastically and vanishes in his usual puff of gray fog.

A ray of sunlight breaks through the rain clouds. "Looks like it's clearing up," Toby observes, looking toward the kitchen window.

"Weather-wise, yeah; this case, not so much," I respond as I stand up and begin to clear the lemonade glasses from the table.

Chapter 9

"All right, kids, why don't you head on home? We can deface Nathan's tombstone after lunch," Monsento says bluntly, placing the dirty glasses into his kitchen sink. He's trying to hide it but I can tell he's worried, just like I am, about UnderWorld retribution, in spite of the treaties of 1412 and 1508. But what choice do we have? We can't take the chance that the UnderWorld recaptures Nathan and finds out Zeaflin helped break him out of prison. Sure, Zeaflin is strange and semi-dead but the boys are both fond of him.

Monsento looks out the kitchen window over his sink. "There are some dark clouds heading our way so this lull won't last long," he tells us. "I suggest you get going before it starts raining again."

Heeding his warning, the three of us head for the kitchen door and out to the back stoop to pull on our boots and rain jackets, unpleasantly damp from this morning's rainstorm. Billy turns back to Monsento, who is still peering out his kitchen window at the sky. "I'll leave my cell on, Mr. Monsento. Be sure to call us when you're ready to head to the cemetery," he requests. Monsento gives him a nod of assent so with a quick wave goodbye, we step off the stoop to head for home.

———◆———

"Those clouds sure look dark. My place is closest so why don't you guys come to my house for lunch? We can play video games while we wait for Mr. Monsento to call," Toby says.

"Sounds good to me," Billy replies.

"My parents don't expect me home until seven so sure, let's do that," I agree. A splatter of rain falls from an overhead tree branch and hits the top of my head, so I pull my hood up and pull the drawstring tight under my chin. A rumble of thunder echoing from the east spurs us to hasten our pace down Locust Street toward Toby's house.

———◆———

The house is dark when we step inside. "Mom's working the day shift today," Toby explains. He motions for us to hang our rain gear on a hook by the door and flips on a lamp next to the sofa. I take a look around. It's been a long time since I've visited Toby's house. It's just as I remembered--small and cozy.

A jagged bolt of lightning lights up the sky, followed by a loud boom that causes the three of us to jump, then the sky opens up and the rain pours down in sheets so hard the outside world becomes a blur. "Better call your folks or they'll worry," Toby advises and heads off toward the kitchen. Billy and I step to opposite sides of the living room to make the phone calls to inform our parents that we are spending the afternoon at Toby's house. After we both hang up, Billy and I head into the kitchen to find Toby. He is smearing mustard onto three bologna sandwiches.

"Pour us some soda, will you, Abby?" Toby requests.

I make a face. "Soda doesn't go well with bologna, Toby."

"OK, then pour me and Billy some soda and help yourself to whatever you think goes good with bologna," he responds.

I pull the cola bottle from the refrigerator and hand it to Billy before I dig around to find the milk. Billy pours out two glasses of soda and puts them on Toby's small two-seat kitchen table before passing me a glass for my beverage. Another flash of lightning lights up the sky.

"I hope this lets up soon. I really don't want to visit a graveyard in a downpour with thunder and lightning," I say, chewing on my lower lip.

"Aw, don't be such a girl, Abby. I think it would add to the ambivalence," Billy replies.

"I think you mean ambiance," I correct automatically, taking one of the sandwich plates from Toby.

"That's what I said," Billy retorts.

Toby grabs a folding chair from his kitchen pantry and sets it next to the other two chairs at the little table. Then we all sit down and eat in silence, listening to the rain beat against the window panes of Toby's tiny kitchen.

———•◆•———

After lunch and a brief argument over who washes and who dries the dishes–Billy and me, respectively–we finish cleaning up the kitchen and adjourn to the living room. Toby is just finishing hooking up the *Wii* to the television set when a cell phone buzzes. Billy rushes over to his rain coat and pulls his cell from the front coat pocket to check the caller ID.

"It's Mr. Monsento," he tells us and flips open the clam to answer. I cast a worried look outside. At least the rain has let up; it's now just a steady drizzle.

"Yeah. Uh-huh. Okay, Mr. Monsento, we'll be right over," Billy says. Then he hangs up and turns to tell us what we already know. We're going back into a people cemetery, this time in the rain. Choking down a feeling of dread, hoping that we don't run into any graveyard ghosts *or* get caught vandalizing a tombstone, I put my rain gear back on and follow the boys out the door toward Monsento's house.

———•◆•———

I'm in the middle of looking up Nathan's grave location online when the kids show up at the back door. Before they come inside and start dripping all over my kitchen floor, I hastily scribble down the location—section B, plot 365—onto the palm of my hand and shut down the laptop. I tuck the computer safely into the drawer where I keep my gardening tools and grab my rain coat from the back of one of the kitchen chairs where I'd left it earlier for easy access. I tug the jacket over my shoulders and pull the hood over my head before I step out to join the kids on the back stoop.

"The car is around front, parked on the opposite side of the street," I inform my soon-to-be fellow grave robbers.

"Yeah, we saw it when we walked over here, Mr. Monsento," Billy responds. "Your old blue Buick is hard to miss." I wonder if that's a compliment or not but decide to take it as one.

I hit the electronic door opener as we approach the car, cringing at the thought of those little kid boots anointing the interior carpets with mud and water but realizing there isn't much I can do about it. Guess I can take the car to the gas station on the way back from the cemetery. It has a vacuum that should at least suck up most of the mess.

The kids pile in, with Abby taking shotgun for a change. That puts the two boys in the back seat, possibly preventing another battle over the car radio. I flip on the news and give the boys a warning look through the rearview mirror to forestall any arguments. Neither of them takes notice so I pull away from the curb to begin our drive to the local cemetery, fortunately only fifteen minutes away.

———— ♦ ————

Abby stares pensively out the passenger window the entire drive out. I wish the boys would do the same. But instead they opt to play some inane card game called *Slap Jack*. I've heard of it, maybe even played it as a kid, but the boys appear to have changed it to "slap everything except the Jack card" which gets really annoying after about five minutes, so I turn up the radio to drown them out. Fearing for my sanity, I let out a sigh of relief when we finally pull up the familiar drive of our hometown graveyard, Morton's Cemetery, named after our town's founding father, Zachary Morton III.

I park the car close to the cemetery gate and peer into the gloom of the graveyard. The drizzle and gray clouds give it a dreary look, which I guess is more apropos than a bright sunny day with happy singing birds. I'm hoping the rain has driven the caretaker inside his tiny caretaker office, or maybe we'll get *really* lucky and he's already called it a day. It's almost 2 pm--a little early for caretaker quitting time, but one can always hope.

"See any ghost shimmers?" I ask Abby, who is still staring out the side window but this time is focused on the cemetery. I wonder if she's remembering the last time we were here— when that OtherWorld bounty hunter, Marzee, kidnapped her and dragged her through the graveyard, swarming with hostile, blue, shimmery ghosts. That was one fun day, all right! Abby shakes her head.

"No. Do you?" she asks. "Any of you?" she adds, turning to look at the boys in the back seat. They both shake their heads.

"Good. If none of us see any ghosts, maybe they're sleeping in today; taking a little siesta. It's that time of day, right?" I say, hoping to draw out a smile from Abby and failing completely. Toby takes the bait instead.

"I don't think ghosts take naps, Mr. Monsento. I think they stay awake all of the time." I turn to look at him.

"Is that a fact? And just what makes you think that?" I ask. Toby shrugs.

"We should ask Mary!" Billy pipes in, leaning forward against his seat belt in excitement.

"Yeah, you do that during our next crystal session," I say, popping open the car door and stepping out into the drizzle.

I open the trunk to the car and pull out the small tool box I'd packed earlier today in preparation for our great baby shoe heist, then I motion for the kids to follow me into the cemetery. I sure hope the caretaker doesn't see me carrying this box. There is absolutely no reason I can provide for carrying it into a cemetery that isn't nefarious.

———◆———

"All right kids, we need to head for section B. That's where Nathan's grave is supposed to be located. Anyone see the caretaker?" Monsento asks, looking around the graveyard. "It'd be nice to know where he is before we start prying the shoe out of the tombstone. I'd hate to get caught in the act; he's certain to call the police." We all scan the cemetery but there is no sign of the caretaker so after a quick look at the cemetery map mounted on a plaque just inside the gate, we make our way toward section B to find Nathan's grave.

While there's no sign of the caretaker, I know the ghosts are here; I can sense them. But they choose to stay invisible this time. Or maybe they only become visible when they are agitated, like they were the day Zeaflin visited their graveyard. I really don't know if that's true or not, but I'm glad they are staying hidden and out of our way.

Then I have a horrible thought!

"Guys! What if Nathan came here after Eurynomos left? Won't he be angry if we start prying his baby shoe off his tombstone?" I ask, putting my hand on my chest to calm my racing heart.

Monsento frowns. He was attacked by ghosts during our last visit to this cemetery when they thought he was Zeaflin and tried to possess him. It was a traumatic experience for him and I can see he's mentally digesting the consequences of Nathan catching us trying to steal his shoe. "Zeaflin said he was certain that Nathan isn't in a cemetery," Monsento finally replies.

"Did he say how he knew that?" I ask.

Monsento shakes his head. "No, he didn't. I'd guess it's because Zeaflin thinks Nathan would be a fool to hide in the cemetery a second time after getting caught there the first time he escaped. But to play it safe, we should set up a lookout to keep an eye out for Nathan...or any other ghosts that might be poised to ambush us. Ghosts tend to materialize before they attack so they should be visible," Monsento replies, a slight tremor in his voice.

"Billy's eyes are the sharpest," Toby says. "He was the first to pick out the ghost shimmers the last time."

"All right. Billy will be the lookout," Monsento agrees, still looking nervous.

A tall, gray granite tombstone to the right of our path catches my eye. It has a bronze-colored lump sticking out of the middle of it! In my excitement, I grab Monsento's arm. He jumps at my touch and gives me an annoyed scowl. "Look over there," I say, pointing to the tombstone. "I think that might be Nathan's grave."

The four of us head over to the stone. As we get closer, I read out the carving: "Nathan Hammersly: 1936-1965: Beloved Husband and Father. This is it, guys."

Monsento crouches down to examine the bronze shoe embedded in the granite. "Not sure how easy this is going to be to pry out," he mumbles to himself. "Of course, it's old so maybe the elements have loosened it up a bit."

Monsento opens his toolbox and rummages around before selecting a small crowbar. Then he looks up at Billy. "Go stand over there and keep a lookout for anyone coming up the path, living or otherwise," he commands, pointing toward the small mound of a grave nearby. *It looks to be more recent so the mound must be dirt still not settled around the grave,* I think with a shiver. But that doesn't appear to bother Billy. He heads right over and takes his position on the small hill.

I turn back to watch Monsento pry the shoe out of Nathan's gravestone. The crowbar keeps slipping off the bronze so, with an under-breath curse, Monsento returns to his toolbox and digs around before selecting a small chisel and hammer. "Didn't want to have to do this," he says to no one in particular, then he starts chipping away at the granite around the shoe. I wince at the noise and look around for any possible witnesses. Fortunately, there are none in view. Billy is still on the mound, looking toward the path that leads to section C and beyond.

What we both failed to do was to look at the path behind us…

"What do you think you're doing?" a gruff voice rings out, startling Monsento into dropping his tools to the ground. I turn to look at the owner of the voice with an inward groan. It's the caretaker. We're all speechless, having no other answer except that we are trying to steal Nathan's bronze baby shoe.

Monsento slowly rises from his crouch at the tombstone and turns to face his inquisitor, a short balding man in a long black raincoat. The caretaker rubs at the stubble of the five o'clock shadow on his chin and glances down at Monsento's handiwork. "It's not worth anything, you know," he tells us, with a disgusted shake of his head.

Billy jogs over from his lookout hill. As always, Billy has an explanation, seldom a good one, but at least he is never at a loss for words. "We know, Mr. Caretaker," he responds cheerily, holding out his hand for a handshake. The caretaker ignores his hand and instead just stares at Billy until it becomes awkward. Billy finally drops his hand but keeps his smile pasted on.

"Nathan's wife asked us to bring his baby shoe back to her. She has a grandchild now and she wants to give him this shoe as his fifth birthday gift. You know, in remembrance of his grandfather and all," Billy explains. The caretaker raises an eyebrow.

"Sounds fishy," he grunts. Then he turns to Monsento. "See, I don't much care if you want that worthless hunk of metal but I'll have to explain to the family how it came up missing one day," he says. "That takes time out of my day, and you know what they say: time is money." The caretaker stares at Monsento, obviously waiting for something.

After a brief uncomfortable silence, Monsento digs into his back pocket and pulls out his wallet. Wearing a deep frown, he opens it and pulls out $20, which he holds out to the caretaker. The caretaker looks insulted. Monsento pulls out another $20 and holds out the two bills. The caretaker still looks insulted. "It's all I've got," Monsento says in a strained voice. Billy pulls out a ten note and hands it to Monsento. The caretaker relaxes and takes the proffered money.

"Make it quick now. You're lucky it's raining so we don't have the usual crowd of visitors for a Saturday afternoon," he says and spins on his heel to walk briskly down the path toward the cemetery gate. Monsento lets out a long, heavy sigh.

"Billy, you chisel that thing out. My hands are too shaky now to be of much use," he informs us in a quavering voice. Billy drops down to the tombstone and immediately starts chiseling at the shoe. After what seems like forever, Billy stops chiseling, leans back and grabs the crowbar from the tool chest. It slips easily into the hole he made next to the shoe and with a firm sideways thrust of the bar, Billy succeeds in extracting the shoe from the granite. Monsento quickly picks it up off the ground and drops it into the toolbox.

"Let's go, kids," he urges, his voice still trembling. Our hard-earned prize in hand, the four of us exit the cemetery, a place I'm sure Monsento will never agree to visit again. And that suits me just fine!

Chapter 10

The rain starts to let up after I drop each one of the kids off at their various houses. It's now just an annoying mist on the windshield that makes the wipers a waste of time. After a long and crazy day, I'm glad to finally have a chance to relax in front of the television with a strong cup of *Earl Grey* at my elbow. I nearly had a heart attack when the caretaker caught us in the act of trying to pry that shoe off the tombstone. Lesson learned: don't put Billy in charge as a look-out. I'd understand if he missed spying one of the graveyard ghosts, but a flesh and bone caretaker? Unbelievable! And now I'm out forty bucks to boot. I'm glad Zeaflin paid some money up front or I'd be flat broke. Guess I'll go sell one of his silver coins to Manny's pawn-shop tomorrow to put some money back in my pocket. Hopefully, it will stay there. Lately, it seems that every time I get involved in one of the kid's cases, it costs me money.

I turn on the television, take a sip of steaming hot tea, and settle back in my chair. My eyelids start to droop so I close them and let myself drift off to sleep.

———————• ◆ •———————

I wake up to the smell of coffee drifting into my living room and sit up to look at the clock over my fireplace mantel. It reads 8 am. With a sigh and a stretch, I snap off the TV and rise from my chair to head for the kitchen. Ordinarily, I'd be worried about coffee-brewing burglars but I've grown used to Zeaflin popping in unexpectedly. And since he has been known to lurk around my kitchen, I suspect it's him behind the coffee smell.

He's in the kitchen, as I anticipated. There are two coffee mugs sitting on the table with steam rising from them. Zeaflin's back is turned from me and it appears he is studying my toaster. "I thought you told me I wouldn't like your cooking," I say, expecting to startle him. But Zeaflin is difficult to surprise; he merely turns slowly to face me.

"You wouldn't. But I hear that toast is easy to cook," Zeaflin replies with a faint smile.

"Not with that toaster. The timer is broken so it always burns the bread. Coffee is fine," I tell him, sitting down in front of one of the mugs. Zeaflin sits down in front of the other and stares at me expectantly. He must be waiting for me to imbibe so I take a sip. *Geez, that's awful!* I steel myself against spitting the vile, bitter liquid back into the cup.

"How many scoops of coffee did you add to this? I thought you knew how to make coffee," I say with a grimace. Zeaflin looks puzzled. "Never mind," I tell him and grab both mugs to toss the coffee down the drain. I add some fresh water to the cups and pop them into the microwave. After the water heats, I split what little remains of my previously full jar of instant coffee between the two mugs and sit down across from Zeaflin.

"You're early," I tell him. "I meant five in the evening, not morning. Is that abstract concept of time eluding you again?"

Zeaflin smiles. "Not today, Mr. Monsento. I stopped by to confirm you were able to acquire the personal item and that there were no complications."

"Complications? You mean like my being locked up in a jail cell for vandalizing a gravestone type of complication?" I ask.

Zeaflin's smile droops. "You were caught trying to obtain the shoe?"

"Oh, yes, I was caught in the act, all right, thanks to Billy's keen eye as a lookout," I reply. Zeaflin's frown deepens. "Don't worry. We got your *personal item* for you," I assure him. "I had to pay off the caretaker but I got it."

"That is good news," Zeaflin responds, his smile returning. "Nerjul and I will come by for the summoning of Nathan around five tonight then." He rises from his chair.

"Sure thing," I say, watching him gather up his hat and cane to make his usual hasty retreat out my back door. After he vanishes from sight, I head to the refrigerator to dig out some eggs and bacon. May as well have a decent breakfast to start off the day.

———————— • ◆ • ————————

Just before I'm heading out to meet Billy at Toby's house so we can ride over to Monsento's shop, Dad asks me to help him find his tomato stakes, buried deep in the shed somewhere. By the time I find them, hidden behind a box of Easter decorations, I'm running a little late so I call Billy and tell him I'll meet him and Toby at Monsento's house. Then I run inside to wash the shed dust off my hands before I jump on my bike to ride fast to Monsento's.

When I walk into the salon, the séance setup is in progress. The thing Zeaflin calls a "talisman" is already sitting in the Ocean Breeze scented oil used to disguise its odor and Monsento is getting ready to light it with the small flint lighter at the top of Zeaflin's old cane. Despite Monsento's insistence that the talisman isn't a finger, I'd say it looks exactly like a finger, except that it is missing a fingernail.

Toby and Billy are already seated at the séance table so I head over to sit between them. The bronze baby shoe is on the table in front of Monsento's chair, sitting next to Zeaflin's summoning spell that, to me, looks to be written on thin white rice paper. I get the feeling it's not rice paper though, because Monsento has an aversion to touching it. I try not to think about what else it could be, being a spell from the UnderWorld and all.

The talisman now lit, Monsento sits down and dons a pair of reading glasses so he can read the UnderWorld spell, which is much more complicated than the three-word OtherWorld spell we typically use. Since realm walkers cannot participate in séances (the results would be positively *ghastly*), Nerjul walks over to stand behind Monsento and Zeaflin wanders off to stand by the front door. From what Monsento tells us, Vila should show up soon after we summon the ghost, so Zeaflin must be planning to be the one to let him in.

Toby, Billy, Monsento, and I join hands to form a living circle. We're supposed to close our eyes but I decide I'm going to keep both of mine open this time. My peeking in past séances didn't seem to affect anything so I'm going to watch this entire event from start to finish, even if Monsento disapproves. Sometimes the ghost is angry or upset when we draw it over here, so I hope Nathan isn't too freaked out when he shows up. From what I can tell, it looks like Zeaflin didn't pour out his "spirit retention circle" this time; a type of sand that keeps a spirit inside the circle so they cannot run away. I imagine they're relying on Nerjul to calm the ghost once he arrives.

Monsento starts reading from the parchment. I've heard this spell a few times before so I block out his voice and focus on the shoe instead. In previous spirit summonings, the personal items started moving around and I'm hoping to catch this personal item in the act from start to finish.

The shoe sits perfectly still for the first two readings of the spell but when Monsento starts a third reading, it begins to slowly spin in lazy circles on the tabletop. It takes almost five full readings before the shoe begins to pick up speed and rise off the table. It hovers and spins in place, occasionally wobbling and losing speed, then catching itself and regaining momentum. In the middle of the seventh recitation, the shoe abruptly drops back onto the lace tablecloth with a thud and a thin blue wisp of fog creeps out slowly from inside the shoe. The fog rises in twisting curlicues but instead of dissipating, it accumulates into a small dense cloud about the size of a softball.

The cloud hovers a few inches over the table and begins to float toward Billy and me. When it passes between our heads, I can feel the soft, cool wetness of it. Billy must have felt it too because he opens his eyes but he doesn't see the cloud because it has already passed us by. I twist in my chair to try to track where it's going, but I can't see it unless I let go of Billy or Toby's hand and if I do that, it might break the spell and I'll be given the worst grief. So instead I look at Nerjul, who is still standing behind Monsento's chair. He is focused on a spot directly behind me and he looks like a cat tensed up and ready to pounce. That means the ghost has appeared and he must be directly behind me!

I yank my hands free, drawing out a surprised squeak from Toby, and jump out of my chair. That causes Monsento to stop reading and look up from the parchment in confusion. Then he looks at what is behind me and his face changes to alarm. His expression is hardly reassuring so, with a deep breath, I turn in dread to face the UnderWorld ghost. But it's not Nathan. It's just a little boy who looks to be about five or six years old. His face is a little blurry but I can see that he is very scared. I reach out my hand to touch his shoulder reassuringly but Nerjul grabs my arm in an icy grip to stop me.

"No, no, mustn't touch, Abigail," Nerjul admonishes as he pulls the top off a small crystal vial he is now holding in his other hand.

The little ghost boy is instantly sucked up into the vial and both he and Nerjul vanish in a puff of yellow smoke.

———————•◆•———————

"What's going on? I thought we were summoning Nathan. That was a kid!" Abby exclaims.

"Maybe Nathan is a kid?" Billy suggests.

"A kid who drinks at the Toothy Tavern?" Abby responds with a look of disbelief. "And why did Nerjul take him away? Weren't we supposed to be waiting for Vila?" We all look at Zeaflin, still standing by the front door. He looks completely befuddled.

"That was Nathan's son. What would Nerjul want with Nathan's son?" Zeaflin is asking himself, staring absently into space and tapping his lip with one of his long fingernails.

"Zeaflin? What's going on here?" I ask, snapping him out of his rumination. He draws his gaze to me and shakes his head.

"I have no idea," he replies, before vanishing in a puff of gray smoke, likely to try to follow Nerjul.

A loud rap on my front door, followed by the doorbell, startles us all, including the talisman, which twitches violently at the noise and flops out of its bowl and onto the fireplace mantel. In my hurry to snuff out the talisman flame before it leaves a burn mark in the mantel wood, my hand upends the oil bowl and the Ocean Breeze scented oil spills out of the bowl. It pools on the mantel and flows over the talisman, killing its flame with a sputter. Now extinguished, the talisman gives one final dying jerk and launches itself off the mantel and onto the floor with a splat. The doorbell rings again.

"Should I answer the door?" Billy asks, watching me sop up the spilled Ocean Breeze with a bar towel.

"Why? Did it ask a question?" I snap. That doorbell is starting to get on my nerves!

Another loud rap bangs on my front door, so I slap the oily towel on the mantel and stomp over to the door to yank it open. My favorite OtherWorld bureaucrat, Vila, is standing on my front porch, clad in his customary pale gray suit that matches his hair and eyes. I always liken looking at him to looking at a man through a dust storm. Behind Vila is another bureaucrat, a platinum blonde wearing a powder blue suit with a powder blue tie carrying a small black briefcase. It appears that Vila has acquired a new lackey.

"Mr. Monsento, may we come in, please?" Vila requests. "There is a matter of importance we need to discuss." *That's an understatement*, I think as I step back to let my two OtherWorld guests in.

"You're pretty quick to respond," I tell Vila as he passes by me to assess the room. He turns back to face me.

"UnderWorld talismans emit a very powerful and unique pulse," Vila explains. "And this particular pulse tells us that you must be working with Zeaflin again." He glances toward his sidekick, who has pulled a small notepad from somewhere and is now holding it, preparing to take notes.

"This is my new associate, Azult. He assures me that neither your detective agency nor Zeaflin have filed the appropriate permits to summon a spirit in the living realm." Vila walks deeper into my salon and takes a seat at the séance table. He looks down and a deep frown creases his face. He must be looking at the talisman I left on the floor where it fell, too distracted with trying to save the wood mantel from an oil stain to hide it.

"Who did you summon?" Vila asks Abby sharply.

"We don't know," she replies. "It was supposed to be an UnderWorld ghost called Nathan Hammersly that was supposed to request asylum from you, but it turned out to be a little boy ghost. Zeaflin said the boy ghost is Nathan's son." Vila's eyes widen in surprise and he makes a motion to Azult to start taking notes.

"Zeaflin hired you to summon *Nathan Hammersly* out of the UnderWorld?" Vila asks. He looks troubled. It seems that Vila knows this Hammersly ghost.

"No, not from the UnderWorld, from somewhere here in the living realm. And Zeaflin didn't hire us…well, okay, technically he did because he paid us," I reply for Abby.

"Paid *you*," Abby mutters under her breath. I glare at her.

"Do go on, Mr. Monsento," Vila urges, drawing my attention back to him. "If not Zeaflin, who? Who is the client that Zeaflin paid you to assist?"

"Some UnderWorld realm walker called Nerjul," I reply, trying to block out the sound of Azult's frantic scribbling. It's really very annoying. I turn to address Azult.

"You should ask your boss here to modernize a little, maybe invest in a tape recorder," I suggest.

Azult looks confused. "What is a tape recorder?" he asks.

Vila drums his fingers on the séance table impatiently. "When you're both done discussing electronic equipment, perhaps we can go back to discussing the Hammersly case? Why did this realm walker, Nerjul, hire you to summon Nathan?"

I hesitate. I can't decide how much we should tell Vila at this point. The entire story, including the fact that Zeaflin and Nerjul helped Nathan escape prison? Or maybe some watered-down version? While I'm mulling this over, Abby jumps in.

"To try to get him back before the UnderWorld recaptures him. Nerjul was carrying him out of the UnderWorld when he lost him somewhere here in our realm. They want you to offer Nathan asylum," she responds. Vila gives her a shake of his head.

"Why was he carrying Nathan out of the UnderWorld?" he asks with a furrowed brow, looking over at me. I can't wait to see the expression on his face after I tell him this one!

"Part of a prison break," I reply, watching Vila's eyes bulge with shock. "Nerjul and Zeaflin teamed up to help this Nathan ghost escape the UnderWorld prison after he was given an eternal jail sentence for possessing Nerjul in a past UnderWorld escape attempt—" Vila holds up his hand to silence me.

"*Nathan Hammersly* possessed a realm walker and attempted to escape the UnderWorld?" he interrupts with a look of absolute incredulity. I've never seen Vila so rattled before. He's usually cool as a cucumber.

"Supposedly, yeah," I reply, wondering why Vila keeps saying "*Nathan Hammersly*" with such disbelief. It doesn't seem like such a stretch that a spirit might try to escape the UnderWorld. I sure would. Vila is staring at me impatiently, obviously waiting for me to elucidate further, so I decide to oblige.

"Anyway, this Nerjul character felt sorry for Nathan. He thought the eternal sentence was a tad harsh so he arranged a little jail break with Zeaflin. Zeaflin incited a prison riot to distract the guards and Nerjul allowed Nathan to possess him and carried him out." Now Vila looks completely mystified. Azult scratches frantically on his notepad, trying to keep up, so I pause a moment to give him time to catch up before continuing. "Like Abby said, Nerjul lost Nathan somewhere in the living realm and had no idea where to find him. Zeaflin hired us to obtain a personal item from Nathan's grave so we could summon him here, figuring you'd show up soon after. They planned to request you provide Nathan asylum in the OtherWorld. Except Nathan didn't show up; his son did. And for some weird reason, Nerjul sucked the kid up into a small glass vial and vanished before you arrived. Zeaflin was as surprised and confused as we were. He smoke-puffed out of here, probably to pursue Nerjul and find out what's going on."

Vila stares pensively at me until Azult's scribbling ceases. Then he slowly rises from his chair and motions to his partner, who is now peering over the top of his notepad, pen poised, with a questioning look. "We should go now," Vila says to Azult. "I need to report all of this to Ambrogio immediately."

"*What?* Hold on here! Who is this Hammersly ghost? You seem to know him. Do you know what's going on? Because if you do, we could use your help," I plead.

Vila gives me a dour look. "I can be of no assistance here, Mr. Monsento. At least not yet." Both he and Azult vanish in a puff of blue smoke.

I stare at the dissipating blue smoke and wonder, *Why won't he help now? What use is there in running away to tell Ambrogio? What good will that do?*

Chapter 11

"So *now* what do we do?" I ask Monsento. This case is turning into a complete mess!

Monsento doesn't answer. Instead he just stares at the blue smoke left behind when Vila and his assistant vanished, wearing a confused look on his face. I'm not sure why he thought Vila would help us right away. Vila probably needs to file the appropriate paperwork before he can help. Even with Elizabeth in charge now, I'm willing to bet the bureaucracy is still thick in the OtherWorld. Toby fills in for Monsento's silence.

"We should go back to the cemetery and get one of Nathan's bones. Maybe he can help us get his son back." That draws Monsento's attention, all right!

"No," he responds in a low tone. "No more visits to the cemetery."

"Oh, but Mr. Monsento, how else to acquire Nathan's personal item?" Nerjul asks from behind us. We're so used to Zeaflin sneaking up on us that none of us are overly startled by the unexpected guest. But his sudden appearance right after Vila's departure is worrisome. He might have been watching us, listening in on what we told Vila.

"Explain," Monsento says tersely. Nerjul pulls out a chair and sits at the séance table. He motions for the four of us to join him. "You may wish to be seated," he advises.

"I'd prefer to stand," Monsento responds coldly.

Nerjul shrugs and motions to Billy, Toby, and me. "Perhaps the detectives would like to sit?" The three of us shake our heads so Nerjul shrugs again and settles back in his seat. "As you wish."

"Where is Mr. Zeaflin?" Toby asks, gnawing at his lower lip.

Nerjul smiles. "Oh, Zeaflin is a bit *detained* at the moment. He won't be able to assist us any longer with contacting Nathan," he replies.

Monsento crosses his arms and glares at Nerjul. "Explain," he repeats.

Nerjul laughs softly. "You are a man of few words, I see," he comments, the smile morphing into a grin, exposing sharp incisors just like Zeaflin's. Monsento purses his lips and begins tapping his foot impatiently. Nerjul's grin fades.

"All right, here is your *explanation*, Mr. Monsento. The escape of Nathan Hammersly was a loyalty test, administered by me and failed miserably by Zeaflin."

"Is Mr. Zeaflin in jail?" Toby asks, a tremor in his voice.

Nerjul pivots his gaze to Toby. "No. He is *detained*. Charges of disloyalty have been filed but there will be a trial, of course, before Zeaflin is imprisoned."

I begin to lose my patience. "Who set up this loyalty test? And why did you help with it? And why did you have us summon Nathan's son instead of Nathan? And where did you take his son? *Why* did you take his son?" I ask in rapid-fire succession, beginning to hyperventilate. I feel faint so I yank out a chair and join Nerjul at the séance table.

"I see that you more than make up for Mr. Monsento's lack of verbiage," Nerjul responds with a chuckle. He holds up his hand and makes a fist. "One: the loyalty test was requested by the Underworld ruler." Nerjul pops his thumb out of his palm and into the air.

"Two: why did I help with the test? Partly because my ruler asked me to administer the test but mainly because I also suspected Zeaflin's loyalties lay elsewhere. His methods have always been unorthodox--more OtherWorld than UnderWorld, in my opinion. Just look at his relationship with *you living*." Nerjul snorts in disgust and pops out his index finger.

"Three: why did I have you summon Nathan's son Martin, instead of Nathan? Because Nathan is hiding somewhere in-between realms, a place we cannot summon him from. His son, however, is very easy to summon and he knows where his father is; Nathan's essence is all over the boy so Martin's obviously been visiting him. Besides, the look on Zeaflin's face when the boy appeared instead of

Nathan was priceless. I'd have done it just for fun." Nerjul smirks and pops out another finger.

"Four: where did I take Martin? To the UnderWorld; where else?" A fourth finger pops out from Nerjul's fist.

"Enough with the counting, already!" Monsento snaps. Nerjul shrugs and drops his hand to the table.

"Last, I took the boy because I need leverage to bring Nathan back into the UnderWorld. I originally thought we could just force the boy to tell us where his father is but alas, it appears that Martin cannot speak. So we're going to have to do this the hard way. I will need to hold onto Martin until his father notices he is missing and enters the living realm to look for him." Nerjul looks at me. "Have I answered all of your questions?" I have a lump in my throat so I just nod.

"Excellent! Then can we move on? Time is of the essence; I'd hate to leave that poor boy in the crystal vinculum too long," Nerjul says with false sympathy.

"Move on to what?" Monsento asks, narrowing his eyes.

"Discussing the acquisition of Nathan's personal item. I am afraid I require another summoning to inform Nathan of Martin's predicament and to entice him to return to the UnderWorld prison voluntarily to secure his son's release. Sadly, I have no silver to pay you but I hope that Martin's freedom will be payment enough? Oh! And an expedient recovery of the prisoner will also please the UnderWorld ruler. He just might be inclined to recommend a lighter sentence for Zeaflin if Nathan is returned quickly."

I look at Monsento. What should we do? I don't want to summon Nathan so Nerjul can blackmail him into going back to the UnderWorld prison but we can't leave Martin in Nerjul's vinculum, which I assume is the vial he sucked him into earlier today and not the mathematical symbol. Monsento doesn't look my way. He is staring hard at Nerjul, trying to make sense of this horrible turn of events.

"We'll get Nathan's personal item," Toby says softly, staring down at his shoes. The rest of us don't object. What choice do we have?

"Can we at least talk to Mr. Zeaflin and make sure he's okay?" Billy asks. "Maybe via crystal ball?"

Nerjul shakes his head. "I would not recommend it. Realm walkers cannot be conjured; the orb would explode if you tried," he warns, rising from his chair. "I have some other items that need attending to, so I'll return at six o'clock in three days' time. I believe you living call the day 'Wednesday'. That should provide adequate time for you to acquire the necessary personal item and ample time for Nathan to notice Martin is missing and emerge from in-between. And don't worry. You won't need to dig up Nathan for the personal item. You will find a personal item of his embedded in Martin's tombstone. The Hammersly family had a penchant for adhering family trinkets to their gravestones and Nathan's wife kept up the tradition." With a tip of his hat, Nerjul vanishes in a puff of yellow smoke.

Why did Zeaflin trust this Nerjul fellow? He obviously doesn't share the belief that realm walkers should stick together, having no qualms over setting Zeaflin up for a fall. But why does the UnderWorld ruler think that Zeaflin has conflicted loyalties in the first place? I wonder if he found out that Ambrogio wanted Zeaflin to ascend and work for him instead.

I snap out of my thoughts and notice the kids are all staring at me gloomily, waiting for me to take the lead, I guess. I huff out a tired sigh. "All right, kids. I'll go get Nathan's personal item but I'll have to go after dark when the caretaker isn't around. No way am I going to take a chance on him catching me vandalizing another tombstone. Not that he isn't going to know who did it since I'll be vandalizing the same family plot. We're never going to be able to set foot in that cemetery again." Then I pause to think on that a moment. Maybe that's not such a bad thing...

"I'll go with you," Billy volunteers. "Keep an eye out for any ghosts." I raise a brow.

"You didn't do such a good job the last time," I remind him. Billy's lower lip juts out in a pout.

"I thought I saw a ghost shimmer near the back hedges. I was trying to focus on it when the caretaker snuck up on us," he retorts. I opt to ignore his explanation.

"Besides, I'm not going until midnight and that's way past your bedtime," I add. I'm not desperate enough to take the chance that Billy's mom might wake up and find him missing. Talk about your five-alarm fire!

"I'll go," Toby murmurs. "I can tell my mom I'm staying over at Billy's." Abby butts in.

"No, you can't, Toby. Tomorrow is a school day and your mom will never allow a sleep-over on a school night," she informs him.

"I can handle it," I declare, hopefully with more confidence than I feel. "No big deal." My eyes draw involuntarily toward my bar in the far corner of the salon. There's nothing liquid in the bar now but I sure wish there were. I'm not looking forward to raiding a graveyard by myself and a bracer would help calm my frazzled nerves. I jump a little when I feel a hand touch my arm. It's Abby.

"Why don't you wait until after school tomorrow, Mr. Monsento?" she suggests. "I'll talk to the caretaker and offer him Marzee's gold pin. I think it's worth a fair amount of money so maybe he'll be open to letting us take one more item from the Hammersly plot if I give it to him."

"Abby has a good idea, Mr. Monsento. You shouldn't go alone into a graveyard, chipping away on a tombstone; the ghosts might get mad. You need some backup," Billy asserts.

"There's plenty of time to get the personal item before Wednesday. We can be here by 4 pm tomorrow at the latest, and the cemetery is only ten or fifteen minutes away. We'd definitely be finished before dinnertime," Toby adds.

I think it over. I guess tomorrow afternoon will be fine, providing Abby can convince the caretaker to accept the pin. If there is any way to avoid it, I'd rather not wander a graveyard alone, especially at night.

"Okay, kids, stop by tomorrow after school. We can send Abby in with the bribe first--see if the caretaker will agree to work on the other side of the cemetery for an hour or two," I respond. "Now scoot on home. It's getting late and your parents are going to worry."

The kids make their way to my front door. The two boys exit without even a wave goodbye, looking sad and dejected. Abby hesitates at the door and then turns around. Tears sparkle in her eyes and her lower lip trembles. I wonder if she's worried about Zeaflin. I take a hesitant step toward her, unsure what to do or say, but she swipes away the tears and steps outside, closing the door quietly behind her.

———— ◆ ————

"We should try the Ouija board," Billy is saying to Toby when I catch up to them. "Ask Mr. Zeaflin if he's okay."

"It probably won't work, and if it did, it might be dangerous, Billy," I respond, feeling weary and disheartened. "If crystal conjuring of a realm walker causes the ball to explode, what might happen to the Ouija board? It might catch on fire or something."

Billy frowns but nods his agreement. "I guess you're right, Abs," he concedes. I place an arm around both Toby and Billy's shoulders.

"He's probably fine, you guys. They didn't have the trial yet so they've most likely just locked him up in a room somewhere," I say, struggling to keep my voice steady while pushing images of demonic punishment out of my mind.

"I hope so," Toby replies, gnawing another hole in his lower lip.

"Do you guys want to come over to the tree house?" Billy asks. "I think we should devise a strategy to rescue Martin and stop Nerjul from capturing Nathan."

"Billy, there *is* no strategy we can devise. If Nathan doesn't go with Nerjul, his son will be stuck in some glass vial forever in the UnderWorld," I tell him. "And I'm pretty sure we can't rescue Martin without a powerful spell, like the one Zeaflin gave Monsento when he pulled John out of Halcyon. We don't have one of those. It burned up, remember? We only have Vila's weak spell and Zeaflin's standard spell and those just aren't strong enough."

"I'm going home," Toby says softly, stepping away from my embrace. "We can meet near my locker tomorrow after classes and head for Mr. Monsento's house so we can help him get Nathan's personal item." Toby jumps on his bike and pedals off toward home.

I drop my arm from Billy's shoulder, the friendly gesture suddenly feeling awkward now that Toby is gone. I busy myself with righting my bike and preparing to ride. Billy's sigh draws my attention back to him. "I guess you're right, Abs; there is no strategy. The UnderWorld is calling all the shots now," he says, looking utterly deflated. Without another word, Billy mounts his bike and rides away.

———— ◆ ————

Next week we have our final exams before we let out for the summer and I know I should be studying, which is what I told Mom and Dad I'm doing, but I can't concentrate. I'm too worried about

Martin, trapped in that little vial. And Zeaflin. What does *"detained"* mean in the UnderWorld? Are they trying to force a confession? The pages of my biology book turn into a blur so I snap it shut and wander over to look out the window at the street below. It's twilight and the outside world is a blue-gray haze. There are a couple of teenagers walking hand in hand, enjoying an evening stroll. The girl laughs at something the boy said and leans in to kiss him on the cheek, so I turn away to give them some privacy and flop down on my bed. It's going to be a very long night.

———————— ◆ ————————

It's midnight and the TV has turned to some late-night movie about teenage vampires fighting teenage werewolves, so I hit the off button on the remote and head for the bedroom. I toy with the notion of heading to the cemetery and trying to get the personal item now to spare the kids the trip, but I can't stir up the nerve. I hate to admit it, but I genuinely wish Zeaflin were here. He'd know what to do to fix this mess. Me, I have no idea what is the right thing to do.

I pause in front of the bed. *Maybe I should use the talisman to summon a ghost and draw Vila back here--tell him about Zeaflin's imprisonment...detainment...whatever. Would Vila help us then?* **Can** *he help us?* I shake my head to force out the thoughts. Not that I can summon a ghost on my own anyway. I need the kids and they're tucked safely in their beds. With tomorrow being a school day, I hope they can sleep.

———•———

A loud rap on my front door, followed by my doorbell, wakes me. I flip over to look at my bedside clock; it reads 9 am. Who would visit me so early and with such urgency? The doorbell buzzes again and another rap follows, so I stumble out of bed and toss on a robe to head for the door and my very impatient visitor. Geez, I hope it's not Nerjul! I don't think I can keep my temper under control this early in the morning before coffee. I peek through the peephole in the front door and see a very annoyed-looking Vila standing on my front porch. I fling open the door just before he presses my doorbell again.

"People sleep at night, Vila," I inform him, keeping a check on my excitement that he has returned and might help.

Vila gives me a disapproving frown. "It is not night, Mr. Monsento," he says crisply. I step back to let him in, deciding not to argue.

"Coffee, Vila?" I offer. He shakes his head.

"No. But I imagine you wish for some," he replies with another disapproving frown. I nod and head for the kitchen. Vila follows. While I'm prepping the coffee, I decide to wait to tell him about Zeaflin's "detainment" until after I find out what brought him here. Vila is quick to provide.

"Ambrogio is worried. He has sent me to request Zeaflin come to the OtherWorld for a meeting with him," he says, pulling out a chair at my kitchen table and taking a seat. I put my coffee cup on the table and sit down to bear the bad news.

"Ambrogio is right to be worried. Zeaflin won't be able to attend his little pow-wow. He's being *detained* in the UnderWorld while they gather evidence of his disloyalty with regard to Nathan's prison break," I respond.

Vila raises a hand to his chin and stares down at the table thoughtfully, a furrow in his brow. I wait patiently while he chews this over. He finally raises his eyes to look at me and lets out a heavy sigh. "I don't understand why Zeaflin did this, why he thought he'd be above suspicion in Nathan's escape. Of course, he always was rash. How much does the UnderWorld know?" Then Vila's eyes widen. "How do *you* know Zeaflin is being detained?" I take a sip of my coffee.

"Nerjul told me. Turns out that Zeaflin's buddy Nerjul is no friend after all. He set Zeaflin up at the UnderWorld ruler's request for a little loyalty test. Would Zeaflin help with a prison break or refuse? He didn't refuse. In regard to how much do they know? Obviously everything, since they set him up for the fall." Vila jumps up from his chair abruptly. I jump up just as fast to stop him.

"Don't you leave on me!" I warn him. "I need your help here. Nerjul wants me to summon Nathan so he can bring him back to the UnderWorld prison and he's using Nathan's kid for blackmail. He won't let him go unless Nathan returns to the UnderWorld to take his place. I don't know what to do."

Vila lets out an exasperated sigh. "I cannot help in this matter, Mr. Monsento. However, I would advise you do as Nerjul requests for now. I will return shortly, after I inform Ambrogio of Zeaflin's plight." Before I can object, Vila vanishes with a puff of blue smoke.

———————— ◆ ————————

The school day drags by slowly. Try as I might, I just cannot concentrate on today's lessons. My lack of focus earns me a D on today's vocabulary quiz, as well as a scolding from my English teacher, Mrs. Harris, who mistakes my lack of attention for daydreaming. When the end-of-school-day bell rings, I jam my books into my backpack and rush out before Mrs. Harris can intercept me for another tongue-lashing on my quiz results. I throw a quick glance in her direction on my way out and note her deep frown of disapproval for my poor scholastic performance today. I can feel her eyes follow me out the door and down the hall.

Billy and Toby are already waiting by Toby's locker by the time I wade my way through the crowded hallway, bustling with our excited schoolmates, all blissfully unaware of the afterlife and its tribulations. Ordinarily, the three of us would be chattering away with them since Friday is the last day of school before summer, but not anymore. Not with the horrible task of summoning a spirit to return him to an UnderWorld prison and definitely not with a possible prison sentence looming over Zeaflin's head. Billy and Toby look as miserable as I feel.

"We'd better hurry to Mr. Monsento's," Toby urges. "My mom doesn't have to work tonight so she asked me to come home by 6:30 pm. She invited her friend Alfred over and she wants me to help her make a '*special dinner*' for him." Toby's face puckers up; Billy's face joins it in sympathy.

I lead the way out and we power-walk to Monsento's house. We're almost there when, out of the corner of my eye, I think I see a ghost face peeking out of the bushes of the house next to Monsento's place. I slow down a little to look at the ghost full on but there is nothing there. I consider asking the boys if they saw anything but they're already past the bushes, so I decide it was probably just the glare of the sun in my eyes and hasten my pace to catch up to them.

Even though we're a few minutes early, Monsento is already waiting on the front porch when we walk up the path. He hurries down the stairs to meet us halfway, obviously anxious to get started.

"All right, let's hit the road. Toss your bags into the trunk so I can drop you off home after we collect the personal item," Monsento says rapidly. Then his eyes focus behind us and he raises his arm to give a hearty wave to his neighbor across the street, peeking out from the top of his front bushes. The neighbor doesn't acknowledge the wave. Instead he turns away and vanishes behind the hedge.

"I left the toolbox in the car so we're all set," Monsento continues, in his rapid nervous patter. "Got the pin?" he asks me. I nod. "Good," he says, opening the passenger side door of the car for me to hop in. Billy and Toby slip into the back seat while Monsento hustles into the driver seat. We pull away from the curb and head back to the cemetery in silence.

———————•◆•———————

The boys and I wait in the car while Abby heads for the care-taker's office, carrying the bribe. She returns shortly, looking dis-couraged. Obviously, the caretaker refused our offer. I roll down the window and lean out to hear the bad news.

"He doesn't want the pin," Abby tells me, stating what I've already deduced. "He said 'time is money, not jewelry.' I think that means we need to give him cash."

I sigh and tug out my wallet. I sold one of the silver doubloons Zeaflin gave me for this case, so I have some cash on me. I know better than to ask the kids if they brought any money with them. It seems lately their allowances have dried up. Or maybe they're hold-ing out on me and hoarding all their money in their piggy banks at home.

I pass two twenties and a ten to Abby; she passes the pin to me in return. "You can sell this to offset the expense," she offers.

I give her my best grateful smile. "Thanks, kid. I'll give you what-ever's leftover."

Abby shakes her head. "That's okay," she says before trotting back to the caretaker's office with the three bills.

———————•◆•———————

After about five minutes, Abby returns with the caretaker on her heels. "All set?" I call out my window. She nods, so the boys and I hop out of the car and into the afternoon sun.

The caretaker walks up to me and stops short, giving me a long steady stare with his squinty little eyes, which I defiantly try to return but my nerves are just about shot. He is chewing on a piece of grass so I focus instead on his jaw moving around, like a cow chewing cud. When the caretaker finally finishes staring me down, he spits the shredded grass onto the ground and turns his disconcerting gaze to the toolbox in Billy's hands.

"If one of the visitors sees you chipping at one of the tombstones, you're on your own," he warns.

"Yeah, we know," I respond, anxious to get away from him.

"And I'll have to notify the Hammersly family if you do get caught. They'll probably press charges," the caretaker says.

"Yeah, we get it," I reply. "Come on, kids." I step away from the caretaker and head down the path, not bothering to look behind to see if the kids are following.

As we approach the Hammersly family plot, I look around for any living visitors or ghost shimmers but see no one. This time, I ask Toby to keep watch on the path in front of us and Abby to keep an eye on the path behind, disregarding Billy's indignant glare. I hope the personal item on Martin's grave is small and easy to extract. It's definitely not as large as a shoe, that much I can tell from a distance.

Billy pulls out in front of our troop and strides purposefully toward the gravestone. I think he might still be pouting about the lookout switcheroo, so I decide to let him perform the extraction. And while it won't spare me a citation if we get caught because I'm aiding and abetting, maybe the charge will be more lenient if I let Billy chip away at the granite because I didn't vandalize the grave directly.

When the three of us finally catch up to Billy at the gravesite, he looks at me questioningly. "Do you want me to chisel out the personal item?" he asks. I give him a nod so he drops to his knees to examine the tombstone.

"Is it Martin's?" Abby asks from behind me.

"Yeah," Billy replies and opens the toolbox.

"What's the item, kid?" I ask.

Billy digs through the box and pulls out a small flat-headed screwdriver before answering. "I think it's a watch...a watch *face*, anyway. But it's hard to tell because the glass in front is all scratched up and foggy."

I turn to Abby and Toby. "Go keep a sharp lookout for anybody coming up the path," I tell them. "In both directions," I add. Abby rolls her eyes and follows Toby to the mound where Billy stood the last time we were here. They stand back-to-back to watch for anyone coming up the path in either direction. That covered, I turn away from them to supervise the extraction.

Billy slips the head of the screwdriver behind the embedded object and wiggles the handle back and forth. "Think it will come out?" I ask him. Billy doesn't answer. Instead he grabs a small hammer out of the box and hits the handle of the screwdriver with it. After a couple of hits, the object pops out of the granite and falls onto the grass. It's a watch all right, but definitely not functional now. My guess is that Dad meant to give his watch to his son when he got older but never had the chance.

"Okay, pass it here," I say, holding out my hand to accept the broken watch. Personal item in hand, I want to get out of here as soon as possible so I motion to Billy to pack up the toolbox. After he drops the hammer and screwdriver into the box, the two of us hurry over to join Toby and Abby on the path and head toward the exit to the car. I'm just settling into the driver's seat when a blur of movement outside my driver's side window catches my eye. I jerk away involuntarily, startled.

"What is it, Mr. Monsento?" Toby asks from the passenger seat next to me. "Was it a bee or something?" He looks past my shoulder with a confused expression. I turn back to look out the window with him and see nothing is there.

"Did any of you see a ghost outside my window a moment ago?" I ask. All three kids say no and look outside in all directions. Then they say no again and give me a worried look. Okay, so I must have imagined it. My nerves are completely frayed; I'll probably be seeing vampires in the back seat next. "Yeah, it must have been a bee," I say and fire up the car engine to start our journey home.

After I drop the kids off at each of their houses, I head straight to Manny's pawnshop to sell Marzee's old pin. It takes nearly an hour of haggling until I finally wear Manny down and he agrees to buy the pin from me for two hundred bucks. Not a bad profit for the day. It's only after I sit down to dinner that I realize I forgot to tell the kids about Vila's visit. Not that it matters; it's not like he was much use anyway.

After dinner, I decide to call it a day. It's a bit early for a grown man to go to bed but I can only take so much stress before my body wears out. I slip on my pajamas, throw a robe on, and sink into my easy chair in front of the TV, where I'm sure I'll be fast asleep soon enough.

Chapter 12

There is a soft breeze stirring the curtains on my window when I wake up in the middle of the night. At first, I'm not sure why I woke up but then I hear a fluttering noise, like bird wings, under my bed. I hold my breath. What could be making that noise? I look over at my bedside lamp and consider turning it on. I don't really want to see what's under my bed but I can't just lie here and ignore the whirring flutter, so I reach out and switch on the lamp. The noise stops immediately. I take a deep breath and lean over to look under the bed.

When I do, I come face to face with Martin!

He must be the ghost I thought I saw in the bushes near Monsento's house and that Monsento later saw outside his car window. Has Martin been following us around all afternoon?

I scramble out of bed and pull back the bedspread to look at the ghost boy underneath. "What are you doing here, Martin? How did you escape Nerjul?" I ask in a whisper, flipping off the bed lamp in case Mom or Dad wake up and see my light is on. Martin floats silently out from under the bed, opposite where I am standing. He puts something on my bed and begins to turn into a hazy outline of himself.

"Wait! Don't go! Let me help you," I whisper sharply, stepping around the bed toward the vanishing ghost boy. The haze that was Martin swirls toward my open window and disappears so I turn back to my bed to see what he left there. It's a bracelet, gold in color, with a small pink butterfly dangling off the chain. I open the clasp and place it on my wrist before I walk over to the window and look out at the street. Martin has rematerialized and is standing under the street lamp outside of my house, gazing up toward my bedroom window. When he sees my face appear, he gestures for me to come outside. It's late and I probably shouldn't, but if I don't follow him now he might never come back and we'll lose him. I quickly pull on a pair of jeans, throw a T-shirt over my pajama top and sneak out the back door off the kitchen to join Martin under the street light.

———— ♦ ————

The full moon casts an eerie blue glow over the deserted street as I follow the ghost boy. He stops periodically to look behind him and to urge me to keep following with a wave of his translucent arm. I wonder where he is leading me and whether I should keep following or turn back toward home before I travel too far.

After we walk a little over three blocks, Martin finally stops and waits for me to catch up. Then he points to a house in front of us. I stand beside him and look at the place he has led me to this night:

a standard two-story brick house with a large porch and neatly trimmed bushes planted in front. I see nothing special about it until I notice a frail, gray-haired woman, wrapped in a pink shawl, is sitting under the porch light in a rocking chair. She is bent over, embroidering something that looks like a pillowcase. The woman glances up from her needlepoint, spots us standing on the front path, and gives us a welcoming smile. Then she rises stiffly from her chair and beckons for us to approach. The woman appears to be able to see Martin so I wonder if she's a ghost. If she is, she is very solid for a phantom.

Martin jumps into a run and literally flies up the steps to melt into the woman's arms. She embraces him tightly and then beckons to me again, so I walk up her front path and onto her porch. Martin pulls away and vanishes through the front door of the house, leaving me alone with the old woman.

"It's not every day that Martin brings me a living thing," she says to me with a chuckle. "Usually he collects ghost toads and spirit spiders and drops them on my front doorstep, just to horrify me, I think. But he is a boy, after all, and boys will be boys, living or not." The old woman turns to open her front door, then looks back over her shoulder at me. "There is a chill tonight and I see you have come without even a sweater, child. You must be cold. Why don't you come with me to the kitchen and I'll put the tea kettle on and set out a few cookies."

I'm thinking I should probably go back home in case my parents wake up and notice I am gone, but I'm curious. How did Martin escape the UnderWorld? Why did he lead me here? Is his father here? Based on her age, this woman is probably Martin's mother and she may have some answers, so I nod and follow her into the house.

As I step inside, the first thing I see is a room filled with bulky red velvet couches and chairs, all piled high with deep blue satin throw pillows. There is an Oriental rug with red and green flowers on the floor and a small potbelly stove in the corner. The stove is emitting a soft orange glow from a dying fire and I pause briefly in front of the embers to soak in their warmth while I assess the room. *What a cozy, comfortable space to relax*, I think to myself, wishing we could sit here instead. But the old woman continues walking down the hall that must lead to her kitchen so I hurry to join her before she notices I'm lagging behind.

There are many photographs of a baby with the woman, much younger than she is now, adorning the walls of the hallway leading to the kitchen. Occasionally, the woman is posing with a man that I assume must be Nathan, making the baby in the photos Martin. Just before we reach the kitchen, I catch sight of a photograph of Martin at the age he appears now as a ghost. It must have been taken shortly before he died so I stop to study it. In this picture, Martin is dressed in a snowsuit, watching a man kneeling in the snow tie the laces of his ice skates. I can't make out the man's face but he's probably Martin's father.

The old woman notices I've paused in the hallway and turns back to gaze at the photograph with me. "That was Martin's first time trying to ice skate," she tells me wistfully. "His father bought him the skates as a Christmas present from Santa Claus. When Martin tore open the gift and saw those skates, he was so excited, he just couldn't wait to try them out." I look over at the woman and catch a trace of a tear trailing down the grooves of her wrinkled cheek.

"Did he like ice skating?" I ask, looking back at the photograph. The old woman heaves out a heavy sigh.

"He did…for a short time," she replies and places her hand on my arm to guide me to her kitchen table. I take a seat while Martin's mother fills the tea kettle and places it on the stove. As the water boils, she pulls out a box of ginger snaps and tosses a few of them onto a plate that she then pushes toward me. "Martin's favorite cookie," she confides with a sad smile. "Of course, he can't eat them now but he does like to suck on them every once in a while."

When I reach forward to take one of the cookies, she notices the butterfly bracelet and a stern look replaces her smile. "Martin! Have you been in my jewelry box again?" she calls out to the hall-way behind me. I turn around just in time to catch Martin staring down at his shoes in the kitchen doorway, before he fades away and vanishes.

The teakettle lets out a sharp whistle and the old woman returns to making us tea. I unlatch the bracelet. "I'm sorry," I say, my cheeks burning. "I didn't know it was yours." The old woman puts a cup of steaming tea in front of me.

"However would you know, dear?" she responds, giving me a kind smile. "Martin obviously wants you to have it, child, so go ahead and keep it. I used to wear that bracelet when Martin was just a baby. He really liked that butterfly." Then she laughs softly. "Liked to chew on it, that is. You might still be able to feel the small dents he made in the metal with his tiny teeth."

The woman motions for me to put the bracelet back on, so I do. She's right; I can feel the tiny nicks he put in the metal as a baby. "Thank you," I say. Then I realize we've never introduced ourselves. "My name is Abby Grant."

"And I am Annette Hammersly, Martin's mother, which I imagine you've already inferred." I nod and take a sip of the tea.

"You can see ghosts. I worried I was the only one who could but I suppose it makes sense there would be others. Is yours a natural talent? Mine is not," Annette divulges.

"Nor mine," I reply. Annette cocks her head to one side in curiosity.

"It's a long story," I say, trying to suppress a yawn.

"And the hour is late," Annette observes with a glance at the clock. "Already almost 12:30 in the morning."

Even though it's late and I'm feeling sleepy, I decide I should try to find out why Martin led me here before I head for home. If his mother knows, that is. I don't dare ask her how he escaped the UnderWorld!

"Do you know why Martin led me here?" I ask.

Annette shakes her head. "I imagine he wanted you to meet me. Perhaps he has some affection for you, dear," she replies. Then she sighs. "I'd ask him for you but Martin doesn't speak; he never has.

When he was living, he was diagnosed with autism. Unfortunately, it still afflicts him in the afterlife too."

"I'm sorry to hear that," I say, feeling sad. Poor Martin. I guess we'll never know for sure why he led me to his mother. Maybe he really did want me to meet her because he likes me. He did give me her bracelet, after all.

I take a deep breath and decide it's time to ask about Nathan. If Annette can see and talk to Martin, she must be able to see Nathan too. And if Nathan has come out from in-between to visit his wife, we can arrange for his asylum before Nerjul forces us to summon him on Wednesday.

"Is Martin's father here too?" I ask, watching Annette closely for any sign of discomfort. But she only looks saddened by the question.

"Martin's father, Nathan, is deceased. I've never seen him here-- nor anywhere else, for that matter. I even visited his gravesite several times in hope I might find him there but, while I did see several other ghosts in the graveyard, I never saw Nathan." Annette stares off into space, a faraway look in her eyes. "Never Nathan." Then she looks back at me and a smile crosses her lips. "He must reside else- where--heaven, I suppose."

I swallow down the lump in my throat at the thought of how awful it would be if Annette found out her husband wasn't in heaven all these years but was in the UnderWorld. And imprisoned, on top of that!

I place my tea cup down on the table and rise from my seat. "Thank you so much for the tea, Mrs. Hammersly, but I should go home now. If my parents wake up and find me gone, they'll be so worried."

"Of course, dear. Shall I walk you home?" Annette offers. While I'm a little nervous about walking home alone in the middle of the night, I can't see how a little old lady could provide much protection so I decide to decline.

"That's okay, I live only a few blocks down the street."

Annette frowns. "You'll call me when you arrive home then, won't you? I'll worry the whole night long if I don't know for certain you made it safely back to your house."

"I'll be fine but yes, I'll call the second I get home," I promise.

Annette walks with me to her living room to see me out the front door. As I approach the threshold, a familiar object resting on a side table next to the door catches my eye. My breath seizes up in my throat. That looks a lot like Vila's "lost" OtherWorld talisman, the one Zeaflin gave to Monsento to use!

"Where did you get that?" I ask, trying not to show my excitement. Annette follows my gaze.

"Oh dear! I forgot I left that out," she says with a troubled frown. Then she studies me. "You know what that is, don't you?" I nod but change the story a bit regarding why I know what it is.

"I have a friend who is a medium. He has an object just like that that he uses to summon spirits. He calls it a talisman."

"You're right, dear; it is called a talisman. I use it to summon Martin whenever he goes missing for too long. He does like playing out in the living realm but it's important for a mother to keep track of her boy," Annette declares.

I wonder, *Did Annette summon Martin out of the UnderWorld with this talisman? Can an OtherWorld talisman do that? Could ours?*

"May I see your talisman?" I ask, anxious to examine it so I can report back to Monsento and the boys about my discovery.

Annette walks over to the table and picks up her totem to hand to me. I roll it over in my hand. It has the same three faces carved on it, just like Vila's old talisman. Only this totem isn't ivory; it's some sort of pale gray wood I've never seen before. On the bottom of the talisman there is a symbol, carved deep into the wood. I almost drop the totem in my surprise. The symbol on the bottom of this totem matches one of the symbols carved in Monsento's door! Zeaflin's symbol!

"Are you all right, dear? You look so pale all of a sudden," Annette says, touching my arm lightly.

"Where did you get this?" I ask, trying to calm myself.

Annette smiles cryptically. "I doubt you'll believe me but I'll be happy to tell you the story behind that totem, if you'd like. Tomorrow afternoon, perhaps, over cookies and milk?"

I really don't want to wait until tomorrow to hear how Annette came to own a talisman with Zeaflin's symbol carved on it, but it is getting late and tomorrow is a school day so, with a heavy heart, I agree to come back tomorrow to hear her story.

———•◆•———

The street is spooky without the distraction of following a ghost boy to a place unknown, and I'm glad it's only a few short blocks before I reach the comfort of home. I pull back the outer screen door and open the inner door that leads into the kitchen slowly, taking the time to peer into the gloom. My heart is racing a mile a minute and I can scarcely breathe for fear that Dad might be sitting in the shadows, ready to ambush me with strict questions regarding where I've been at such a late hour of the night. Luckily, his soft snore travels down the stairwell to assure me it's safe. If Mom was awake, Dad would be too, so they both must still be sleeping. I tiptoe up the stairs and slip into my bedroom.

Now safe in my room, I grab my cell phone from the corner desk where I left it to make the brief phone call to Annette to inform her that I made it home safely. After I hang up, I turn the phone off, remove my outer clothes and crawl under the warm blankets of my bed. I need to hurry back to sleep or I'll never be able to wake up in time for the school bus tomorrow. I can't wait to tell Billy and Toby about what I discovered tonight! And I can't wait for the school day to end so I can find out the story behind Annette's talisman!

My excitement keeps me up for several more hours, even though I will myself to calm down and relax. It seems like I've only just fallen asleep when the alarm clock rattles and I have to drag myself into the shower to get ready for the day.

———•◆•———

I look for Billy and Toby on the bus ride to school but they must have decided to walk today. The one day I'm bursting to tell them important news just *has* to be the day they decide not to ride the bus! And since the boys have some sort of field trip out to the natural history museum today, I'm not going to have an opportunity to talk to them now until after the final class of the day lets out. For distraction, I crack open my biology book and try to read chapter twenty before my 1 pm biology class, but I can't concentrate so I put the book back into my backpack and stare out the bus window instead. It's going to be a very long day!

———◆———

I've almost finished solving the last math problem in the back of chapter seventeen when the final school bell rings. All the other kids pile up their books and rush out of the classroom eagerly but I stay the few extra minutes to complete the last equation so I won't have to worry about it as homework tonight. As I gather up my books to put them into my backpack, Ms. Grady walks up to me from the back of the room. Her bulky body blocks out the afternoon sun and casts a deep shadow across my desk.

"You did very well on last week's math test, Abigail; your parents will be very proud. Have you ever considered tutoring some of the less talented students?" she asks in her low, gravelly voice. I look up at her towering form. Ms. Grady is a tall, stocky woman with jet black hair that she wears cropped short like a military man. She is hovering over my desk expectantly, waiting for my answer. I clear my throat.

"Thanks, Ms. Grady, but I'm pretty busy with school and mowing lawns," I reply, standing up from my desk and tugging the backpack onto my shoulders. Behind her, I see Toby and Billy are waiting for me by the classroom door, snickering and whispering to each other. Ms. Grady abruptly spins around. I can't see her expression but the boys immediately stop snickering and a look of fear crosses Toby's face.

Billy gives a cheery wave. "Hi, Ms. Grady. Lovely afternoon, isn't it?" he says with his most charming smile.

Ms. Grady just grunts in reply and turns back to me. "Be careful of the company you keep, Abigail," she advises and with a shake of her head, she trundles to her desk in the front of the room to sit down and grade papers. Now free to go, I rush out to join Toby and Billy, anxious to tell them what I found out about Martin and his mother last night.

"I have something to show you guys," I say, as we begin our walk down the school hall toward the exit. I pause for dramatic effect before I hold out my arm for Billy and Toby to see the butterfly bracelet. They both look at the bracelet with a puzzled expression. Then Billy gives me a bored shrug. "Not really your style, Abs," he comments.

"Martin gave it to me last night," I inform him, giving the bracelet a little shake in his face.

Suddenly, Billy isn't so bored. "He did? How? He's locked away in a bottle in the UnderWorld."

"Not anymore, he isn't. Martin escaped somehow and came to my house in the middle of the night. He made some noise, which woke me up, and I found him hiding under my bed. When I tried to talk to him, he left this bracelet, turned into a haze, and flew out my bedroom window," I respond.

Billy's face drops into a frown. "Martin got away? Nerjul might find out he escaped and come looking for him. You should have stopped him, Abby." I give him a long, cool stare.

"And how do you think I'd have gone about stopping him?" I retort, half-tempted not to tell him about last night. Billy opens his mouth to respond but I quickly interrupt with my news.

"Martin didn't get away, Billy; I followed him to his mother's house. She's still alive, although pretty old now." Billy and Toby stare at me, both speechless.

Billy recovers first. "Is Nathan there?" he asks.

I shrug. "I didn't see him and Martin's mother said she hasn't seen him either. She even went to the cemetery, looking for him at his gravesite, but he wasn't there."

"Martin's mother can see ghosts?" Toby asks, his eyes wide with surprise.

"She sure can. She said she saw some ghosts at the cemetery and she sees Martin too. In fact, she can summon him whenever she wants using a totem talisman just like Vila's, except hers is wood.

I think that may be how Martin escaped Nerjul--his mother summoned him out. *And* I think her talisman used to be Zeaflin's talisman," I tell them, enjoying the look of shock on both boys' faces. Then Billy decides I must be mistaken.

"Mr. Zeaflin doesn't use a totem, Abby. That's an *OtherWorld* talisman," he scoffs.

"Well, this totem has Zeaflin's symbol carved in the bottom," I rebut. "Anyway, Martin's mother invited me to come back to hear the story behind how she acquired it. If you two promise to behave, you can come with me."

"Sure," Billy quickly replies. "I want to see this supposed totem of Zeaflin's first-hand." "Me too," Toby adds. But at least he looks like he believes me.

———— ◆ ————

Mrs. Hammersly is on the front porch when we arrive, sipping from a steaming cup of what is most probably tea. She watches us come up the front path and onto her porch before speaking. "You've brought some friends. How lovely," she declares.

Billy steps forward and offers her his hand. "I'm Billy and he's Toby." Billy gives a half-nod toward Toby.

Mrs. Hammersly takes Billy's hand and allows him to pump her arm in a quick handshake. "I am most pleased to meet you, Billy and Toby. I am Annette Hammersly," she says, before giving me a troubled look that I think might be concern over discussing Martin and the talisman in front of the boys.

"Billy and Toby can see ghosts too, Mrs. Hammersly. In fact, the three of us run a detective agency for ghosts in the StopOver of the OtherWorld," I explain.

Annette looks at the boys and then back at me. "I've never heard of such a thing," she responds. "How amazing. And you are not afraid of the ghosts?"

Billy lets out a short snort. "We know how to handle ourselves," he replies haughtily.

Annette gives Billy an amused smile. "I am certain you do. Why don't you all come inside for some milk and cookies? I'd love to hear more about your detective agency and how you came about seeing ghosts." She gestures toward the front door of her house.

———•◆•———

After we are all settled in with the cookies and milk, I decide to take the lead. "Mrs. Hammersly–"

"Please call me Annette," Martin's mother interrupts.

"Annette, could you tell us the story behind your talisman?" I ask.

"And can we see it?" Billy adds, still unconvinced that Zeaflin once owned a totem talisman.

Annette hesitates a moment before she rises from the table and heads down the hallway toward the back of her house. After a few minutes, she returns, carrying the small wooden totem I'd seen the night before. She hands it to Billy.

"Please be careful with it. It is how I bring Martin home when he's outside playing and is gone for too long."

Billy turns the totem over in his hand, examining it closely. Toby leans in and points to the symbol carved in the bottom. "Abby was right, Billy. That's Mr. Zeaflin's mark," he affirms.

Annette looks confused. "Whose mark, dear?"

"Mr. Zeaflin is a friend of ours. He's an UnderWorld realm walker," Toby replies.

Annette gives him an indulgent smile and shakes her head lightly. "If your friend is from the UnderWorld, then you must be mistaken, dear. This totem was given to me by an angel. Martin's guardian angel, to be precise."

Chapter 13

The three of us are stunned. Now we simply must hear her story! I lean forward in my chair, almost knocking over my milk glass in my excitement. "Please go on, Mrs....I mean Annette," I implore.

Annette sighs. "It's a rather sad tale but I will share it with you. After all these years, I've had no one to whom I could tell this story. No one who would believe me anyway..." She trails off with a distant stare.

"We'll believe you," Toby says quietly. Annette looks back at the three of us and, with a smile of gratitude, she stands up and heads into the hall behind us. She returns with a photograph of Martin and his father– the one where Martin is going ice skating for the first time– and places it in the middle of the table for us all to see.

"This photo was taken the day that Martin died, a Christmas day so many years ago," she tells us in a voice laced with sorrow. "He was so anxious to try out the new ice skates that Santa brought him, so we agreed to take him out right after breakfast. We bundled Martin up in his little snowsuit and put on his little mittens, taking care our dear boy would stay warm. It was a very cold day, so Nathan and I never suspected that the lake ice wasn't thick enough yet for ice skating. I took this photo," Annette pauses to run a finger over the picture glass, "just before they slid their way over to the lake shore." Billy reaches out and gently touches Annette's hand. She looks up at him and smiles wistfully before returning her gaze to the photograph and continuing her tale.

"Nathan took Martin out onto the ice, holding his hand to keep him from falling down. It was awkward going in the beginning; never having been on ice before, Martin was all scrambling legs and arms. But Nathan eventually succeeded in leading Martin to the middle of the lake, where the ice was smooth as glass, and hand in hand, the two of them began to glide. It was then I heard a horrible cracking sound I hope to never hear again. I jumped up and yelled for Nathan to hurry back to the shore, but it was too late. Nathan plunged through the ice and Martin immediately followed. I ran full out, not caring if the ice gave way under me, slipping and sliding my way toward them, but by the time I reached the hole they fell into, they were gone. In my desperation, I dove into the icy water. The cold of it took my breath away and I felt faint." Annette abruptly stands up from the table and looks out her kitchen window, hugging herself with her arms as if still feeling the chill of the water.

"Did you die?" Toby asks in a hushed voice. I give him a light punch in the arm.

"She's not a ghost, Toby," I scold. Annette turns back to look at us. Her eyes are red and watery.

"No, I did not die but I wished I had. A local fisherman, trying out a little ice fishing that day, saw me dive into the water. He pulled me from the lake and brought me to his shed, where he wrapped me in a heavy blanket. I don't remember much after that. I might have fainted, or maybe I was in shock. I'm not sure how I got home but I imagine the fisherman must have carried me and then called for a doctor because I woke up that evening in my bed, with a nurse sitting in a chair beside me. I became hysterical, begging them to go rescue Martin and Nathan but of course, it was much too late. They sent divers down to retrieve the bodies the following day." Annette heaves out a heavy sigh and sits back down at the table.

"And that's when Martin's guardian angel appeared?" Billy asks.

Annette shakes her head. "No. He didn't appear at all, dear. He came to me in a dream I had after I visited the lake a few weeks later. By that time, the nurse had gone and I was all alone. They wanted to call my mother to ask her to come stay with me, but I told them I had no living parents. I didn't want company, I wanted Martin and Nathan. So I waited for the nurse to leave and I went to the lake to join them. But by then the ice was thick and I couldn't break it, not even with a shovel."

I put my hand on my chest and swallow down the lump I have in my throat. This is all horribly sad and I can feel my eyes start to sting. I look over at Billy. He is staring uncomfortably at his milk glass. Toby is chewing at his lower lip and a small droplet of blood is welling up where he must have bitten too hard. Annette shakes her head as if trying to shake away the bad memories and then reaches for a cookie.

"I'm sorry, children. This is not a tale for young people," she says, biting into the cookie with a snap.

Billy looks up from his milk glass. "That's all right, Annette. You said Martin's guardian angel came to you in a dream that night?" he prompts.

Annette nods. "Thwarted by the thick ice, I returned home. I was so angry, so *frustrated*. I saw the sleeping pills the nurse left behind for me and swallowed the few that remained in the vial. There weren't enough of them for me to join Martin and Nathan but they did put me into a deep slumber. It was then that Martin's guardian angel visited me in my dreams."

Annette takes another bite of her cookie and pushes the plate toward me. I reach forward, never taking my eyes off Annette. My hand fumbles around the plate until it homes in on one of the ginger snaps. I robotically bring the cookie to my mouth and chew.

"He was a beautiful angel, with gold-colored eyes and silky black hair that hung past his shoulders. He was wearing a gray-colored suit with a green tie and there was a fedora on his head." Annette chuckles. "Certainly not the attire I'd expect from an angel. But when he smiled, I lost all doubts. This angel's smile was simply amazing. When he smiled, he had this glow about him, like the warm glow of a candle in a cold, dark room. We walked together through a field of tall grass where the air smelled of honeysuckle—"

"What's honeysuckle?" Toby interrupts. I throw him an annoyed look but Annette merely smiles.

"A type of flower, dear," she replies before picking up from where she left off. "While we strolled, the angel told me he was Martin's guardian and that he was sorry for failing to protect my boy from the lake. He said he met with the OtherWorld ruler, which I assumed was angel-speak for heavenly God, and pleaded for Martin to be allowed to live. Unfortunately, the ruler refused to bend the rules; Martin had died and there would be no resurrection. So Martin's angel said he would arrange for my boy's spirit to reside in the living realm with me instead. I told him I doubted I'd be able to see Martin and keep track of him if he was a ghost, at which the angel laughed and told me to look for a stone and a wooden totem he called a talisman when I awoke. If I added my blood to the stone, he explained, I would be able to see Martin. And with the talisman, I could summon Martin to me whenever he strayed too far from home."

"Was the stone pearly white with a sharp edge?" I ask breathlessly.

Annette tilts her head to one side. "You have one too?" she asks. I nod. "Where did you get yours? From your guardian angel?"

I feel a laugh swell up in my chest. "We got ours from Zeaflin, and he's definitely no angel," I reply. Toby gives me a punch in my thigh under the table.

"Mrs. Hammersly's stone is a magic stone that helps her see ghosts, just like the one Zeaflin gave us, Abby," Toby retorts angrily. "So he obviously *used* to be an angel!"

"It sure sounds like our stone, Abs," Billy says. "Maybe Toby is right."

I stare at Toby, trying to fathom how Zeaflin could possibly have ever been an angel. He looks more like a cross between a zombie and a vampire. And then it hits me. That time in the columbarium when Zeaflin reached out to stroke my hair, he called me Annie. I thought he was just confused and misremembered my name but he must have been thinking about Annette. He apologized for failing me, which at the time seemed a strange thing to say since he hadn't exactly *failed* me; he'd only made me angry. But if Zeaflin was Martin's guardian angel and if he still feels responsible for Martin's death, then his comment makes perfect sense.

"Did you used to call yourself Annie?" I ask Annette. She gives me a puzzled smile at what must seem an odd question to pop out of nowhere.

"At one time I did, but I haven't called myself Annie for many years now, dear. That is a young girl's name and I am a little too old for it now," she replies.

That clinches it! Zeaflin must be Martin's guardian angel...or rather, he was. I wonder what happened after Zeaflin visited Annette in her dream to cause him to switch from an angel of the OtherWorld into an UnderWorld bounty hunter?

I pop out of my thoughts to discover Annette is looking at me, still wearing her puzzled smile. She must be waiting for me to explain why I asked her if she used to call herself Annie. Fortunately, Billy isn't interested in why I asked and interrupts to bring the conversation back to the night of Annette's dream.

"Where did you find the stone and totem?" he asks, drawing Annette's attention away from me.

"On Martin's bed, next to his favorite teddy bear," she replies. "There was a scroll with a spell of some sort and instructions explaining how to summon Martin should he wander too far or be gone too long."

Somewhere down the hall, a clock chimes five times. I look at my watch in disbelief that it's already 5 pm and time for us to head for home. I stand up from my seat. "We had better get going, guys, or our parents are going to wonder what happened to us," I tell the boys before I turn to Annette. "Thank you for the milk and cookies. And for telling us about Martin and his guardian angel." Billy passes Annette her totem and we all walk to the front door. With heartfelt goodbyes, the three of us step outside into the late afternoon sun and head down the path.

We're nearly halfway down the block when Annette calls out after us, "Please come visit again soon! I'd like to hear about how you all came to be detectives for ghosts." I feel my cheeks flush and look around to see if anyone has overheard Annette but luckily, no one is around to hear her strange request.

"Do you think Mr. Zeaflin's talisman is how Martin escaped Nerjul? That Annette summoned him out?" Toby asks. He seems excited for some reason.

"Maybe," I reply. "How else could he have escaped?"

Toby lets out a bubbly laugh. "That's it!" he exclaims. "We can summon Mr. Zeaflin out too, using Vila's talisman! Mr. Monsento has Zeaflin's old cane for the personal item!" I look over at Billy, whose eyes have widened in a "eureka" moment.

"That's a great idea!" Billy declares, giving Toby a high-five. But I think of Zeaflin's red glowing eyes that day in the columbarium when Marzee angered him, and I have my doubts. I think Zeaflin might be something more than just a ghost like Kayla and something more than just a realm walker like Marzee. They were summoned without any trouble, but Zeaflin...I'm not so sure what he is and I worry it might not be safe.

"Guys, we don't know what might happen if we try to summon Zeaflin. He's *different* from the more conventional spirits," I point out. "Besides, we'd need a spell, a powerful spell, which we don't have."

"But Annette must have a spell like that if she pulled Martin from the UnderWorld. We can ask her if we can borrow it," Toby replies.

I shake my head. "Toby, I really don't want to try to summon Zeaflin without knowing if it's safe for him *and* us."

"We can ask Vila; he'd know if it's safe," Billy replies. "Let's go to Mr. Monsento's house and see if he'll conjure Mary. We can have Mary ask Vila if it's safe to summon Zeaflin from the UnderWorld."

I think about this. I'm a little afraid of what the UnderWorld will do if we summon Zeaflin away from them; they're sure to know who did it and send someone. Of course, supposedly that someone would be Nerjul. While I'm considering the consequences of summoning Zeaflin, Toby and Billy move forward with their plan.

"Mom is working late tonight so I can go to Mr. Monsento's house right now and ask him if he'll conjure Mary for us. But I think we'll need a third in the conjuring circle. Can you slip away, Billy? Maybe say you're having dinner at my house, keeping me company until my mom gets home?"

"Great idea, Toby. For extra insurance, I'll add that we have some homework we should do together," Billy replies, giving Toby a sly smile. Then he turns to me. "We'll give you a call, Abby--let you know what we find out."

I'm concerned but since Vila will know the plan, he should be able to advise what the UnderWorld might do if we summon Zeaflin out. Besides, he'll probably need to process the paperwork for Zeaflin's asylum in the OtherWorld...that's if Zeaflin agrees to reside there on a permanent basis. He did once mention he has no interest in Halcyon, which is likely the best part of the OtherWorld to spend eternity.

While I'm thinking all this over, the boys give me a quick wave goodbye and peel off in the direction of Monsento's house. I turn away and head for home.

———— ◆ ————

The beef stew is bubbling so I ladle it out into a bowl, pour myself a glass of iced tea, and sit down to eat. No sooner do I pop the first spoonful in my mouth than I see movement in my backyard. It's Billy and Toby. *What brings them here?* I wonder. *Shouldn't they be home eating dinner?* I stand up to let them in.

"What brings you kids out here?" I ask the boys as they step through the door. "The summoning isn't until tomorrow."

Billy grins. "We have a plan, Mr. Monsento," he says. "Martin's mother has a spell and talisman that can summon ghosts out of the UnderWorld. We think we might be able to use them to summon Mr. Zeaflin out too." *Are these kids pulling my leg here?*

"And exactly what makes you think Martin's mother, and I presume by Martin you mean Martin *Hammersly*, has a spell and talisman?" I ask, thinking the stress of all this must have made the boys go off their rockers.

"We saw it...well, the talisman, at least. Martin's mom, Annette, summoned Martin out of the UnderWorld, although I don't think she knows that's where he was when she called him. He's at her house now...I think so anyway; we didn't see him there but Abby did," Toby responds.

I hold up a hand to interrupt. "Hold on a second. Abby found out where Nathan Hammersly lived?"

Toby nods. "Yeah. Martin somehow knew where Abby lived and he visited her house last night and led her to his mom. Abby took us to meet her this afternoon, just before we came over to see you," he replies. My heart dances a jig over the news that the kids know the location of Nathan's family abode. If he came out from in-between, Nathan is certain to have visited there!

"What about Nathan? Was he there too?" I ask with bated breath. But Billy shakes his head.

"I don't think so. Nathan's wife said she's seen other ghosts here in the living realm but she hasn't seen Nathan; she could be fibbing though. Anyway, even if he isn't with her, it's possible she might know where he is."

I mull this over. If this Annette does know where Nathan is, odds are he told her he escaped from an UnderWorld prison and not knowing us from Adam, she probably won't trust us enough to tell us where to find him. The question is, if she really can summon ghosts out of the UnderWorld, why didn't she summon her husband out too? Surely in all the years Nathan resided in the UnderWorld, she would have tried to summon him at least once. I decide the kids must be mistaken; Martin must have escaped some other way. Maybe Nerjul had a change of heart or, more likely, he didn't push the stopper of the vial down tight enough and Martin was able to uncork it and slip out. Of course, that doesn't explain how Martin got out of the UnderWorld. I'd bet that's a difficult place to leave without a hall pass.

"And guess what?" Toby exclaims with a big grin. "Annette's totem talisman has the exact same mark as one of the symbols that Mr. Zeaflin carved into your door. She said she got her totem from Martin's guardian angel, so we think that maybe Zeaflin was once an angel or something and he gave her the totem." *Say what now??*

I sink down into one of my kitchen chairs and stare up at the boys. Billy picks up where Toby left off without giving me a chance to recover from the shock. "Anyway, we came here to see if you'd conjure Mary for us so we can ask her to contact Vila before we set up a séance to call Zeaflin. Abby's worried something bad might happen if we try to summon Zeaflin so we thought we should ask Vila first if it's okay for us to do that or not." Billy stops talking and looks at me expectantly. I struggle to recover my composure so I can become the voice of reason since the boys seem to be fresh out of sanity today.

"Okay. Let's say for the sake of argument, that Martin's mother *does* have a talisman and spell that will pull Zeaflin out of the UnderWorld; what do you think is going to happen when…IF…we do that? One, they'll know we did it and heaven help us then. And two, they'll just drag Zeaflin right back anyway, probably after they smite us with hellfire," I say.

Toby huffs in annoyance. "One, so what if they know we did it? Nerjul said they can't do anything to us because of one of their treaties, remember?" he retorts.

"Yeah, the treaty of 1508," Billy interjects.

Toby nods vigorously. "Yeah, that one. And two, the Otherworld can give Mr. Zeaflin asylum."

I reach over and take a swig of my tea to moisten my suddenly very dry throat and give myself a chance to think. If we do rescue Zeaflin, and if Abby didn't have a break with reality and truly did see Martin in the living realm, Nerjul will have no cards left to play. Providing the OtherWorld takes in Martin, Nathan, *and* Zeaflin, that is. As for this "Zeaflin was an angel" nonsense the kids have dreamed up, I'm going to let that slide because that's just plain crazy talk.

"Okay, kids. Let's conjure Mary and ask her to send Vila over here, pronto. We should probably discuss this with him face to face," I say. Thus far, Vila's been reluctant to help but maybe the boys can convince him where I've failed.

"Thanks, Mr. Monsento," Toby murmurs, his defiance fading.

"And since this is your idea, you can lead the conjuring, kid," I tell Toby. Billy frowns but doesn't object. "And you get to try to convince Vila to help. I didn't tell you before but he came here yesterday morning. He knows all about Zeaflin and Martin's *detainment* but still he refused to provide any assistance beyond smoke-puffing back to the OtherWorld to update Ambrogio."

I sweep my hand toward the door that leads to my salon and wait until the boys exit before grabbing my stew and popping it into the refrigerator. If Vila does heed our request for a meeting, this could take a while.

While we eat dinner, Dad and Mom are discussing where we should travel for our summer vacation next month. I'm doing my best to act like I'm paying attention but my mind keeps wandering back to Annette and Zeaflin.

Was Zeaflin truly Annette's angel? It sure sounds like he was, so what happened? Did Martin's death spur him to leave the OtherWorld? If so, why? Martin is living as a ghost with his mother, exactly as he arranged, but that apparently wasn't enough to soothe Zeaflin's feelings of guilt.

"Abby?" Mom says, interrupting my thoughts. Both Mom and Dad are staring at me.

"Uh, sure. Philadelphia sounds good," I respond. I'm pretty sure I heard them mention Philadelphia.

Mom gives a little half-nod of approval. "We hadn't considered Philadelphia. That sounds like a good place, don't you think, Sam?"

Dad looks perplexed. Then he smiles at me. "We were suggesting Dallas but sure, I can see where you might mistake that for Phillie," he says with a chuckle. I feel my cheeks turn red.

"Sorry, Dad," I mumble. "I was thinking about final exams at school. They start the day after tomorrow." Dad gives me a sympathetic smile. I decide to use that excuse to head for my bedroom early.

"May I be excused? I think I should study a little more."

"Go ahead, kiddo," Dad responds cheerfully.

"Don't study too late, Abby. A good night's sleep is very important!" Mom adds.

———•◆•———

Alone in my room, I start thinking about Annette again. If Vila does agree we can summon Zeaflin, we're going to need her spell and maybe even her totem. I'm not sure Monsento's OtherWorld totem is strong enough. Sure, the UnderWorld finger talisman *might* be powerful enough but it's best not to take any chances. I glance at my bedside clock. 6:30 pm. *Could I sneak out? But what if Mom or Dad come up here and see me gone?* I grab my cell phone from the top drawer of my writing desk and dial Billy's number.

The phone rings a couple of times before Billy answers. "What's up, Abs? We're getting ready to conjure Mary," he says irritably.

"Could you call me on my home line--pretend you need help with a math problem or something? I need an excuse to get out of here so I can go to Annette's house and ask her for her spell and totem. Nerjul comes by tomorrow night so we need to hurry this up," I tell him in a near whisper so my parents don't overhear should they come up the stairs for some reason.

"Too dangerous, Abs. Remember the time you pretended you were going to hang out with my sisters? You know, when we hid in Mr. Monsento's bushes instead? Your parents checked up on you and found out you lied and—"

I cut him off, my cheeks burning hot. "I don't need a reminder about how I got us all in trouble that night," I respond sharply. "Could you *at least* ask Monsento to head over there after the conjuring and get the items? We're running out of time."

"What's the deal here, Billy?" I hear Monsento ask in the background.

"It's Abby. After the conjuring, she wants you to go to Annette's house and get her spell" comes Billy's distant reply.

Monsento's exasperated sigh travels through my cell receiver. "And her totem," I hastily remind Billy.

Billy's muffled voice says, "And she wants you to get Annette's talisman too."

"Swell," I hear Monsento grumble. "Then get over here so we can get this conjuring over with."

"Gotta run," Billy says and hangs up the phone. I stare out the window a minute before heading for my desk to try to study for the upcoming exams.

Chapter 14

"What did Mary say?" I ask, snapping out of my connection with her through the crystal ball.

"She said she'll head over to the Department of Living Affairs right away and ask Vila to come over here," Billy replies. I look at the clock over my mantel--7:00 pm already, better hurry. I turn to Toby.

"You stay here in case Vila arrives while we're gone. Billy and I will go visit this Annette and see if she'll be willing to let us borrow her spell." Not that I'm convinced that she has a spell powerful enough to rescue Zeaflin, but the kids seem to think so. Plus, there is still the mystery of how Martin got out of the UnderWorld, so who knows? Maybe they're right. Only one way to find out. I grab my car keys and usher Billy out the door.

I park the car at the curb in front of a brick house with a wrap-around porch that Billy indicates is the Hammersly abode. Billy jumps right out but I take a moment to look around. A furtive movement in the front bushes catches my eye. It's Martin. He is hiding in the shrubbery, watching Billy walk up the path. So Abby was right; Martin did escape the UnderWorld. I hop out of the car to catch up to Billy, who hasn't noticed Martin yet.

"The ghost kid is hiding in the front bushes. No, don't look! You might scare him off," I whisper sharply. We walk up the porch steps, taking care not to look in Martin's direction. Our footfall draws an old woman to the screen door. She recognizes Billy but gives me a perplexed look.

"Are you Billy's father?" she asks.

"He's the medium for our detective agency," Billy replies for me. "May we come in for a second? We have something we'd like to ask you." Mrs. Hammersly steps back from the screen door and gestures for us to come inside.

"Would you like a cup of tea?" she offers, her gaze behind us. We both turn and see that Martin has come inside with us. He darts past us and vanishes through the living room wall.

"Martin," I say, to let her know I can see him. That might help break the ice. It works. Annette relaxes and a pleased smile crosses her face.

"You are certainly a talented medium, if you can see him," she declares. "Most mediums only pretend to see ghosts."

"True, but I'm a special kind of medium," I reply, before I get straight to business. "Mrs. Hammersly, the kids tell me that you can summon Martin with some sort of spell and totem. Is this true?"

Annette's smile quickly morphs into a frown. "Why do you ask?" she responds, looking nervously over at Billy.

"We have a friend we might need to summon here. He's trapped in the UnderWorld and we'd like to use your spell and totem to pull him out," I explain.

"His name is Zeaflin," Billy adds. "We told you about him this afternoon."

Annette's frown deepens. "I'm sorry. My spell and talisman can't pull your friend out of the UnderWorld, or any other place, for that matter. I've tried to summon my husband with it many times, but it always failed," she responds. That is bad news. Nathan was probably in the UnderWorld when she tried to summon him, so her spell must not be very powerful after all. Maybe it can only draw a spirit already in the living realm.

"When was the last time you summoned Martin, Mrs. Hammersly?" I ask, to put a final nail in this coffin.

"Sunday night, I'd say around 10 pm. He was missing the entire day and I was worried," she replies.

Okay, no final nail yet. Sunday night was the night Nerjul kidnapped Martin. That would mean a hasty escape on Martin's part, so maybe Mrs. Hammersly's spell *is* a potent one.

"Can I see your spell and totem, Mrs. Hammersly?" I request, thinking I should be able to at least determine if her spell is similar to the complicated one I used last summer when I pulled that John Johnson ghost out of Halcyon for Zeaflin.

Annette hesitates, then heads down the hall. She soon returns holding a small wooden statue and a rolled-up parchment tied with a blue ribbon. She hands both to me and motions for Billy and me to take a seat on the sofa. I sink down onto the plush velvet, set the totem on the cushion next to me, and unfurl the parchment. Billy scooches over to look over my shoulder.

"What's it say, Mr. Monsento?" he asks, his head bumping into mine as he tries to get a closer look. I lean away from Billy and read over the spell. It's complicated all right, full of all kinds of tongue twisters and in some sort of bizarre language I've never seen before. I look up at Annette.

"I can't read this language. Can you? Do you know what this says in English?" I ask her. She shakes her head.

"I do," a cool voice echoes out from the front door. "May I come in, Mrs. Hammersly?" Vila requests.

"Mr. Vila!" Billy exclaims. He jumps up from the couch in his excitement, causing the totem on the seat between us to fall to the floor with a thud. I pick it up and rise to greet Vila, while Billy starts yammering at him about summoning Zeaflin. Vila stares down at the babbling boy with tightly pursed lips and a deeply furrowed brow so I decide to intervene and place a hand on Billy's shoulder to silence him.

Billy turns around to look at me. "What?" he asks, innocently. I give him a shake of my head and hold up the parchment for Vila to read.

Annette interrupts. "Who is this gentleman?" she asks, with a worried frown. Vila ignores the parchment I'm holding out for him and instead steps toward Annette.

"Mrs. Hammersly, I am Vila, an agent from the OtherWorld Department of Living Affairs." Annette gives him a skeptical look.

"He really is," I affirm. "Trust me on that one."

A sudden look of fear crosses Annette's face. "Has he come to take Martin away?" she asks, sinking down onto her sofa.

Vila takes a seat next to her. "Not at all," he assures her. "I am here because Ambrogio has sent me to help Martin and your husband Nathan." Annette looks at me questioningly.

"Ambrogio is the OtherWorld ruler...or rather, he was. He's abdicated his throne--right, Vila?" I say.

Vila frowns my way. "It is still transitional," he points out curtly.

"I don't understand," Annette says, visibly troubled. "Why does the OtherWorld ruler think Nathan and Martin need help? What sort of trouble are they in?" She looks at me again. I decide to let Vila bear the bad news. Vila glances at me to check if I'm going to answer her, while I look away to study a nearby painting of red poppies in a blue vase. Vila takes the hint.

"I hate to be the one to tell you this, but Nathan was a prisoner in the UnderWorld prison, Mrs. Hammersly. He escaped and the UnderWorld is trying to recapture him using Mr. Monsento here."

Hold on a minute. That sounds bad!

"I'm helping under duress," I hastily point out, giving Vila an indignant glare. Annette's hand flutters to her breast and her eyes dart from me to Vila.

"Nathan was in the UnderWorld? But *why*? He was a good man," she responds, her voice faltering.

"Yes, he was a good man. He still is. Unfortunately, as payment for the talisman and spell you possess, the UnderWorld ruler demanded a pure soul," Vila explains. "Nathan volunteered to go to the UnderWorld and be that pure soul."

Annette's face turns ashen. "The spell and totem are from the UnderWorld? They are the devil's work?" she gasps.

Vila looks irritated by her question. "No. They are the work of an old colleague of mine called Zeaflin. What you possess is one of his most powerful spells for summoning a spirit. In fact, it is so powerful that it does not require a personal item, and it appears it can even draw a spirit out of a vinculum in the UnderWorld detention center," he replies.

"Why did Zeaflin give it to Nathan's wife?" I quickly interject before Annette can ask about the vinculum thing. It's probably not a good idea to tell her right now that just recently, Martin was a prisoner in the UnderWorld too.

"Because he was Martin's guardian angel--right, Mr. Vila?" Billy pipes in. Vila cringes at the word "angel".

"More accurately, Zeaflin was assigned to look after Martin by the long-since dissolved Department of Living Aegis. The living called those agents guardian angels." Vila eyes Billy and puckers his lips. "Apparently, they still do. But that is not an official OtherWorld designation," he clarifies before turning back to answer me. "Zeaflin gave this spell to Mrs. Hammersly because he felt he had failed her when her son fell through the ice and drowned. Aegis agents cannot anticipate everything and Ambrogio did his best to assure Zeaflin of this, but Zeaflin was adamant that he set things right. First, he requested resurrection, something the OtherWorld had not done for thousands of years. Naturally, Ambrogio refused. We just don't do that sort of thing anymore; it causes too much distress to the living, who prefer a natural order in their realm. Thus, Zeaflin took matters into his own hands and created the spell and the talisman you now hold in your hand, Mr. Monsento, and requested permission to give them to Martin's mother so she could keep him with her in the living realm."

Now *I* need to sit down. I'm sinking into the chair across from Annette and Vila when a cell phone suddenly whistles out a merry tune. The music startles everyone except Vila, who only looks annoyed by the disruption. Billy mutters a quick "sorry" and pulls the phone out of his jacket to answer the call.

"Hi Mom. Yeah, we're almost finished with our homework." He pauses. "No, you don't need to come pick me up; Toby's mother can drop me off when she gets home." He pauses again, glancing at the three of us staring up at him from our seats. "Okay. Bye Mom," he concludes and flips the cell closed.

"That was my mom," Billy tells us, as if it wasn't obvious. "I have to go home now but I'll stop by your place, Mr. Monsento, in case Toby is still waiting there for Mr. Vila to show up. Could you text me what you find out here?"

"I don't text, kid," I reply. "I'll send you an email."

"Before you leave, young man, in answer to your question regarding summoning Zeaflin out of the UnderWorld; yes, Zeaflin, like any other realm walker, can be summoned." Billy perks up before Vila delivers the bad news. "But no, Mrs. Hammersly's spell won't call him. Her spell and totem are specific to Martin and they are the only items currently in existence powerful enough to pull a spirit from the UnderWorld detention center." Billy's face falls.

"We'll figure something else out, kid," I reassure him. "Now scoot on home before your mom gets worried." Billy gives Vila a discouraged look and, with a wave of his hand, he reluctantly exits to head for home. Vila waits until Billy vanishes down the porch steps before he continues from where he left off when the cell phone rang.

"The permission to give such powerful spiritual items to one of the living was not granted but Zeaflin was always a bit of a rebel. He defied Ambrogio and gave the items to Mrs. Hammersly anyway."

I'm stunned. Well, not by the fact that Zeaflin was a bit of a rebel; I'd be surprised if he wasn't. But I *am* surprised Mrs. Hammersly didn't run in the opposite direction when Zeaflin showed up at her door. To put it kindly, he's a bit of an odd character, with his pasty skin, pointy teeth and long, sharp fingernails.

"You weren't *afraid* of him?" I can't help asking her. "The Zeaflin I know is very weird, in manner and appearance." Annette looks bewildered. She gives me a shake of her head and looks at Vila questioningly.

"Zeaflin has changed, Mr. Monsento. His time in the UnderWorld has taken its toll, both physically and mentally. The Zeaflin you know is not the Zeaflin of the OtherWorld," Vila informs me.

"All right, so what happened? How did Zeaflin go from being an Aegis agent in the OtherWorld to a realm walker in the UnderWorld?" I ask. "Did Ambrogio banish him or something?"

Vila looks appalled. "Certainly not. The first time Mrs. Hammersly used Zeaflin's '*gifts*', the Underworld ruler became aware of their existence and, to put it mildly, he was very unhappy. As part of the truce of 1198, only generic spells and talismans that require a personal object are permitted to be created and used. The skill to make those items is relatively simple and it is common knowledge within our two realms. But the items Zeaflin created for Annette were generated using an ancient OtherWorld magic, unknown to the UnderWorld and thus banned by the aforementioned truce in order to keep a balance of power between our two realms. As anticipated, when the UnderWorld ruler discovered that not only were the forbidden items created, but they were given to one of the living to use, he was livid. And exacerbating the matter further, the only way Zeaflin could have given his items to one of the living would be through a visit to the living realm, breaking yet another truce--the one of 1412. The UnderWorld ruler demanded requital and, as you are already well-aware, disobedient OtherWorld spirits are to be sent to the UnderWorld."

"Yeah, Zeaflin mentioned that. He and Nerjul also mentioned the truce of 1412, saying it banned demons and angels from visiting the living realm," I reply. Knowing how Vila feels about the epithet, I add, "Which one was Zeaflin at the time?" Vila lets out a frustrated sigh.

"The truce of 1412 banned demons and *Aegis* agents from the living realm, Mr. Monsento. I've tried to explain to Zeaflin that words matter, that using the term angels to describe Aegis agents only encouraged the living to call us so. But Zeaflin always enjoyed the vernacular of the living and insisted on using their term for us. He apparently still does."

"So does Nerjul, it would seem," I observe.

"Yes, I'm certain the other UnderWorld realm walkers find the term amusing too. Zeaflin promotes its use, no doubt," Vila says irritably. While I always enjoy antagonizing Vila, I move the conversation back on course.

"So Ambrogio asked Zeaflin to go to the UnderWorld then?" I ask.

Vila shakes his head. "No. Zeaflin volunteered. I believe he was still upset over Ambrogio's refusal to reanimate Martin after he fell into the lake and was already considering transferring to the UnderWorld. When Ambrogio reprimanded Zeaflin for creating the taboo objects and subsequently giving them to Mrs. Hammersly without permission, Zeaflin finally lost his temper. He ranted on about there being too many decrees in the OtherWorld and he left. We tried to stop him but perhaps it was for the best. Zeaflin was very talented with the living but he always did stretch the rules. I'm not certain he ever belonged in the OtherWorld, although Ambrogio seems to think otherwise."

I glance at Annette. "And what about Nathan? You said the UnderWorld ruler insisted on a pure soul? Zeaflin wasn't enough?" I ask, hoping the reminder that Nathan was in the UnderWorld doesn't upset Annette further. She remains silent, staring dully at Vila. I'm worried the shock of all this may be too much for an old woman like her. Vila apparently has no such worries. A grim smile passes briefly across his pale face.

"The UnderWorld had Zeaflin dead to rights, Mr. Monsento. After all, he broke OtherWorld law. However, because Ambrogio didn't send Zeaflin to the UnderWorld immediately as required, the UnderWorld ruler was uneasy. He decided a little leverage was needed to assure that Zeaflin didn't have a change of heart and return to the OtherWorld, where Ambrogio would be certain to provide him refuge. Therefore, the UnderWorld offered to forgive the creation of the forbidden spiritual items and permit them to remain with Annette in the living realm if a pure soul accompanied Zeaflin." Vila places a hand on Annette's arm, who flinches slightly at his touch. He likely thinks it is a comforting gesture but it's probably more like being touched by an ice cube, him being undead and all.

"Ambrogio refused to transfer a pure soul and relations between our two realms were strained until your husband stepped in, Mrs. Hammersly. He knew how heartbroken you were over losing Martin as a living boy and he knew you'd be doubly-heartbroken to lose him again as a ghost boy. Hence, Nathan volunteered to travel to the UnderWorld with Zeaflin, diplomacy was restored, and you were permitted to keep the forbidden talisman and spell until you pass on and can accompany Martin to the OtherWorld. After which, it was agreed the spell and talisman would both be destroyed."

Annette looks very distressed. I don't think she needs to hear any more of this so I decide to press Vila regarding his assistance with Nathan and Martin. "You said you came here to help Nathan. Want to fill us in on how you plan to do this?" I ask, opting to omit mentioning Martin. I'd rather we skip discussing why Martin needs help too.

Vila raises a brow. "I am surprised you don't already know the answer to that, Mr. Monsento. You have Nathan's personal item, do you not?"

"Sure. You want me to summon him for you?"

"Of course. Tomorrow afternoon, before Nerjul returns, you will summon Nathan for me. I'll come by your séance parlor at 4 pm, as I should have the paperwork for Nathan's asylum request completed by then. I'll bring the documents with me and he can sign them when he arrives," Vila replies. He rises from the sofa.

"Mrs. Hammersly, rest assured your husband will soon be safe in the OtherWorld. But may I request you bring Martin to the séance?

I think it is time for him to come to the OtherWorld; he has been in the living realm for far too long. His father can take care of him in the StopOver until you join them."

Annette looks at the living room wall Martin vanished through earlier. "I will miss him but I agree he has been here too long and should go on to heaven." Vila purses his lips tightly over the word "heaven" but says nothing. "I've been worried that Martin has been fading over the years. It is more difficult to see him now than when I was younger. Of course, maybe that's due to old eyes..." She trails off and then brightens. "Nathan and Martin will be very happy to see each other after all this time so yes, I will bring him to the séance tomorrow."

"Shall we?" Vila says to me, sweeping his hand toward the front door.

I stand up and dig into my jeans pocket for my wallet to pull out a business card to hand to Annette. She is still a bit pale but looks to be recovering from her shock. I guess being visited by an "angel" and being able to keep your dead boy around the house dulls one's sense of consternation. Annette glances down at the card. "My address is on the card," I tell her. She nods and rises slowly from the sofa to see us to the door.

———◆———

As we approach my car, I decide to ask Vila if the OtherWorld knew Zeaflin's items could draw a spirit out of a vinculum. I got the impression Vila didn't know until now. If so, that might explain why Nerjul hasn't figured out that Martin isn't still inside his vial.

"Say, Vila, did you know that Annette could pull Martin out of Nerjul's vinculum?" I ask. Vila stops just shy of my car and turns to look at me.

"No, Mr. Monsento, I did not. While it was common knowledge that Martin could be drawn out of an UnderWorld prison using Zeaflin's creations, none of us had any inkling Martin--or any other spirit, for that matter--could be drawn out of a vinculum. It has a very strong spiritual force and no magic in our realms has ever been powerful enough to break it. Zeaflin must have been tinkering with some of the ancient OtherWorld spells in his spare time and created something very special."

I think this over. Zeaflin once told me he was a "medium, of a sort" when he was alive so that would explain his skill in concocting spells and things that summon spirits. Now I only have the mystery of the comment he made that he was also a "tailor, of a sort." I come out of my thoughts and see that Vila is staring at me.

"Is there something else you need answered before I depart? You appear confused," he says. I decide not to pursue that train of thought any further and instead ask what prompted Vila to agree to help with this case.

"I was wondering why Ambrogio finally agreed to let you help us with Nathan. Why the change of heart?" I ask.

"Nathan volunteered to live in the UnderWorld but it was agreed that it would only be until Annette ascended. At that time, the forbidden objects would be destroyed and Nathan would return to the OtherWorld to join his family. Therefore, one does have to wonder, after so many years of residing peacefully in the UnderWorld, why Nathan tried to escape before Annette ascended, knowing full well that he would be imprisoned for it and his transfer to the OtherWorld nullified. We would like to know what drove him to such an imprudent action. And while Ambrogio is hesitant to spark the ire of the UnderWorld ruler, he cannot allow a pure spirit like Nathan to be locked away in the UnderWorld prison indefinitely, where his soul will most certainly be irreparably tainted. In this, he must intervene."

"And what of Zeaflin? Is Ambrogio going to help him too?" I ask.

Vila stares hard at me. "Zeaflin is no longer a pure soul, Mr. Monsento," he replies coldly. I open my mouth to retort, pause, and then realize I have no rebuttal. While I'm trying to think up an argument for saving Zeaflin, Vila considers his argument sufficient and looks toward Annette's house. The porch light is switched off and the front room is dark so the old woman must have gone to bed. I hope she can sleep.

"Annette's time draws near," Vila informs me. "Soon she and Martin will be safe in the OtherWorld, both finally out of reach of the UnderWorld. And while I'm not certain of it, I suspect the UnderWorld is concerned that Zeaflin was planning to carry Nathan out to join his family after Annette died. And if he did accompany Nathan to the OtherWorld, Zeaflin might leave too, having no pure soul to watch over in the UnderWorld. That is most likely the reason for this loyalty test offering him the opportunity to help Nathan escape prison. Given Zeaflin's history with the Hammersly family, it was a difficult test to pass."

"Okay, so if this all plays out as the UnderWorld ruler planned and Zeaflin is found guilty—"

"Oh, he will be," Vila interjects.

"Then he'll be in jail, right? How does an imprisoned realm walker benefit the UnderWorld? They'll have lost him either way, right?"

Vila gives me a nod of agreement. "True, but I'd say they'd rather lose Zeaflin to prison than to Ambrogio. It is a rare individual who possesses the potent magic of creating spells capable of drawing a spirit without a personal item, let alone one that can summon a spirit out of anywhere, including the highly-fortified UnderWorld penitentiary. I'm sure the UnderWorld would prefer such a talented individual not reside in the OtherWorld. And when they find out Zeaflin's items pulled Martin from a vinculum, they will be all the more determined to keep Zeaflin in their realm. Of course, Ambrogio would never *encourage* Zeaflin to create another of these forbidden objects, but the UnderWorld ruler has a history of trust issues."

"Is that a fact?" I respond and motion for Vila to get into the car so I can head for home. He shakes his head.

"I prefer to walk. I'll see you tomorrow afternoon at 4 pm." Vila turns on his heel and walks away down the street. I watch until he disappears around the corner of the block before jumping into the car to head for home.

————— ◆ —————

I keep the email to Billy short, merely asking him to relay to the other kids to stop by my shop after school. I'd prefer not to put into writing all the crazy things Vila told me; I can brief the kids when they arrive. There should be plenty of time to update them before Vila shows up for Nathan's summoning.

By the time I hit the send button and shut down the laptop, it's 9 pm. The rumble in my stomach reminds me that I have some stew in the refrigerator, so I get up to pop it into the microwave. While I eat, I think about Annette. Her time is near, Vila said. I wonder how near? Something tells me very near. Maybe that's why Ambrogio agreed that Vila can help now. Well, help Nathan anyway. It doesn't sound like they can help Zeaflin. I feel a strange sinking feeling in my gut as that fact hits home. How are the kids going to handle it if Zeaflin is imprisoned? Try as I may to push the thought out of my head, it sneaks in anyway...*How am I going to handle it?*

Chapter 15

"Abby! It's time to get up!" Mom calls up the stairs. I roll over and look at the bedside clock with a groan. Eight o'clock already?

I didn't sleep well last night, fretting over whether we can help Zeaflin or whether he'd even allow us to help him. He refused to be purified in our last case, after he was stabbed with a small dagger called a phurba. If he hadn't fought it off, the phurba would have cleansed his soul and made him suitable to move to Halcyon. That was the perfect opportunity for Zeaflin to return to the OtherWorld, but he stubbornly refused to allow the purification to take hold. Of course, he didn't have a possible prison sentence hanging over his head that time.

Today is Wednesday, the day Nerjul returns to force us to summon Nathan for him, and yet another reason to be worried. With a wide yawn, I roll out of bed and head for the shower, then trudge downstairs to breakfast. I hope Mom and Dad don't notice the heavy bags under my eyes. If they do, I'll tell them I'm worried about my final exams tomorrow.

I scarf down my breakfast, keeping my eyes focused on the cereal bowl to avoid eye contact and possible questions over my bloodshot eyes. Fortunately, Dad keeps his nose buried in the Daily Times and Mom is too busy tidying the kitchen to notice anything amiss. I'm just dropping my bowl and juice glass into the sink for Mom to wash when Billy and Toby show up at the screen door off our kitchen.

"Hi Mr. and Mrs. Grant," Billy calls out in greeting before turning to me. "Say, Abby, Toby's mom agreed we could eat dinner at his house tonight so we can study for finals together. Did you ask your parents yet?" I slap my forehead. I completely forgot to clear with Mom and Dad about coming home late tonight. Thank goodness for Billy's quick thinking! Toby's mom works the late shift on Wednesdays so we'll be free and clear.

"I'm sorry, I totally forgot. Is it okay, Mom and Dad?" I ask in my sweetest pleading voice. Dad looks over the top of his newspaper at Mom. She's usually the decision maker for my outside activities during the school year. I look at Mom. She is frowning thoughtfully, likely weighing the pros and cons of my "studying" with Billy and Toby, who tend not to be as focused as I am during intellectual pursuits.

"Mom plans to roast a chicken. *And* she baked a pie yesterday," Toby says to insert some guilt into the decision. Mom looks at Dad but he's already gone back to his newspaper, so she makes the executive decision and nods.

"Be sure you come home before dark," she advises.

"Will do! Thanks Mom! Thanks Dad!" I exclaim. I give them both a quick peck goodbye and rush out to join the boys.

"What'd you find out?" I ask as we begin our walk to school.

"Lots," Billy replies. "Most of it is bad news though. Zeaflin can be summoned but we can't use Mrs. Hammersly's talisman and spell to summon him out. They're specific to Martin." My heart drops into my shoes.

"Can Vila help? Maybe he can make a totem specific to Zeaflin?" Toby suggests. Billy's face lights up and he holds up his hand for a high five. The two boys slap hands in the air.

"Awesome idea, Toby! Mr. Monsento asked us to stop by after school. Let's ask him to contact Vila through Mary--see if he'll come back here and make the totem," Billy responds. The boys look relieved but I'm still worried. Maybe Vila will refuse to make one. Or maybe he can't.

"So, Vila confirmed that Zeaflin is Martin's guardian angel. Or rather he was, I guess. He made the spell and totem for Annette after Ambrogio refused to raise Martin from the dead," Billy tells me. Toby doesn't look surprised so he's probably been filled in about all of that beforehand. Or maybe he already believed Zeaflin was Martin's angel without Vila's confirmation.

"I told you the totem was his," I can't resist saying. Billy rolls his eyes but doesn't fight back. Of course, he has no argument; I did tell him the totem was Zeaflin's.

"So how did Zeaflin go from being a guardian angel in the OtherWorld to a bounty hunter in the UnderWorld?" I ask.

Billy shrugs. "I have no idea. I had to leave before Vila told the whole story about Zeaflin. Mr. Monsento stayed behind so he might know. Anyway, we can find out more after school," he replies.

We walk on in silence. The boys seem to be so focused on Zeaflin that I wonder if they've thought about Nerjul at all. I sure have. He's coming back tonight, expecting us to summon Nathan. That's if he hasn't already discovered Martin escaped. If he has, he might just show up early.

We enter the school hallway, where we all agree to meet at the front door when school lets out so we can head immediately over to Monsento's house. Then I split off to attend my first class of the day--Social Studies with Mr. Kruger. I hope I can concentrate on my lessons today!

———— ◆ ————

The end of the school day bell rings. I quickly toss my backpack onto my back and rush for the door. But before I can make good my escape, Ms. Grady's cool voice rings out across the classroom. "A word, Miss Grant?" With an inward groan, I turn back and walk reluctantly to her desk at the front of the room, while the other kids brush past me and file out of the classroom.

"Yesterday's math quiz results were abysmal. Is there something wrong at home?" Ms. Grady asks. Abashed, I shake my head. After a brief pause, Ms. Grady continues. "Your final exams are tomorrow.

Are you ready for them?" I swallow hard and nod. Ms. Grady eyes me closely. "Because I'd hate to see another poor test result," she says, looking down at me from over the top of her glasses. "Fortunately, the failed math test was merely a quiz and doesn't hold much weight in your final grade for the year, but tomorrow's tests are very important." Suddenly Ms. Grady's expression turns dark and her eyes focus behind me.

"Do you find something amusing, Mr. Miller?" she calls out.

I turn to catch Billy plastering on his most charming smile. "No ma'am, I'm just happy today is all," he responds cheerfully. Ms. Grady lets out an annoyed grunt in reply.

"May I go now, Ms. Grady?" I manage to squeak out. "I'd like to get started studying now."

Ms. Grady peers down at me. "See that you do," she responds with a deep frown in Billy's direction. I rush out the door, nearly colliding with Billy in my hurry to get away from her disapproving stare.

———•◆•———

"Where's Toby?" I ask, looking around the deserted hallway.

"He's waiting by the front door. We were wondering what happened to you so I offered to check," Billy replies.

"I'm glad you did or I'd have never gotten away. I don't know why Ms. Grady always picks on me," I say with a moan.

Billy laughs. "Because you're her favorite." I stick my tongue out at him and march ahead to find Toby, sitting on the steps just outside the school door. He stands up to join Billy and me and the three of us begin our walk to Monsento's house.

———— ◆ ————

Today is Wednesday, the day we stand up against the UnderWorld and send Nathan off to the OtherWorld instead, and I'm too nervous to sit still. Since the detectives are in school and can provide no helpful distractions, I busy myself in the back garden, pulling the weeds I've neglected this past month. I'm kneeling over, cursing under my breath at the tiny pricks and scratches my rose bush is inflicting on my hands and arms when I feel a sudden chill run down my spine. I twist my head and look down to see a translucent bluish hand resting on my shoulder. I jerk away in surprise and pitch forward, giving the attacking rose bush fertile ground on my face for fresh scratches.

"Oh dear! I'm so sorry, Mr. Monsento! We didn't mean to startle you," Annette says, materializing to help pull me out of the bush. I tug free of the rose thorns and rise to my feet to look at my two spirit visitors: Martin, and now, Annette. Vila was right, her time really was near. *But why are they here? It can't be four o'clock already.* I look down at my watch--nope, not yet. Unless my watch has stopped–like my heart almost did when I saw that ghost hand–it's only 3:30 pm. May as well address the elephant in the room.

"You've...er...passed on," I say hesitantly. Annette smiles but says nothing. "You're a little early. Vila and the kids won't get here until around four," I tell her.

She nods. "I know. But I have something I'd like to show you." Annette motions toward my kitchen door. I raise a questioning brow and lead the way into my house.

Okay, one shock in an afternoon is one too many but now I have the pleasure of a second surprise: a man ghost, sitting in a chair at my kitchen table. This ghost has a pale gray glow about him instead of the usual blue I've seen in all the other ghosts I've encountered. I look back questioningly at Annette, who is walking through my screen door to join me in the kitchen.

"Mr. Monsento, it's time you met your quarry: Nathan Hammersly," she says with a mischievous smile.

"You knew where he was all along," I declare, unsure of why that surprises me. She is his wife, after all. But Annette shakes her head.

"No, I didn't. Martin did though, didn't you, dear?" she says to the ghost boy, who gives a quick nod to his mom before he pulls away from her to jump onto Nathan's lap. Nathan wraps his arms around Martin in a ghostly embrace and looks up at me.

"Martin traveled in-between realms to play with me every day but I asked him never to tell Annie. I felt it a necessary precaution should the UnderWorld decide to send someone to question her," he explains.

"Fortunately, they never did," Annette interjects.

"Thank goodness for small favors," Nathan responds, giving his wife a brief smile before continuing his narrative. "When a few days went by with no visit from Martin, I started to worry. It was risky but I took the chance and left in-between to go look for him at our living house. And there I found Martin, sitting on my old bed watching over Annie. She was almost gone when I arrived, so I sat down on the bed with Martin and we both held Annie's hand until she passed on. It took a few hours but she finally awoke as a ghost and suggested we come here immediately to wait for Vila so he could take us all to the OtherWorld."

Martin starts to struggle so Nathan releases him and the boy vanishes through the wall of my kitchen to head for my salon. "Hey! He won't mess with my séance stuff, will he?" I ask, alarmed at the thought of ghost boy handprints all over my tarot cards and crystal ball; spirit essence can be gooey. Annette passes through the wall to keep an eye on the kid so I decide to take the opportunity to grill Nathan over what prompted him to try to escape the UnderWorld so many years after he had volunteered to go there. From what Vila says, not even the all-seeing Ambrogio knows the answer to that question.

"So why'd you possess Nerjul and force him to break you out of the UnderWorld that time at the tavern and start this whole mess? I was told you went there so Annette could keep Martin around. You were lucky that the UnderWorld didn't demand Ambrogio take Martin away because you didn't keep your side of the bargain and stay in the UnderWorld like you said you would," I say, deciding to give him a scolding for his lack of foresight.

Nathan frowns. "I didn't break the bargain and I certainly never possessed Nerjul. He said I did but that's a lie."

"Now there's a surprise--Nerjul as a liar. What's the story then?" I ask. "What really happened?" Nathan sighs and rises from the table to look out my kitchen window. He keeps his back to me, his gaze focused outside, while he relates what occurred the day of his first UnderWorld escape.

"I was living as peaceably as any spirit can in a crazy place like the UnderWorld when, a few living weeks back, Zeaflin visited me at my usual table in the corner of the Toothy Tavern. I'd seen him here and there but this was the first time he'd ever directly approached me. He came to tell me that Annette's ascension was near and I would soon be free to return to the OtherWorld to join her. He seemed to be in a hurry so I gave him a thank you nod and watched him make a hasty retreat out the tavern door."

"That sounds like Zeaflin, all right. Always in a rush, never time to tarry," I comment. Nathan laughs lightly before picking up from where he left off.

"It was mixed news. While I was sad about Annie's pending death, I was happy we would all soon be together as a family, so I ordered a cocktail to celebrate. I was savoring that drink when Nerjul showed up at the tavern. I watched him play cards for a while, watched him lose, and then I ordered another drink, paid for by the winner of the poker game. My drink choice is a bit unusual for the UnderWorld but I happen to like the UnderWorld version of a mint julep, so that's what I ordered. That drew Nerjul's attention to me sitting in the shadows. He came over to congratulate me on my pending transfer to the OtherWorld and asked if he might join me for a drink. I wasn't surprised that Zeaflin knew about Annie; he was once an OtherWorld agent and he probably has a sense for such things. But I wondered why Nerjul knew. I decided maybe the OtherWorld briefs all realm walkers about upcoming spirit arrivals, regardless of what realm the walkers reside in. Anyway, I saw no harm in letting Nerjul join me at the table so I shrugged and he took the seat across from me. We were silently enjoying our drinks when the piano player started up some stupid song mocking me. Nerjul gave the piano player a withering look and suggested we take a walk. I agreed, figuring I'd be safe from any further teasing if I was accompanied by a realm walker; the other spirits knew better than to mess with one of them. We didn't get very far from the tavern when Nerjul sucked me up into some sort of vial I'd never seen before and tucked me into his pocket."

"Nerjul tells that part of the story a little differently. He said you possessed him and forced him to carry you out of the UnderWorld," I respond. Nathan turns away from his nature-gazing out my kitchen window and looks back at me, wearing a deep scowl.

"It was all a setup to get me arrested. I was in his pocket, not his mind, when Nerjul dissipated to the living realm. Once we arrived there, he uncorked the vial I was in and tossed it through the gate of the cemetery where I was buried. Fortunately, I slipped out of the vial just before the glass shattered against a tombstone, but I was trapped in the graveyard. That is, until some dark blue creature with sharp teeth wearing a ratty old fur showed up and dragged me out."

"That was probably Eurynomos. It's supposed to be some sort of corpse eater," I tell him.

Nathan grimaces. "That must be why it smelled so bad. Anyway, whatever it was, it brought me back to the UnderWorld, where I was immediately thrown into prison. They claimed I possessed a realm walker and used him to escape the UnderWorld. I explained what happened but they didn't believe me. They said it was my word versus a senior realm walker. You can guess who they believed."

"Well, that clears up a few things," I say. "But what brings you here so early? You realize that Nerjul might come here, don't you? He's due to arrive at six but he might come sooner and if he does, you're going to be caught. Vila is working on getting the asylum papers together but he's not due until four. Maybe you should take your family in-between realms until Vila gets here, just to play it safe."

"That's okay, we can wait here. I doubt Nerjul will show up before six. He is a creature of habit and I'd say right now, he is probably in the Toothy Tavern. It's his favorite haunt and it's unlikely he will forgo his afternoon cocktail to visit you early."

"He might visit me early," I say in a low voice to keep Annette from hearing, "if he discovers Martin escaped his crystal vial. Nerjul locked him up in one of his little glass bottles to blackmail you into going back to prison voluntarily."

Nathan takes in a sharp breath. "The fiend!" he exclaims.

"Yeah, imagine that...an UnderWorld bounty hunter with a lack of morals," I say sarcastically.

"I knew Nerjul was unscrupulous--he's a senior UnderWorld realm walker and I doubt he got the promotion by being sweet and cuddly--but I never thought he would stoop so low as to kidnap my son."

"I don't think anything is too low for Nerjul. So what's the deal with the prison break?" I ask. "Why did you go along with it? I mean, Nerjul set you up to go to prison, so why did you trust him to help break you out? Or did he force you out again?"

"Force me? No, he didn't *force* me," Nathan spits out angrily. "But given a choice between eternal prison in the UnderWorld or possible escape to the OtherWorld, trusting him was a chance I had to take. Sure, I didn't know what Nerjul's end-game was but if I ever wanted to join my family, what other choice did I have? Once inside Nerjul's mind, though, I could see the deception. He had no intention of taking me to the OtherWorld. It was all just a ruse to entrap Zeaflin. Nerjul planned to make a roundtrip right back to the UnderWorld, so I jumped off in-between realms. I knew they'd have a difficult time finding me there."

"They're going to put Zeaflin on trial, you know, for helping with your escape," I say.

Nathan hangs his head and sighs. "I know. Is Ambrogio going to try to help him?"

"Not currently. But something might be arranged if it becomes necessary," Vila responds from behind me, spooking me with the sudden intrusion. I spin around in my chair to give him an exasperated look. What is it with realm walkers and their incredible sense of timing?

"Well, well. Excellent timing there, Vila," I tell him. Vila steps inside the kitchen and points at the wall clock.

"It is 4 pm, is it not?" he states before he looks back at Nathan. "I am pleased you have come out of hiding, Mr. Hammersly. You have spared us all a summoning, which I always find to be quite taxing."

"*You* find them taxing? I'm the one who does all the work," I mutter. Vila's back stiffens but he ignores my aside and blathers on.

"I have brought papers for your asylum request, Nathan, that require your signature. Once they're signed, you'll be given indefinite refuge in the OtherWorld." Vila pulls a tightly-rolled silver-colored document out of his suit pocket and hands it to Nathan, along with a short feather quill and a small pot of what looks to be gold-colored ink. Then he turns to address me.

"Are Annette and Martin here yet?"

"They're in the salon, probably messing around with my tarot cards," I respond.

Vila studies me a moment. "What happened to your face?"

I reach up to feel several scratches on my chin and nose. "Had a run-in with a rose bush," I reply.

Vila glances down at the scratches on my hands and arms. "It would appear the bush won the battle," he observes, reaching out to take the now-signed asylum documents from Nathan.

"Yeah, I think it did," I agree before I add, "You do know Annette is deceased, right?" Vila looks at me like I just asked if the earth is round.

"I believe you already know the answer to that question, Mr. Monsento. Now, shall we go find Annette and Martin so I can escort the Hammersly family to the OtherWorld? Ambrogio has many questions he would like to ask Nathan."

"Whoa! Hold on a minute here! What do I do when Nerjul shows up here at six?" I ask, panicked over being left with the job of dealing with an angry Nerjul alone. "I thought you were at least going to stick around until then and tell him about the asylum thing."

"I imagine you can just as easily inform Nerjul that the Hammersly family is under the protection of the OtherWorld now. As a realm walker, he will be well-versed in diplomacy," Vila replies.

"Why don't you drop off the Hammersly family and come back here to inform him yourself?" I suggest, not savoring being the bearer of news that's sure to enrage a senior UnderWorld realm walker.

Vila sighs impatiently. "All right, Mr. Monsento. I will send a herald with a formal proclamation to inform the UnderWorld of the Hammersly asylum. I cannot guarantee that Nerjul will not pay you a visit but at least he will be aware of the situation beforehand," he responds and then motions for us all to head into the salon to join Annette and Martin so he can whisk them away.

Vila is instructing the Hammersly family to join hands, preparing to realm jump them into the OtherWorld, when the three detectives finally arrive at my porch steps, fifteen minutes late. Abby enters the salon first and lets out a gasp when she sees Annette is a ghost. Then she lets out another gasp when her eyes fall on Nathan. Billy grasps her arm to pull her aside so he and Toby can step inside and see what all the fuss is about.

"Wow! Annette...you're a...a...ghost," Billy stammers.

"Great observation skills there, Billy," I say.

"Oh Annette! I'm so sorry," Abby cries out, tears welling up in her eyes. Annette steps forward and places her blue-hued hand on Abby's shoulder.

"It's all right, dear, I've lived a full life and I'm happy to be deceased. Now we can all be a family together in the OtherWorld," she says.

Abby swivels her gaze to Vila. "You're going to take them there? Elizabeth is providing asylum for Nathan?" she asks, with wide eyes. I'm not sure why the kid is surprised. It would be a tad harsh if they didn't.

"Elizabeth *and* Ambrogio, yes," Vila clarifies. "Shall we?" he says to Annette, holding out his hand to beckon her back into the ghost circle so he can carry them off.

Annette asks for a moment and turns back to Abby and the boys. "I'm so glad I was able to see you children again before we left for the OtherWorld. I never did have the opportunity to hear the story about how you three became detectives for ghosts, but maybe I'll be in need of your services one day and I can hear about it then."

Martin tugs his hand away from his father and runs to Abby. In his hand is what looks like a small ladybug pin. He holds it out for Abby to take. Abby looks at Annette questioningly. "Go ahead and take it, dear. I have no use for it now," Annette says, then laughs softly. "Actually, I haven't had any use for it for years."

After a brief hesitation, Abby takes the pin from Martin and pins it on her sweater. "Thank you, Martin and Annette. I'll think of you both whenever I wear it," she responds, her eyes becoming teary again.

Martin spins around and runs to his mother. She grasps the ghost boy's hand to draw him into a circle with her, Nathan and Vila, and after a chorus of ghostly goodbyes (except Vila, of course, who only gives us a curt nod), the Hammersly family fades to a pale gray mist to begin their journey to the OtherWorld StopOver and beyond.

Chapter 16

"All right, kids. You'd better hit the road and head for home. Vila said he'd send a herald to inform the UnderWorld of the Hammersly asylum so Nerjul is probably going to be paying me a visit real soon," I warn my companions.

"You shouldn't have to face him alone, Mr. Monsento," Billy responds.

"Billy's right," Abby chimes in.

"Yeah. Billy and Abby aren't expected home until after seven tonight and my mom is working, so we can wait here with you," Toby says, putting in his two cents.

I shake my head. "It could be dangerous. Nerjul might flip out when he discovers Martin has escaped and he and Nathan are now beyond his reach."

"All the more reason for us to stay," Billy contends. Abby and Toby nod in agreement. I give them an arched brow.

The Fantastic Phantasmic Detective Agency And the Woebegone Oddity of the Underworld

"And exactly what do you three kids think you can do if Nerjul goes savage?" I ask. Not that I'm thrilled with facing an irate UnderWorld realm walker alone but I can't see how the kids will be of much help.

"If Nerjul goes 'savage', what makes you think he won't decide to pay us all a visit? I think it's better we face him down together as a team rather than individually. And I surely don't want him coming to *my* house where my parents might see him," Abby responds.

I think this over. Yeah, she's probably right. Nerjul just might go to the kids' homes in his rage after he finishes with me and if my neighbor can see Zeaflin, no doubt the kids' parents will be able to see Nerjul. We'd better settle this here and now.

"Okay, okay. You can stay," I concede, uncertain if I'm making a good decision but grateful for the company.

"Great! I'll make dinner while we wait," Billy exclaims. He wanders off toward my kitchen, oddly cheery for someone who could soon have a run-in with an enraged UnderWorld realm walker. I look at Abby and Toby. They aren't nearly as cheerful as Billy but they are definitely resolute over staying for a possible confrontation. Abby gives me a worried look before she steers Toby to the kitchen to join Billy in scrounging up some food for supper.

———— ◆ ————

While Billy and Toby attend to cooking dinner, I tell the kids what I found out from Vila about Zeaflin's fall from grace and why Nathan volunteered to join him. I tell them the real story behind

Nathan's first "escape" attempt and relate Vila's theory regarding the possible reasons behind this setup to test Zeaflin's loyalty after so many years of him working as a faithful UnderWorld bounty hunter. The kids are quiet until I finish, then Billy speaks up.

"Do you think Mr. Zeaflin might agree to go to the OtherWorld now? I mean, if he isn't convicted, that is," he asks.

"I don't know, kid. Vila seemed to think he would have, but it's too late for that now. Unless they exonerate him, which I doubt," I reply.

"What will they do if he's found guilty?" Abby asks anxiously. I think it's best not to hypothesize what constitutes punishment in the UnderWorld, so I just shake my head.

"I don't know," I reply, wishing I had something more positive to tell her. Toby and Billy are facing the stove but I can tell by their drooped shoulders that they are as upset as Abby about Zeaflin's misfortune. I decide it's time to redirect.

"What's on the menu tonight, boys?"

Billy turns away from the stove to face me. "You didn't have much to choose from, Mr. Monsento, but we dug up a box of mac and cheese and a couple of cans of peas," he replies with a shrug. Abby scrunches her nose in disapproval.

"You really should take better care of yourself," she lectures me. "Fresh fruits and vegetables are important for a man your age." *A man my age?*

"Like I have time to grocery shop while I'm summoning ghosts and retrieving personal items for you kids," I retort. Toby places a couple of plates of macaroni and cheese mixed with peas onto the table in front of Abby and me.

"I like boxed mac and cheese," Billy confides, carrying two more plates to the table. "Mom always makes homemade mac and cheese. Its good, I suppose, but I like the vibrant orange cheese of the box kind better."

"You actually like the orange powder? I don't think it's even real cheese, Billy. I think it's more like powdered milk with orange dye," Abby responds, looking down at her plate and pushing the fluorescent noodles around with her fork. Ignoring her warning, the boys and I dig into our bountiful feast. After a brief hesitation, Abby gives in and joins us.

Midway through our meal, the doorbell buzzes. I look up at the kitchen clock and see it's already 6 pm. Nerjul is right on time. But if he's ringing the doorbell, maybe he's not all that angry then. I take in a deep breath.

"This is it, kids," I say, struggling to keep my voice even. I rise from the table to go answer the door. Billy, Toby and Abby walk silently behind me.

———— ◆ ————

I take up the rear behind Billy and Toby as we follow Monsento to the door to face Nerjul, or whatever UnderWorld monster Nerjul might have sent our way after finding out Nathan gained asylum in the OtherWorld and he doesn't need us anymore. I know he can't send a demon but he might send that flesh-eating creature, Eurynomos. Maybe it doesn't eat just corpses.

Monsento peeks through the peephole in his front door. "Not Nerjul. Looks like some sort of ghost," he tells us in a near-whisper before he opens the door to greet his guest.

The ghost standing on Monsento's porch is dressed in somber tones: a black tie, a gray shirt and a black three-piece suit that makes him look like a phantom mortician. In his left hand, he is carrying a black leather briefcase that appears to be as solid as any "living" briefcase I've seen, but that's the only part of this ghost that looks tangible to me. Unlike most of the ghosts I've met outside of a cemetery thus far, this one is gauzy and fuzzy around the edges and has the same faint gray glow around him that Nathan had. In fact, this spirit reminds me of the photographs of ghosts I've seen published in the National Jabberer. I always thought those photos were fake black and white images intentionally taken out of focus, because that's how everyone expects a ghost to look--gray and blurry. But now I wonder if they were actual photographs of ghosts like this one. He may be fuzzy but if I focus hard on his face, I can see that this ghost has short black hair slicked back with some sort of oil or gel, a broad nose and pencil-thin lips.

The ghost looks us all over before he selects Monsento to address. "Arthur Monsento?" he asks in a reedy voice. Monsento nods. The ghost gives him a tight-lipped smile, causing his thin ashen lips to almost disappear. "I am Ravat, the attorney assigned to Zeaflin's defense. May I come in?" Monsento, at a loss for words, nods again and steps away from the door. The ghost enters the salon and looks around the room until his eyes rest on Monsento's crystal ball, sitting in the middle of the séance table.

"I suggest you put that ball away somewhere safe, Arthur Monsento. When the prosecutor comes to visit, he may decide to confiscate it as evidence."

Monsento gives Ravat a bewildered look, then clears his throat nervously. "Evidence of what?" he asks.

Ravat looks at Monsento with a raised brow. "The ball is Zeaflin's, is it not?"

"Was Zeaflin's, yeah. It's mine now," Monsento replies.

Ravat nods knowingly. "Yes, he mentioned that he gifted it to you after he broke your living crystal ball. Currently, only I know this. However, if the prosecution becomes aware of this gift it could be used as evidence that some of Zeaflin's benevolent OtherWorld qualities have been returning. Hide the ball. It radiates an UnderWorld aura and will definitely provoke questions if the prosecutor sees it."

Monsento frowns. "I think Nerjul knows about the crystal ball. He made a comment to Zeaflin about it when he first visited me. Something like how sentimental Zeaflin was to give me his old ball."

Ravat closes his eyes and rubs his temples in a circular motion. "Why-oh-why did they pick me for this case? They had so many lawyers in the UnderWorld to choose from but it just had to be me," he groans. We all wait around in astonishment while the ghost struggles to compose himself. Several minutes tick by before Ravat finally drops his hands and opens his eyes, picking up from where Monsento left off. "All the more reason for you to hide the ball, Arthur Monsento. Better yet, go buy a new one and replace this one with a living model. The prosecutor will think Nerjul was mistaken when he sees your ball is useless." Then Ravat looks over at me and points a hazy finger in my direction.

"The girl might be trouble," he declares. I feel a surge of anger and confusion.

"What do you mean by that?" I demand.

"Your affection for Zeaflin--more evidence of reversion to his OtherWorld self," the ghost replies. Now that makes me really mad!

"Why does everyone keep saying I have affection for Zeaflin?" I snap. "He's creepy and he's weird and he's dead!"

At first Ravat looks taken aback, then he smiles broadly, displaying perfectly even teeth that radiate the same gray glow of his face. "That's the spirit! Keep with that if they ask you to testify," he exclaims. My anger melts into fear.

"What do you mean by that? They're not going to ask us to go to the UnderWorld, are they?" I ask, my voice faltering. I glance at Monsento and the boys, who all suddenly look very pale.

Ravat's broad smile droops. "Request, yes. But they *will* issue a subpoena if you refuse," he replies. "The prosecutor most likely will insist on your testimony."

"See here now," Monsento objects. "We're not going to the UnderWorld, subpoena or no subpoena. What if we're defense witnesses instead? That makes more sense, right? You can interview us here and submit our statements to the court."

Ravat shakes his head. "There is little defense you or the children can provide, Arthur Monsento. By agreeing to assist in the Hammersly prison break, Zeaflin showed reckless disregard for UnderWorld law and blatant disloyalty to the UnderWorld ruler who writes those laws. His guilt is almost impossible to refute; Nerjul's sworn testimony in this matter has been particularly *damning*."

"Sounds like they've already determined that he's guilty, so what use are you then?" Monsento asks abrasively.

"My use, or rather my *role*, is to provide counsel to you that may help minimize Zeaflin's sentence after the guilty verdict is rendered. After that occurs, the prosecution will subpoena you and the young people here to testify as character witnesses. Your testimony will be crucial in determining whether Zeaflin can be rehabilitated and become a functioning member of UnderWorld society again. I am here to advise what you should and should not say to increase his chances for a lighter sentence," Ravat replies.

"We're not going to the UnderWorld," Monsento repeats sharply.

Ravat gives him a half-shrug. "That I will leave between you and the prosecutor. As I said, I'm only here to provide advice regarding your testimony about Zeaflin's character. Shall we sit?" he suggests abruptly, gesturing toward Monsento's séance table.

My legs are trembling and my knees feel weak so I take the lead, and the four of us walk to the table to be counseled on what we should say to convince the UnderWorld that Zeaflin is still be impure enough to be rehabilitated back into a loyal UnderWorld citizen.

———————— ♦ ————————

Abby leads our down-hearted walk to the séance table, with the ghost taking up the rear. While I have no intention of traveling to the UnderWorld, subpoena or no subpoena, it's probably a good idea to listen to what this ghost suggests we say if the prosecutor shows up at my door, which it sounds like he will.

Ravat walks through the back of one of my séance chairs and takes a seat to join us at the table. He materializes, changing from a blurry gray-glowing ghost into a distinct gray-glowing man, and lifts his briefcase up to place it on the table in front of him.

"Mr. Ravat?" Toby speaks up tentatively. "Is Mr. Zeaflin all right?"

Ravat curls his lip. "No, he is not. He is too pure and a danger to us all in the UnderWorld. But if your question refers to Zeaflin's physical state, other than being undead, he is fine. We are not barbarians in the UnderWorld; we have official procedures in place for this sort of thing." He flips open his briefcase to extract a notepad and pencil. "Let's start with you, shall we?" Ravat suggests, pointing his pencil at Toby, whose eyes widen with fright.

Billy jumps in for the rescue. "You can start with me," he says.

Ravat looks Billy over, then shakes his head. "I like to start with the most difficult witnesses and I suspect you'll be the easiest to counsel." Ravat looks back at Toby. "Zeaflin informed me about the dinner invitation. Unfortunately, he also told Nerjul about it back when he mistakenly thought Nerjul was a reliable confidant."

"Toby rescinded the invitation," I quickly point out. The ghost smiles.

"Very good. And why did you rescind your offer, young man?" he asks Toby. Toby squirms in his chair and looks down at his hands, lying palms-down on the table.

"I dunno. Mr. Zeaflin seemed happy about the dinner invitation at first but after we finished the Belial case with him, he acted like he was going to decline. I thought maybe he changed his mind and didn't want to meet my mom after all," he mumbles, "So I told him Mom already had a boyfriend. But she doesn't; Alfred is just a family friend."

Ravat looks horrified. "No, no, no!'" he cries. "That will never do!" Toby's face flushes.

Billy jumps in for the rescue again. "I dared him to ask Zeaflin to dinner. It was all just for a bit of fun, to see if Toby would have the nerve to do it. Toby took the dare but we never expected that Zeaflin would actually accept his offer."

Toby looks up to glare at Billy. "I'm not saying that. It'll hurt Mr. Zeaflin's feelings."

Ravat narrows his eyes. "*Mister* Zeaflin's feelings are not at issue here, young man; his eternal well-being is. If the subject comes up, stick with Billy's story. It has a fine nuance of contempt and mean-spiritedness the UnderWorld judge will appreciate. Oh, and lose the Mister. He is only Zeaflin, an undead, creepy creature of the UnderWorld to you," he instructs sternly. Toby looks distressed but doesn't object any further. "Good," Ravat says with an approving nod. "We have the two boys covered with the dinner invitation dare." The ghost lawyer looks over at me and appears to be studying me. I give him a raised brow.

"What? I can think of something bad to say about Zeaflin on my own," I tell him. Ravat returns my raised brow with his own. He says nothing so I guess he's waiting for me to elaborate. I search my brain. Zeaflin's pulled a few things over on us in the past but I think of one in particular that I've only just realized. While I'm digesting this epiphany, Abby fills the silence with her astute insight.

"I don't think Mr. Monsento will be able to come up with anything. He's on a first-name basis with Zeaflin, after all," she declares haughtily.

"And you're *not*?" I counter. While Abby tries to think up a snappy comeback, I share my revelation.

"I *do* have something, something bad that Zeaflin actually did. And it's not the time we thought he kidnapped John," I hastily add, seeing Abby preparing to interrupt. She closes her mouth and gives me her undivided attention. "That time at the cemetery with Zeaflin, when the two of us went into the graveyard together to help Elizabeth leave the columbarium, Zeaflin gave me his cane. He told me it was for my protection from the crazed cemetery ghosts that were all riled up because a realm walker was in the vicinity. But you know what I think? I think Zeaflin gave the cane to me so the ghosts would think I was him and attack me instead, allowing him to just waltz on through to the columbarium unharmed." Abby and the boys look shocked, but Ravat claps his hands together approvingly.

"Excellent! It shows devious forethought on the defendant's part," he exclaims merrily. "And yes, you are probably correct, Arthur Monsento. Realm walker personal objects exude an aura that the graveyard ghosts were certain to pick up on. Zeaflin knew this and must have decided to let you provide a distraction." I scowl, not very happy about the deception. I'm going to have a little chat with Zeaflin about that when this is over. If I get the chance, that is.

There is a sudden rap on my front door. Ravat quickly tosses his notepad and pencil into the briefcase, snaps it shut and dematerializes back into his original wispy self. Guess he figures the guest is human and he can hide in plain sight that way. I give him a frown.

"That could be Nerjul. If it is, you're going to send him away, right?" I say.

The ghost shakes his head. "Nerjul is not allowed to pay you a visit. The prosecution would be furious if he did because it could be construed as attempting to tamper with your testimony." I fail to see how the prosecution wouldn't see Ravat's visit as tampering with our testimony but maybe that's how defense cases work in the UnderWorld.

The unexpected visitor loses patience and lays into the doorbell. Only one "person" I know is that impatient. I rise to answer the door. Sure enough, on the front porch stands Vila, looking as sour as usual. I motion for him to come inside.

"What brings you here, Vila? I thought you weren't coming back," I say.

"Ambrogio sent me back here immediately. There is an important matter he would like us all to discuss," Vila explains. Then his gaze falls on the translucent ghost sitting at my séance table and he steps briskly past me to approach Ravat. "Ravat, are you the prosecutor or defense attorney in this case?"

Ravat gives Vila a cheerless smile. "I have the dubious honor of defense for this particular case. Which, of course, was doomed from the start—"

"Maybe it was doomed from the start because of your attitude," Abby scolds.

Ravat shakes his head. "No. It was doomed the moment your realm walker friend accepted Nerjul's offer to assist with a prison break. Thanks to his foolishness, the best I can do for defense is submit a request for a lighter, or at least shorter, sentence. But to do that, I have to demonstrate the defendant can be rehabilitated."

"And exactly how do you plan to go about that here? Shouldn't you be working on that with Zeaflin?" Vila queries.

"I am coaching his character witnesses." Ravat sweeps his hands to indicate the four of us living and lets out a heavy sigh that sounds more like a low, spooky moan. "It is a good thing I am here, or I fear Zeaflin's sentence would have been more severe."

"Indeed? And are they coached to your satisfaction?" Vila asks, looking skeptically at Toby. Toby shrinks farther down in his chair.

Ravat moan-sighs again. "As well as they can be." One hand materializes and picks up the briefcase, then Ravat rises from his seat. "I should be going now. Do me a favor and don't corrupt my witnesses." Vila gives Ravat a silent stare until the ghost breaks eye contact and vanishes into thin air.

Chapter 17

Vila steps over to the séance table where the boys and I are sitting and pulls out a chair. He takes the seat next to mine and motions for Monsento to join us. With a weary sigh, Monsento crosses the room and sits down next to Toby.

"Have you come to help us, Mr. Vila?" Billy asks. "Mr. Zeaflin's lawyer said we're going to be subpoenaed and forced to testify in the UnderWorld."

"Can they do that?" I add, gnawing on my thumbnail nervously. Visiting the OtherWorld was one thing, but I truly do *not* want to see what the UnderWorld looks like! Vila frowns at me.

"They can. Of course, the OtherWorld Department of Living Affairs can demand your testimony be recorded here in the living realm instead, but we would prefer not to exercise that option," he replies before he turns to answer Billy. "And no, I have not come to help you, young man. I have come to ask for your help instead."

Vila reaches into his coat pocket and pulls out a small, curved dagger. He places it reverently onto the lace tablecloth on Monsento's séance table and we all lean forward for a look. The dagger is three-sided with three faces on top, just like the phurba Elizabeth gave to Monsento for purifying Marzee, a corrupted OtherWorld mercenary. Fortunately, after Monsento stabbed her (but only in the hand), Marzee accepted the purification and ascended to Halcyon in tiny droplets of light. Elizabeth's phurba was brass and very plain but this dagger is silver and ornate, with intricate carvings of exotic-looking birds on the blade and blue and red gems embedded in the eyes of the faces. *Is this Vila's personal phurba?* I wonder.

Monsento frowns deeply. "You want me to go to the UnderWorld and stab Zeaflin with that, don't you?" he says anxiously, looking up at Vila. A small bead of sweat rolls down the side of Monsento's temple and his hands begin to tremble.

Vila shakes his head. "Because you are a medium and may try to smuggle some spiritual object in to pass to Zeaflin, I'm afraid the bailiff may search you before allowing you to enter the courtroom. But Abigail, being a girl, will likely not be searched." I let out a horrified gasp. *Vila wants me to stab Zeaflin??*

"I can do it!" Billy offers quickly

Monsento stands up abruptly and bangs his hand on the table. "Whoa there! **No one** is going to the UnderWorld and **no one** is stabbing Zeaflin!' he bellows. Vila gives Monsento a cool stare until he sits back down at the table.

"Allow me to elaborate. This is Ambrogio's personal phurba and he specifically requests Abigail assist in this matter. In regard to going to the UnderWorld, as I said, we can certainly demand your testimony be recorded here in the living realm. However, if we do this, there will be no hope of saving Zeaflin from UnderWorld prison. Even if your testimony sways the judge to be more lenient, Zeaflin will still be sentenced to at least one millennium in Malebolge."

"What's Malebolge?" Toby asks in a small voice.

"One of the levels in the UnderWorld prison. From what I've been told, it is essentially a concentric series of deep ravines surrounding a funnel-shaped stairwell that provides the only access to the lower levels. It is also one of the most secure areas, being deep inside the prison," Vila replies.

"And what will happen to him there?" Monsento asks, his hands starting to tremble again.

Vila sighs. "I can only speculate. It's likely the longer Zeaflin resides there, the more tainted his essence will become. If he stays there long enough, he may even transform into a demon. However, I'm not certain what ultimately becomes of the creatures that inhabit those dreadful caverns, having never had the honor of conversing with one."

"And... if I stab Zeaflin with this phurba... he'll ascend?" I ask haltingly, my heart hammering against my chest, making it difficult to breathe.

Vila rubs his chin thoughtfully. "It is Ambrogio's phurba, one of the most powerful phurbas in existence, so I imagine Zeaflin would have a difficult time resisting it. Of course, Zeaflin is known to be very stubborn and he may be able to resist purification long enough for the UnderWorld to administer treatment. Therefore, after he is impaled, it is imperative you convince Zeaflin to accept the purification, Abby. Ambrogio selected you to wield his phurba not just because you are female, but also because he believes Zeaflin will listen to you."

I stare down at Ambrogio's phurba in a daze. Visit the UnderWorld? Stab Zeaflin? Okay, technically he's already dead but I saw what Elizabeth's phurba did to him the last time he was stabbed and fought off purification. It wasn't a pretty sight, all yellow pus and putrefying skin. I look up at Vila, then around the table at Billy, Toby, and Monsento, my heart pounding wildly.

"If we go to the UnderWorld," I say slowly to keep my voice steady, "what will we see?" I reluctantly draw my eyes back to Vila, dreading his answer.

"I will be carrying you straight to the courthouse so all you will see is a courtroom, very much like one of your living courtrooms. The UnderWorld doesn't waste their imagination on mundane trivialities like trials and hearings so they tend to keep their courtrooms simple. They save their creativity for the punishment stage of the proceedings," he responds with a bleak smile.

"Will we be safe there?" I ask, watching Vila closely for any sign of worry. He is completely unreadable.

"The living are under the protection of the Department of Living Affairs, as I have earlier stated. So yes, you will be safe," he declares.

"And after Abby stabs Zeaflin? Are we going to be safe *then*?" Monsento asks crossly. "Seems to me that's going to make the UnderWorld pretty mad, don't you think?" Vila drums his fingers on the table in front of him and frowns at Monsento.

"Yes, Mr. Monsento. They will undeniably be *pretty mad* but they must respect the authority of the Department of—"

"Living Affairs. We get it already," Monsento growls.

"Besides, you will all have diplomatic immunity. Ambrogio will designate you living Ambassadors for the OtherWorld and I will carry the paperwork with me to the hearing as proof. There will be no repercussions for any of you," Vila continues, unfazed by Monsento's ill humor.

"I'll do it. I'll stab Zeaflin," I blurt out before I lose my nerve. Then I look around the table again. "Toby, Billy, and Mr. Monsento can give their testimony here. I'll say I want to see the look on Zeaflin's face when they sentence him so I want to testify in person." Monsento, Toby, and Billy start to object all at once.

Vila puts up a hand. "If you please!" he says loudly, shocking everyone into silence. Then he looks over at me and shakes his head. "If I file the paperwork requiring the living testimony be recorded in the living realm, it will apply to all of you. I cannot file for an exemption and I certainly cannot file for an exemption on such a weak premise that you, of all people, have malice for Zeaflin. Your affection for him will be obvious, even to the most inattentive judge." Billy snorts out a muffled laugh until Toby's rib jab silences him.

I stare in amazement at Vila, completely baffled. Why does everyone keep saying I have affection for Zeaflin? Do I? A small voice whispers inside my head, *"Of course you do."*

———— ◆ ————

Abby looks confused by Vila's statement but it comes as no surprise to the rest of us. Ever since our little visit to the OtherWorld, Abby has shown an interest in "saving Zeaflin's soul" and getting him to leave the UnderWorld. Looks like she finally has the opportunity.

I'm not pleased about the kids visiting the UnderWorld. Okay, I'm not pleased about *me* visiting the UnderWorld either. But if Vila can assure our safety--and he seems to think he can--and all we'll see is a courtroom, I suppose we should do it to help Zeaflin. We'd never forgive ourselves if he turned into a demon like Belial. Although come to think of it...with his blood red lips, sharp teeth and long fingernails, maybe he's already halfway there.

Billy interrupts my thoughts. "We'll all go, Mr. Vila. Right, Toby? Mr. Monsento?"

Toby gives an almost imperceptible nod of his head. Now four pairs of eyes are boring into me, waiting for my reply. I glance over at the bar in the corner of my salon, craving the familiar warmth of scotch that might lessen the tension I feel in my chest. But it's not there, so instead I take a deep breath and give a nod of assent toward Billy.

"Good. Once the prosecutor executes his subpoena, the OtherWorld will be notified and per standard protocol, an agent of the Department of Living Affairs will be assigned to accompany you to the UnderWorld. I shall be that agent." Vila turns to Abby. "Keep Ambrogio's phurba safe until the day of the hearing. Be certain to wear a dress with deep pockets to hide the phurba well. I will arrange for you to testify last, providing you sufficient time to draw close enough to Zeaflin to perform the purification." Abby nods, wide-eyed and pale.

"Maybe Abby should pass me the dagger, Mr. Vila," Billy suggests. "Being a girl, she might not be strong enough to push the blade in."

The color instantly returns to Abby's face. "It's not about *strength*, Billy. Remember? A phurba doesn't even have to be sharp to penetrate," she retorts.

Vila holds up a hand to call for a truce before Billy can respond. "Ambrogio requested Abby specifically," he reminds the boy.

Abby sticks her tongue out at Billy, who gives her a very fake shrug of nonchalance. "*Fine*. If you want to stab Zeaflin so badly, then you can do it," he concedes with a touch of snottiness that betrays his annoyance with the girl. Vila rises from his chair and grasps his walking stick.

"One word of advice. Keep your answers brief to any questions the prosecutor might bring to you here. Your goal is to convince him that your testimony will damage Zeaflin's chances for a light sentence. To do that, you will need to give the prosecutor the impression that Zeaflin is regressing back to his pure OtherWorld self. Therefore, if there are any *positive* things you can say about Zeaflin, do try to slip them into the conversation. But only enough to convince the prosecutor that it is worth his while to subpoena you. Once on the stand, you can say whatever negative things Ravat suggested." With that parting message, Vila abruptly disappears in a puff of blue smoke.

"It's getting late," Abby says softly, her defiant expression fading into one of misery.

"I can drive you all home," I offer and stand up to head over to the hall closet so I can grab my jacket.

Toby looks at Abby and shakes his head. "Billy and I can walk home, Mr. Monsento. You should drive Abby, though, or she'll be late," he responds. The kid must want me to talk to Abby alone. *But what is it he wants me to say? What can I say?* I watch helplessly as Toby and Billy make a hasty exit from my salon, leaving me alone with the girl. "Looks like it's just you and me, kiddo," I say, motioning toward the front door.

After I lock up the house, Abby and I make our way down the path in uncomfortable silence and hop into my car. While I fire up the engine and pull slowly away from the curb to begin our journey, I glance over at Abby. She is staring pensively out the side window. I struggle to figure out what I'm supposed to say to alleviate the anxiety she must be feeling over being assigned the task of stabbing Zeaflin with the phurba. I know how it feels, having been recruited to stab Marzee with one of those things. We are almost to her house when Abby speaks up.

"I'm scared, Mr. Monsento. I'm scared Zeaflin won't listen to me if I ask him to ascend after I stab him. I know Ambrogio thinks he will, but what if he won't?" I pull the car over and kill the engine. A small tear traces its way down Abby's cheek as she looks up at me. Several more tears threaten to follow it. I draw in a nervous breath.

"Look, kid. You once told me that maybe Ambrogio knows how everything will turn out or that maybe his will makes events unfold." I pause, becoming a bit confused about what I was trying to say.

"His will shapes events outside of his control," Abby corrects with a hint of a smile.

"Okay, so maybe that doesn't quite apply here since he seems to be in control, taking matters into his own hands by giving you his phurba." I pause again, lost.

"Maybe it does apply," she responds.

I give her a shake of my head, not following. "How do you figure?"

"This event *is* outside of Ambrogio's control, Mr. Monsento; it's entirely in Zeaflin's control. We may be taking Ambrogio's phurba to the UnderWorld to purify him, but it's ultimately Zeaflin who will decide if he ascends or not," Abby explains. She looks out my windshield at the street outside. The streetlamps are turning on, one by one, down the block. "I have to go! I promised I'd be home before dark." She pops open the car door and runs to her house.

I stare after her, thinking, *No, Abby, I get the feeling this upcoming event will be entirely in your control.*

———————— ◆ ————————

——— ◆ ———

Almost two days have passed with no visit from the UnderWorld prosecutor--or the kids, for that matter. They had their final exams yesterday, only a day after Ravat and Vila's visit, and I worry what effect the looming subpoena might have had on their tests. If I remember correctly, they only have a half-day of school today and are then free for the summer. Unless they flunked their tests, that is. If so, they might need to attend summer school.

With a sigh, I wander into the kitchen and pour myself an iced tea before I plop down onto a chair at the table. A movement catches my eye. There is someone standing outside my kitchen door. Like Ravat, he has a pale gray glow about him so he's undeniably a ghost. But unlike Ravat, he has arrived in a tangible form. This ghost has pasty white skin with oily brown hair that hangs down to his shoulders, and he is dressed in a tan suit with a red tie over a crisp white shirt. Very dapper. The ghost's eyes meet mine. They are penetrating orbs of ice blue that freeze me in place. My visitor flashes me a quick smile before he reaches up to rap on the kitchen door window. Even though I anticipate the knock, it still causes me to jump a little in my chair. I stand up to open the door.

"Arthur Monsento?" the ghost inquires.

"That'd be me. And you must be the prosecutor I've been told to expect." I look down and notice that he is carrying a small black briefcase, almost identical to the one Ravat brought with him. Must be standard issue for UnderWorld lawyers. I look back up. The ghost is smiling at me again but something isn't quite right; his teeth are too even and they are way too white. I stare at the teeth, trying to figure out how an UnderWorld spirit could have such perfect dental care.

"I am indeed the prosecutor. May I come in?" the ghost asks, walking past me, not waiting for my answer.

"Yeah, sure, come on in," I say, belatedly. A thin, gray phantom I didn't see at first trails behind the prosecutor. It is dressed in a cloak with the hood pulled over its face so I can't quite make out its features, but its eyes glow a sickly yellow hue from inside the depths of the hood. It passes me a rolled parchment with a skeletal hand.

"This is your subpoena, as well as the young people's subpoena. I am certain Ravat has informed you of my interest in your testimony as character witnesses," the prosecutor says as he pulls out a chair and sits down. The creepy hooded ghost skeleton floats over to stand behind his boss. Trying to ignore the glowing eyes boring into me, I unroll the parchment and read over the subpoena.

```
The   UnderWorld   summons   Arthur   Monsento,
Abigail Grant, William Miller and Tobias Moore
to  testify,  at  a  time  and  date  to  yet  be
determined,  as  character  witnesses  for  the
defendant, Zeaflin.
```

There is a small silver drawing of a justice scale in the top left corner of the paper. In the bottom right corner of the page is a small red stamp that looks like a two-pronged pitchfork. The other bottom corner bears an image of a small pointy helmet with wings painted in gold.

"Fancy," I say, tossing the document onto the table and taking a seat across from the prosecutor. "And you are?" I ask, keeping my focus on the less spooky creature in my kitchen.

The ghost in the suit frowns. "You may call me Mr. Prosecutor. Unlike the defendant, I have no need or desire to establish a relationship with the living," he responds. I blink at him, shocked by his rudeness.

"Okay, *Mr. Prosecutor*. You've served your subpoena. What else do you want?"

"Just a few preliminary questions answered to help me assess your usefulness as a witness. A mere formality," the prosecutor replies.

I lean back in my chair and cross my arms. "Shoot," I say.

My seated guest gives me a perplexed look. "I have no gun and certainly nothing to shoot at," he replies. Now I'm perplexed. *Is he serious?* The prosecutor sits silent. We both stare at each other until I decide I must need to explain.

"It means ask away," I say.

The prosecutor furrows his brow and gives me a frustrated head shake. "I do wish the living would just say what they mean. I can't be expected to keep up with their ridiculous slang, can I?" he laments. The ghost skeleton behind him lets out a low, bone-chilling moan of commiseration.

Mr. Prosecutor pulls out a notepad and pen. "Let's start with your relationship to the defendant. You are his medium, correct?"

"When he pays me to summon spirits for him, I am," I reply.

"And you agree to work for him in full awareness that he is from the UnderWorld?" I shrug. He leans forward and locks onto my eyes. "Why, Arthur Monsento? Why would you agree to work with a creature from the UnderWorld?"

I hold eye contact. "He pays well," I reply. Then I remember I need to convince the prosecutor that I can be useful to him. "And he makes me coffee sometimes. I kind of like that." The prosecutor's eyes narrow and he scribbles down my comment. Then he looks back up at me.

"I have been told that you have Zeaflin's crystal ball, that he gave it to you. Is this true?" he asks.

"I have an ordinary living model. Hold on, let me go grab it for you." I stand up and head into my salon to grab the crystal ball I picked up at the *Party Shoppe* on Locust Street yesterday. Fortunately, they carry costumes and accessories year-round. Of course, the ball I picked up isn't crystal—it's plastic—but that should make it even more convincing that it's a cheap orb and not Zeaflin's.

I grab the ball from its stand and spin around to head back to the kitchen but the prosecutor has decided to follow me here, instead of waiting at my kitchen table. No hooded skeleton ghost is behind him this time so hopefully its job was just to hand me the subpoena and go back home afterward. I walk over and pass the ball to my "guest". He rolls it in his hands and gives me a look of disgust.

"I'm surprised your human clients are convinced by such a cheap prop, Arthur Monsento. But then again, living creatures are known to be most gullible."

"Is that a fact?" I retort, struggling to hold my temper in check.

"It is a well-known fact, yes," the prosecutor replies, passing the ball back to me. Then he tucks his notepad into his front pocket and gives me a long stare. "One final question, if I may?"

"Sure. Knock yourself out," I say, drawing out a fresh look of confusion from my visitor. "It means go ahead," I elucidate. The prosecutor lets out a small, tired sigh and closes his eyes. After a brief moment, he pulls himself together and looks at me.

"Are you friends with the defendant? Is he your *friend*?" he asks pointedly. This is it! The answer to this question could clinch the enforcement of that subpoena; I just need to answer it nebulously enough. I let out a fake cough and pretend to be nervous.

"I don't know; it's hard to say. We living tend to believe that because we think we are friends with someone, they are friends with us. You know, because we're just so darned *gullible* and all."

The prosecutor looks confused. I wait him out, hoping he interprets my answer to mean that I think Zeaflin and I are compadres. After a minute or so of digesting my comment, the attorney gives me a brief nod.

"Thank you for your cooperation, Arthur Monsento. I should like to interview William Miller next. Is he here?"

"Does it look like he's here?" I ask sarcastically, sweeping my hand to indicate the empty room.

"No, it does not. Is he here?" I stare at the prosecutor. He is obviously completely clueless. Then again, he is a lawyer.

"I'll call him. What about the other kids? You want to interview them too?" I ask, wandering over to grab my cell phone from the side table next to the front door.

"No. I see no need to interview the girl or the other boy, Tobias, prior to their testimony in the courtroom. I am sure they will perform admirably." He gives me a confident smile.

"Is that a fact?" I respond.

The prosecutor frowns thoughtfully. "No, I don't think so. I think it's more of an opinion…" He trails off with a befuddled look on his face.

———— ♦ ————

Billy answers the call on the second ring. "What's up, Mr. Monsento?" I can barely hear him over the hullabaloo in the background.

"Billy! Get off that telephone and clean up this mess! I'm telling Mom and you're going to get it this time!" a girl shrills in the background. "Don't you walk away from—" Then I hear a door slam and footsteps pounding on stairs.

"You there, kid?" I ask.

"Yeah, Mr. Monsento. I had to get away from Suzy and Luanne or I'd never be able to hear you. They knocked over a lamp, chasing me around the living room and are trying to make me clean it up. Like it's my fault they're so clumsy." Curious as I am, I resist asking why his sisters were chasing him around the living room.

"Look, Billy. The prosecutor is here and he wants to interview you. Can you come over here, pronto?" I ask, casting an eye on my visitor. He has migrated over to my tarot card table and is starting to play with the deck.

"No problem. Want me to call Toby and Abby?" Billy asks.

"No, just you," I reply. A muffled woman's voice travels through the line. "Billy, would you come down here, please!"

Billy huffs out an angry sigh. "I'll be there as soon as I can, Mr. Monsento," he promises and then hangs up. Sounds like Billy might be a little delayed so I head over to distract Mr. Prosecutor.

"Billy is on his way but might be a few minutes. Want a reading?" I ask.

The ghost looks surprised by the offer. "I'm not sure. I've never had one before. The cards are supposed to tell the future, are they not?"

"More like probable outcomes," I reply. "Look, how about I give you a quick reading before Billy gets here? It just takes three cards—past, present and future." I eye the prosecutor closely. He looks hesitant but if I can get him to accept a reading, maybe I can plant some over-confidence in him in regard to Zeaflin's case. "Seriously, it will only take a few minutes," I add, taking a seat at the tarot table. My "client" pauses, then takes the seat across from me. He gives me an expectant look.

"What do I need to do?" he asks.

I push the cards his way. "Shuffle the cards and then give them back to me," I direct. Mr. Prosecutor performs a lame half-shuffle, dropping a few of the cards to the floor. I lean over, pick them up and push them back into the pile. He starts to shuffle the cards again.

"No! Er...no, that's okay. You've shuffled them well enough," I tell him. It's just too painful to watch. I take the deck from him and splay the cards across the table. Then I pile them back together and pull out three cards randomly, laying them out in a neat line.

"Past. Present. Future," I say, jabbing my finger on each card to indicate which card stands for which timeline. Then I flip over the Past card: the Five of Wands. Interesting. I work on interpreting this card for him.

"You have struggled mightily to obtain your position as an UnderWorld litigator. You have had much competition from the many lawyers who have descended, but you prevailed and are reaping the rewards of a most successful career." The prosecutor leans back in his chair and smiles so I guess I've "divined" correctly.

I flip over the Present card: the Star card, reversed. I strive to keep my expression neutral. If I recall correctly, the reversed Star can be read as arrogance and impotence. I can't tell him that so I opt for the non-reversed interpretation.

"The Star card in the present position indicates bright prospects. If you succeed in winning your current case, your career will further flourish." I glance up at my client. He is still smiling but is now leaning forward in anticipation of his future reading so I flip over the Future card for him: the Tower. I widen my eyes in surprise. The prosecutor picks up on my reaction.

"Is something wrong?" he asks, his smile sliding into a worried frown. I instantly put on a poker face.

"No, not at all," I reply casually. "The Tower card is a very lucky card, is all. It predicts your future will be one of continued success and that you will be content in all aspects of your..." I trail off. I was going to say life but that isn't exactly the correct word here. "Eternal existence," I conclude.

The prosecutor relaxes and his pleased smile returns. I battle against smiling myself. The Tower card is one of the worst cards you can draw. Many interpret it to be a card predicting adversity and unforeseen catastrophe. This could be a good sign. Maybe Abby is going to succeed in stabbing Zeaflin and convincing him to ascend, pulling the rug out from Mr. Prosecutor here. I'm sure he would find *that* conclusion to his case a catastrophe.

I'm racking my brain, trying to figure out how else I might entertain my guest, when the front door opens and Billy steps inside the salon. He hesitates a moment when his eyes rest on the ghost seated at my tarot card table. Then his face lights up and he crosses over to stand next to me. "Are you reading the tarot cards, Mr. Monsento? Can I watch?" he asks.

"Sorry, kid, you missed it," I tell him, causing Billy's beaming face to drop into a pout. I nod toward the visitor sitting on the other side of the table. "This is the prosecutor for Zeaflin's case."

Billy reaches forward to shake the prosecutor's hand. "I figured that much out, Mr. Monsento," he replies, still waiting for the ghost to reach out for the handshake.

Mr. Prosecutor is leaning back in his chair, cringing away from Billy's hand with a curled lip of disgust. "I'm sorry, but I don't touch the living. I find the feel of their flesh quite unappealing," he states bluntly.

Billy blinks rapidly, drops his hand and looks at me, slack-jawed. Yeah, this ghost is brutally honest, all right. I rise from my seat to offer it to Billy, who sits down and gives his attention to the rude ghost across the table.

"Just a few questions, William Miller, and I'll be on my way," Mr. Prosecutor says, jumping directly to the matter at hand. "Tell me about the defendant, Zeaflin."

Billy shrugs. "He's our client." The prosecutor makes a "go on" gesture with his hands. Billy shrugs again. "He's a repeat client," he elaborates. The prosecutor makes another "go on" gesture. Billy glances at me, standing behind the ghost. I give him a half-eye roll and make my own "go on" gesture.

"Um, he pays well?" I raise a brow at Billy. *Seriously?* Never at a loss for words, this kid chooses *now* to become succinct? The prosecutor lets out a frustrated sigh.

"Tell me about how you *feel* about him. Your *relationship* with him," he clarifies. Billy looks up at me. I mouth the word "character witness" to remind the kid of his role here. Billy looks back at the ghost.

"He's pretty cool—"

"Of *course,* he's cool," the prosecutor interrupts. "He is undead. But you say you consider Zeaflin to be attractive? In what way?" Billy looks up at me, his lips twisted to one side and brow furrowed with confusion.

"Pretty cool means interesting and fun," I interpret. The ghost rubs his forehead and groans. "Yeah, I know. You wish the living would just say what they mean," I say with mock sympathy before I explain to Billy, "Mr. Prosecutor is a literal kind of guy, kid."

The ghost composes himself and drops his hand. "Please elaborate then. What is fun and interesting about the defendant?" he asks.

"He's from the UnderWorld; he can dissipate and vaporate; he's a snappy dresser. Oh, and I like his long fingernails and sharp teeth. They're totally wicked!" Billy exclaims.

"He means awesome," I interject hastily. The prosecutor rubs his forehead again. Then he rises slowly from the tarot table.

"I believe I have all I need, Arthur Monsento and William Miller. An agent from the UnderWorld will contact your OtherWorld representative shortly with a date and time for your testimony," the ghost says, leaning down to pick up the briefcase he'd placed on the floor next to the table when we began our tarot reading.

"Sure thing," I respond and wander over to open my front door for the specter.

"Yes, Arthur Monsento, it is absolutely a sure thing," Mr. Prosecutor agrees. I stand by the door to watch him walk down the front porch steps. He vanishes into thin air before he reaches the sidewalk.

Chapter 18

"He was weird, huh, Mr. Monsento?" Billy remarks. He looks down at the three tarot cards I'd pulled from the deck for Mr. Prosecutor. "What'd his cards predict?" he asks. I point at the Tower card.

"Deception and ruin," I reply, unable to keep a smile off my face. Not that I'm a firm believer in fortune telling, but it's possible the spectral energy of Mr. Prosecutor might have drawn some magic into the tarot cards. Billy looks surprised, then he grins.

"Cool!" he exclaims. My smile fades. Sounds like we'll be visiting the UnderWorld soon. Geez! I hope they don't have demon deputies or goblin stenographers in their courthouse. We never asked who or what worked there.

"You okay with going to the UnderWorld, kid?" I ask. "It could be a scary place, in spite of what Vila says."

Billy misinterprets my concern for a joke and laughs. "Yeah. Imagine a room full of prudish, rude, literal ghosts carrying briefcases; that *is* some scary stuff." I study Billy a moment. He is either one brave kid or a very reckless one.

"Would you read my cards?" Billy requests.

I shake my head. "Not today, kid. I need some alone time before the UnderWorld sends for us, okay?"

Billy cocks his head to one side, confused by my sudden anxiety. I come to the decision that Billy is more reckless than brave. "Scoot," I tell him. Billy rolls his eyes and heads for the front door. Before he exits, he turns back to me.

"It's going to be okay, Mr. Monsento. The cards say ruin for the prosecutor, not for us. I bet if you read my cards, you'd see that this is all going to end happily." Billy steps outside and closes the door behind him.

I conclude that Billy isn't reckless; he's an optimist. He believes his tarot reading will predict success in saving Zeaflin, but suddenly I'm not so certain. Catastrophe and ruin could be events the prosecutor is witness to, not events specifically catastrophic for him. Sometimes the mystery of the future is best left unseen.

———————•◆•———————

It's a nice June afternoon, with a bright sun and a light breeze, so I decide to take a walk to get out of the house and think things over. I don't know much about Zeaflin but one thing I do know is that he has a strong dislike for the OtherWorld, so it's a complete unknown if he will accept purification and ascend there. And that's *if* we succeed in smuggling in the phurba and *if* Abby will have the opportunity to use it and *if* she is brave enough to perform the task. That's an awful lot of ifs.

My feet automatically draw me to Teddy's Tavern, a place I haven't visited for almost a year now. I hesitate, unsure if going into the pub is a good idea, before I pull open the heavy wood door and step into the cool, dark interior of the bar. Teddy is standing behind the counter, pulling a beer for a customer who is watching a baseball game on the TV posted on the wall over Teddy's head. Outside of him, there are no other patrons. The nice weather must be keeping the tavern's usual Friday afternoon crowd away.

Teddy notices me standing by the door and gives me a hearty wave of greeting. "Arthur Monsento!" he calls out. "Now there's a face I haven't seen in a long time. I was beginning to worry that something might have happened to you." Too late to back out now, so I head over to grab a stool at the far end of the bar, away from the sports fan. Teddy grabs a glass and pours me my usual: a single malt whiskey, neat.

Remembering Zeaflin's preference, I shake my head. "Put some ice in it, will you, Teddy? It's difficult for my friend to drink scotch neat."

Teddy arches a brow. "You meeting a girl here, Arthur?" His amused smile causes the corner of his eyes to crinkle.

"Not exactly," I reply.

"That's a pity," Teddy remarks. He drops some ice into the scotch and places the drink in front of the stool next to mine. Then he looks at me questioningly.

"I'll take a cola," I say.

"On the wagon, huh? Okay, one cola coming up."

A brief flash of sunlight lights up the bar behind me, announcing that Teddy has another customer. I'm not in a small talk kind of mood so I think I'll drink my soda quick and move on before it gets too crowded in here. Fortunately for me, Teddy promptly returns from the soda tap with my cola. He passes me the glass but his eyes are focused over my shoulder.

"Your friend is here," he tells me. I look in the mirror hanging behind the bar and see Vila, taking the seat in front of the drink I ordered for Zeaflin. *Is he here to tell me it's time to go to the UnderWorld?*

I look at Teddy. "Put a shot of rum in this cola, will you?" I request, with hope that the rum might calm my suddenly trembling hands. Vila and I sit in silence until Teddy pushes a shot glass of rum my way and wanders off to stand near his other customer. He watches us from the far end of the counter with a worried look on his face.

"You here to take us to the UnderWorld?" I ask hoarsely, dropping the rum into the cola and taking a deep pull. The heat of the rum warms my stomach and my hands become steadier. Vila places his finger into Zeaflin's scotch and swirls the ice cubes around before picking the drink up and holding it high in a cheers gesture.

"I didn't take you for a drinking man, Vila," I say, watching him gulp the drink down in one go. Vila places the glass down and looks at my reflection in the mirror.

"I am not, Mr. Monsento. But since your usual drinking companion is occupied at the moment, I can fill his role for you today. And no, I am not here to take you to the UnderWorld. I am here because I believe you could use some company." I nod and stare back at Vila in the mirror.

"So, what shall we talk about?" Vila asks congenially. I'm speechless. This is not the Vila I know at all. To help alleviate my discomfort with this suddenly companionable Vila, I motion for Teddy to bring us another round.

Vila looks over at the television screen. "Sports, perhaps?" he suggests.

"Sorry, I don't follow sports," I reply.

Vila smiles briefly. "Nor do I," he confesses. We sit in awkward silence until Teddy drops off the drinks and moseys back out of hearing range, then I ask Vila if Ambrogio sent him here.

Vila nods his head. "Even though the Department of Living Aegis has been abolished for some time now, I was your assigned Aegis agent when you were a child so Ambrogio thought me the most suitable individual to provide counsel to you. He believes you could use an adult to talk with regarding the upcoming events."

I think about it. "Maybe," I concede.

Hold on a second...did Vila just say he was my guardian angel??

I turn in my seat to look at Vila head on. He is slamming his scotch down like it's water and he's been lost in the desert for a month. For someone who isn't a drinking man, I'd say Vila could drink me under the table.

"You were my guardian...er...Aegis agent?" I ask Vila timidly. Surely I misheard.

"This surprises you?" he responds.

"Yeah. No. I-I don't know," I stammer.

Teddy gestures to Vila to ask if he'd like another drink. Vila declines. I take a pull on my own drink to clear my head and find my lost sense of reality. Once I locate it, I look at Vila through the mirror again. Ambrogio is right. I would like to talk with an adult, even if he's a stuffed shirt like Vila, to discuss what's been worrying me since I started on the stroll that led me to Teddy's place. Does the future card for Mr. Prosecutor portend catastrophe and calamity for him when Zeaflin ascends or calamity in the courtroom after Zeaflin is impaled and catastrophe for us when he refuses to be purified?

"Okay, you're here so let's talk then. If Abby stabs him, do you think Zeaflin is going to agree to ascend? Because I'm not so sure he will; he didn't the last time he was stabbed with a phurba," I point out.

Vila gives me a tight-lipped smile. "You forget that Nathan Hammersly was still in the UnderWorld at that time, and there was no threat of Malebolge over his head then either. Zeaflin is very stubborn but he isn't a fool. He knows full well the UnderWorld prison is not a happy place. And while he may find our bureaucracy frustrating, it is difficult to believe he would choose Malebolge over the OtherWorld."

"Okay, so he'll agree to ascend. But he can't do that without Abby stabbing him. Do you think she's up to the task? Do you think she'll be able to stab Zeaflin?" I ask Vila's reflection.

"Yes, Mr. Monsento, I do believe she will successfully wield Ambrogio's phurba. We have both seen Abby in action during the battle with Belial's prison guards. She was a strong girl then and she is a strong girl now. She will perform what is necessary when the time calls for it." Vila gazes back at me in the mirror. I say nothing, so he takes advantage of the lull in conversation to bear his news.

"The UnderWorld contacted my department today. They have requested I escort you and the detectives to their courthouse for your testimony tomorrow morning, 10 am living time. Will you and the children be ready by then?"

"Do we have a choice?" I ask.

"Yes. But I think we should stick with the date and time selected by the UnderWorld to avoid the additional paperwork of requesting an extension." I stare at Vila's reflection, trying to determine if he's joking with me, but he appears to be serious. That, or he's got a great deadpan delivery.

"I will arrive promptly at 9 am," Vila continues, "to provide you some time to visit with Zeaflin before the hearing, if you'd like. The children, however, will not be allowed to visit him."

"Yeah, I'd like to see him beforehand. Thanks," I reply. Since I'll have an opportunity to talk to Zeaflin before our testimony and because Vila is in a friendly mood, I take a chance on asking him for a favor.

"Mind if I ask you something, Vila?"

"That is what I am here for, Mr. Monsento."

"Do you know Zeaflin's name--you know, before he became Zeaflin? He said he forgot it because he drank from some river in the UnderWorld."

"Lethe," Vila says.

"Last name or first?" I ask.

Vila frowns at me. "The name of the river is called Lethe, the river of forgetfulness. I do not know Zeaflin's previous name."

"Could you find out? Maybe ask Ambrogio? If Zeaflin refuses to ascend, I'd like to at least let him know who he was, in case he becomes a demon in Malebolge and forgets who he is," I explain.

I finish my rum and cola and signal to Teddy to write up the tab. While Teddy preps my bill, Vila rises from his barstool. "All right, Mr. Monsento. I will ask Ambrogio who Zeaflin was in life. He does not usually share such information but perhaps he will make an exception for Zeaflin, given the circumstances." Teddy brings me the bill so I pull out my wallet. He watches Vila exit his tavern before he takes the money for our drinks.

"You have strange friends, Arthur. That guy looks like he came straight out of a *Batman* cartoon," Teddy says. I give him a bemused look. "You know the *Gray Ghost*, don't you? He was one of the good guys," he elaborates.

I shake my head. "Never heard of him. But that's certainly an apropos nickname for my friend."

"Don't be a stranger, huh, Arthur?" Teddy calls out as I head for the door. I give him a nod and step outside to begin the long walk home, where I'll soon have the pleasure of contacting the kids to inform them that tomorrow morning, we'll all be dissipating to the UnderWorld.

———————— ◆ ————————

Dad and I are in the backyard, planting carrot seeds, when Mom sticks her head out the backscreen door off our kitchen. "Abby? Billy is on the telephone," she calls out. I take a deep breath and head into the house. *Is this it? Has the UnderWorld issued their subpoena?*

"What's up, Billy?" I ask, trying to keep my voice neutral. Mom breezes past me and heads for her sewing room off the dining room, leaving me alone in the kitchen.

"Mr. Monsento called. The UnderWorld has issued their subpoena and we're supposed to report for testimony tomorrow at 10 am," Billy relays. My heart starts to pound in my chest.

"Okay," I manage to choke out.

"But Mr. Monsento asks us to arrive by 9 am because he wants to visit with Mr. Zeaflin before the hearing," Billy continues.

"Okay," I rasp out. Then I clear my closed throat. "Can we visit with him too?" I ask, thinking maybe I could stab him before the hearing and get it over with quickly.

"Sorry, Abs. Mr. Monsento said only adults are permitted to visit the prisoners," Billy replies. I heave out a heavy sigh that Billy picks up through the phone line.

"Don't worry, Abby. Mr. Monsento read the prosecutor's tarot cards and he predicts catastrophe for the prosecutor. So this is all going to work out okay, you'll see." I don't believe in tarot cards and especially not tarot cards interpreted by Monsento, but it appears that Billy does.

"I'll be there by nine," I say and place the receiver gently down in its cradle. I turn around and see Dad standing just inside the screen door, wearing a frown of concern. "Bad news, Pumpkin?" he asks.

Even though I feel just awful about it, I dig up a little white lie. "Mr. Monsento threw out his back yesterday. He's doing well, but Billy and I thought we might visit with him tomorrow morning for a few hours--see if he needs us to run any errands for him. If it's okay with you and Mom," I respond, my cheeks starting to burn with remorse over my untruth at such a terrible time as this. Dad doesn't notice my reddening cheeks and instead walks over to give me a brief hug.

"That's very nice, Pumpkin. Maybe your mom can put together a care package for him and you can take that over when you visit?" Dad suggests, pulling back and giving me a smile.

"Uh, sure. I think he'd like that," I reply, feeling very uncomfortable.

"I'll talk to her about it a little later. In the meantime, how about we go back and finish planting those carrots?" Dad says cheerfully, tossing an arm around my shoulders to lead me back outside to the garden. Grateful for the distraction, I focus on digging the neat little rows for Dad to sow his carrot seeds. After that, we move on to planting the cucumbers.

It's suppertime by the time Dad and I finish the garden. I do my best to eat the delicious food Mom cooked--pot roast with green beans and potatoes--but my appetite is off. While I'm forcing a few forkfuls of dinner down, Dad is asking Mom about the care package. Mom looks at my mostly full plate and notices I'm not going to eat my usual two servings of pot roast.

"Abby appears less hungry tonight, so I can pack up the leftover pot roast for her to bring to her ailing friend," Mom says. Then she frowns. "Are you feeling okay, honey? You usually just gobble down my pot roast." I look up from my plate.

"I'm fine, Mom," I reply, stuffing another forkful into my mouth. "Just not as hungry tonight. I ate too many gummy bears after lunch today."

Mom purses her lips in disapproval. "Please don't talk with your mouth full, Abby," she scolds. "And next time, you should eat a piece of fruit if you're hungry and it's close to dinnertime. Candy is a very unhealthy snack." I look down at my plate and try to appear contrite.

"May I be excused?" I ask. "I just cracked open that new *Nancy Drew* book Dad picked up for me last week and I'm anxious to see how this latest case plays out." Mom gives my now half-full plate a frown but nods her consent.

———————• ♦ •———————

Safe in my room, I flip on the side lamp, grab the *Nancy Drew* book, and lie down on my bed with the pillow propped up. I know I'll never be able to concentrate but if Mom or Dad come upstairs, it's best to keep up the pretense that I'm up here reading. I open the book to page sixty and stare at the jumble of words while I think about tomorrow.

Will I succeed in smuggling in Ambrogio's phurba? If so, will I find the opportunity to stab Zeaflin with it? If the opportunity does arise, will I lose my nerve and have to pass the dagger to Billy instead? Will Zeaflin agree to ascend if Billy stabs him? Will he agree to ascend if I stab him?

I flip a page of the book and force myself to read. I'm almost to the end, having little idea what I've just read, when Mom pokes her head into the room to warn me it's almost 11 pm and well past my bedtime.

Chapter 19

I sleep poorly, tossing and turning and fighting with my pillow and blankets, waiting for morning to arrive. When the sun finally does creep out over the horizon, lighting the sky with a pale pink hue, I stagger out of bed and take a cool shower, letting the water run down my face to wash away the fuzziness I feel from lack of sleep. After my shower, while I brush my hair, I peer into the bathroom mirror at the red-haired girl with deep bags under her eyes.

"Can you do it? Can you actually stab Zeaflin?" I ask my reflection. The girl in the mirror just stares back wearily, refusing to answer, so I head for my bedroom closet and the deep-pocketed dress I selected to wear to Zeaflin's hearing today.

I pull the dress over my head and step in front of the full-length mirror hanging inside the closet door to look myself over. The dress is pale yellow with fine white lace sewn around the scoop-neck collar and elbow-length sleeves. While it may not be the height of fashion, it does at least have a heavily pleated skirt that should hide the phurba well. I twirl around once and make an assessment. This is a dress I haven't worn in a while and it's a little short now, so I grab a pair of shorts to put on underneath in case the skirt of the dress becomes too revealing when I lunge toward my victim and give him a good stab in the back. A dark smile briefly passes the face of the girl in the mirror when she realizes that she'll be stabbing Zeaflin in the back both figuratively and literally.

The phurba is in my desk drawer, wrapped in a hand towel. I wander over to remove it from its wrapping and run my finger along the dull three-sided blade. It may be dull but it is metal and it tapers to a point like a real knife does, so it should drive home easily. Unless I hit bone. I swallow down the nausea welling up with that horrible thought and tuck the phurba into the right-hand pocket of my skirt. Then I head back to the closet mirror and twirl around again. The dagger is surprisingly light and doesn't weigh down the right side of the skirt like I thought it would. I can tell something is in my pocket but I know it's there; I don't think anyone else will notice. I hope not, anyway.

With a sigh, I dig out my shiny black dress shoes, low-heeled because I'm a practical kind of girl, and slip my feet inside. Then I grab a yellow scrunchie out of the hair accessory box sitting on my bedside table to tie my hair back in its usual pony-tail. Now dressed, I take in a deep, rattling breath of nervousness. It's time to go downstairs and face Mom and Dad.

I can smell Mom frying bacon, meaning I'll need to whip up an appetite for a hearty breakfast that I don't feel I can eat. I slip into the

kitchen unnoticed and stand for a moment to look at my parents…
well, what I can see of them, that is. Dad has his nose in his newspaper and Mom has her back turned and is indeed frying up some
bacon and eggs. I draw in another deep breath and pull out my seat
at the kitchen table. The sound of my chair sliding across the floor
tiles alerts my parents of my arrival.

"Good morning, Abby," Mom and Dad say in unison. They both
laugh at the dual greeting. I force a smile and reply in kind.

"My, Sweetie! I haven't seen you in that dress for a year or two. It
still fits you?" Mom asks with disbelief. Then she looks down at the
hemline and her smiling face immediately drops into a frown. "The
skirt is a little short, don't you think?"

"I put shorts on underneath. I thought I'd try out a new style--
throw Billy and Toby off a bit. They're sure to tease me about wearing
a dress today," I reply, working hard to draw my lips into a mischievous grin while I slip into my chair and scooch it close to the table.
Mom furrows her brow but lets the dress issue go. Instead, she turns
back to scoop a couple of the fried eggs out of the pan and slide them
onto the plate in front of me. Next, Mom adds two strips of bacon
and a slice of toast and pushes the plate toward me before turning
back to prep her and Dad's bacon and eggs. I look down at the daunt-
ing pile of food and force myself to grab my fork and dig in heartily.

After we finish breakfast, I help Mom with the dirty dishes.
By the time the cleanup is complete, it's time for me to head over
to Monsento's house so Mom passes me the leftover pot roast care
package, wrapped tightly in aluminum, and I give her and Dad a hug

goodbye. I hope Vila is right and all I'll see is a boring courthouse with blurry gray ghost lawyers, but in case he's wrong, I hold my parents in the hug a little longer than usual, having no idea if I'll still be the same Abby when I return.

———— ◆ ————

I stare at the steam rising from my fourth cup of coffee in a daze. I've been awake since 6 am and I'm feeling the caffeine jitters, but it was either coffee or scotch to keep me occupied while I wait for the kids and Vila to arrive. After significant internal debate, I decided it's probably better to testify sober, so coffee it has been.

A loud rap, followed immediately by the doorbell, announces Vila has arrived so I rise from the kitchen table to go open the front door for him. I'll never understand why Vila almost always rings the bell and waits for me to let him in while Zeaflin usually just danced on in like he owned the place. Not that I'm complaining, mind you. It's bad enough being startled by Zeaflin; the last thing I need is for Vila to pick up the habit and begin appearing behind me unannounced.

I open the door and, sure enough, there stands Vila, wearing his customary gray suit paired with his usual dour visage. But unexpectedly, the three detectives are standing alongside him. Abby is in a yellow dress with a heavily-pleated skirt. She probably chose it because the folds hide the lump of the phurba in her pocket, but the dress is a mite short for her, I'd say. Abby is holding a mysterious aluminum package that smells suspiciously like food and I wonder,

*Is she is worried about the food in the UnderWorld prison and bring-
ing Zeaflin a care package?* That thought brings on a sudden jab of
regret that I didn't think to pick up a bottle of scotch for him. Zeaflin
probably could use a little pick-me-up before his sentencing hearing
today.

I step back to allow my four visitors to enter the salon and close
the door behind them. Then I glance at the clock over the mantel: 9
am. No surprise there; Vila is always punctual. I turn my head just in
time to catch Vila looking me over, wearing a deep frown. I'm in my
best navy blue suit with complementary tie but I still feel self-con-
scious under Vila's scrutinizing gaze.

"Mr. Monsento," Vila says, as way of greeting.

"That'd be me, all day, every day," I respond. Billy muffles a laugh.
That boy is undeniably one very easy audience.

"Exceptionally droll repartee, Mr. Monsento," Vila comments
stiffly, apparently not so easy. He reaches into his suit coat pocket
and extracts the small notebook that he always seems to carry with
him. "I have brought the information you requested," he tells me and
flips open the notebook. He tears out one of the pages and holds it
out toward me.

I take the paper from Vila's hand and look down at Zeaflin's original name, written in a flowing cursive script that is likely Ambrogio's
handwriting. Billy darts over and reads off the page in my hand.
"Lucius Tailor. Who's that, Mr. Vila?"

"Lucius Tailor is Zeaflin's living name. Realm walkers adopt new
names when they are initiated into the fold," Vila replies.

Billy lets out a low whistle. "Cool!" he exclaims. "Why did you ask for his living name, Mr. Monsento?"

Vila answers for me. "Zeaflin does not recall his living name, young man. Mr. Monsento would like to provide it to him out of some sort of sentimental impulse."

"Is that a fact?" I retort, but begrudgingly realize he's right; I am becoming an old softie.

As if to emphasize that point, Abby reaches for my arm and gives it a gentle squeeze. "That's very nice of you, Mr. Monsento. I'm sure Zeaflin will appreciate the reminder," she says, giving Vila a scowl.

"No doubt he will," Vila responds with a touch of contempt, his eyes focused up toward the ceiling.

Abby holds her foil parcel out toward me. I give her a questioning look. "It's a care package from my parents. They sent you some leftover pot roast from last night," she explains.

"And why would they do that?" I ask, thinking that's a very strange thing to do.

Abby sighs. "I told them you threw your back out," she replies.

I stare hard at the girl, trying to comprehend why she'd tell them I threw my back out and why her parents would think that food would cure the problem. "Why'd you—" I begin to ask, but Vila cuts me off.

"While the discussion of damaged backs and dinner packages makes for riveting conversation, perhaps we should consider beginning our trip to the UnderWorld instead?" he suggests. "Unless you'd prefer to discuss beef roast over visiting with Zeaflin, Mr. Monsento? I certainly would not fault you if you choose the former."

I study Vila. *Is he trying to be funny?* Vila stares back at me blankly, his face dead serious, so I shake my head and say, "No. Let's go," before I grab the care package from Abby's hands and rush off to drop it into the refrigerator. After I hurry back to the salon to join the others, Vila motions for us all to join hands in a circle so we can begin our travel to the realm of the UnderWorld.

———— ◆ ————

Soon after we join hands in a circle with Vila, we all turn into hazy figures that look like millions of tiny water droplets molded together into two men, two boys, and a girl. Ordinarily I'd be scared but this is the same thing that happened to us during our last realm jump with Vila, only that time we were dissipating to the OtherWorld. Light fades in and out of our circle as we enter and exit several in-between realms on our way to the UnderWorld. I'm curious whether one of those realms might be where Nathan hid before he entered the living realm for Vila to provide him asylum.

It doesn't seem to take long to travel to the UnderWorld, and we soon arrive in what appears to be an empty conference room. I'm surprised Vila is familiar enough with the layout of the UnderWorld to land us in its courthouse so precisely, not to mention into an empty room on top of it. It makes me wonder if he's represented other living people in an UnderWorld court case before us. Or maybe he visits the UnderWorld in his free time for a little change of scenery.

Vila was right, at least in terms of this room; it is very much like one you might find in the living realm, although it's a bit on the old-fashioned side. In the center of the room is a long pinewood table with six orange-colored, hard-plastic chairs arranged around it. There is an empty whiteboard with red markers sitting on the shelf below and a beige rotary-dial telephone mounted on the wall next to the door. There is also a tall bookshelf, crammed full of what appears to be law books. One of the book titles I can make out from where I stand reads "Legal Loopholes of the UnderWorld". Outside of a garish ceiling lamp comprised of three yellow light globes with bright orange metal leaves curling around them, this is a very dull room.

Monsento tugs his hands free from Vila and Billy and sinks down into one of the chairs at the conference table, looking green around the edges. I feel a little lightheaded too so I pull out the chair next to Monsento and join him at the table to wait for the feeling to pass. I glance up at the boys. The trip doesn't seem to have bothered them at all; they both look pert and alert. Lucky them!

"They have telephones in the UnderWorld?" Toby asks, looking over at the phone on the wall.

Vila follows his gaze. "No, they do not. However, since conference rooms in the living realm typically contain a telephone, the designer of this room probably felt it necessary to include one in his conference room too. From the style of it, he must have based his model on a living telephone created in the 1970s."

"Is everything styled on the 1970s, Mr. Vila?" Billy asks.

"Most likely. Modernization isn't a strong attribute of the UnderWorld."

"Swell, so we'll be getting a blast from the past, huh?" Monsento says.

"Cool!" Billy exclaims.

"Are all the ghosts here going to be wearing bell bottoms and peasant shirts?" Monsento asks sarcastically.

Vila gives him a humorless smile. "Only the décor will be so dated. Unlike OtherWorld spirits, the UnderWorld ghosts update their garb regularly. In that regard, they are as narcissistic as living beings," he explains.

"Is that so?" Monsento says.

"It is surely so, Mr. Monsento," Vila responds. "Have you recovered from your travels now? Shall we take a step outside and arrange your visit with Zeaflin? Time waits for no man, living or otherwise."

With a nod, Monsento rises from his chair. I stand up slowly with him, feeling the blood drain from my face. Every passing moment brings me closer to stabbing Zeaflin, and I do my best to push away the thought. But even when I don't think about it, my stomach still twists in knots with the ticking of the clock. Of course, it's difficult not to think about what I've been assigned to do because the weight of the phurba keeps tugging my dress slightly to the right, providing a constant reminder of what lies ahead.

Monsento takes a deep breath to steady himself. "Sure. Let's go," he finally replies to Vila. Then he looks at me. "You ready, kid?" I'm worried my voice will crack so I just nod, and we all fall into line behind Vila to make our way to the conference room exit and into the great unknown.

———————— ◆ ————————

Billy and Toby step immediately through the threshold, obviously eager to see the retro UnderWorld courthouse. Monsento is next in line but instead of boldly stepping out, he hesitates and pokes his head out the door to check for danger. "All clear," he tells me and Vila before he joins the boys, waiting just outside the conference room door. I look over at Vila. He is shaking his head in disgust, likely annoyed that Monsento thought he might be leading us directly into a hostile UnderWorld ghost mob.

I step out after Monsento and pause to look around. Our conference room opens into a long, ordinary hallway with many closed doors along both sides. The rooms are all labeled with a number posted on a sign next to the door. The room we walked out of is labeled with the number 102. I don't see any other identification outside of the numbers on the wall next to the doors so maybe these are all conference rooms just like ours.

The hallway is very attractive, with floors of highly polished white and rose marble tiles and a heavily sculpted ceiling of deep-tiered octagons, painted gold. There are ornate brass lamps along the wall on both sides of the corridor, casting a soft warm glow that is surprisingly pleasant for a building in the UnderWorld. All together as a group, we make our way down the hall in silence, with

Vila taking the lead. As we pass each door, I keep a wary eye for any demons that might suddenly jump out at us but fortunately, we complete our journey through the corridor unseen and unmolested.

We soon arrive at a spacious atrium where the four hallways of the courthouse converge. This center room is beautiful, with gray marble walls and tall white columns spanning four floors high to a skylight that must be at least a hundred feet above us. A green marble staircase spirals up the far end of the atrium to provide access to the floors above. Each upper level along the stairway is lined with a black wrought-iron rail, decorated with the image of either a large winged helmet or a two-pronged pitchfork in the center panels.

It is in this grand room we find the UnderWorld courthouse spirits. There must be hundreds of them, all with a gray glow about them and all in a hurry, either rushing up and down the main staircase or hustling down the other three halls off the atrium. Most of the male ghosts are dressed in well-fitted suits with ties of various styles and colors, while the lady ghosts are wearing either stylish pantsuits or designer dresses with matching high heels. If they weren't casting an eerie gray glow, you could easily mistake these spirits for living lawyers and their staff. Most of the ghosts ignore us but a few pause to stare our way in curiosity and whisper to each other as we pass by. Vila disregards them all until he finally comes to a stop in front of a spirit wearing a guard's uniform, standing next to a door with a sign reading "Courtroom 5".

"We are here for the Zeaflin sentencing hearing," Vila announces.

"Courtroom eight," the guard responds brusquely, giving us all a quick once-over.

"One of the living here would like to visit with the defendant beforehand," Vila tells him.

The guard looks at me and the boys, then back at Vila. "No kids," he orders and walks briskly down the corridor behind us--the same empty hall we just traveled through.

"What's the deal?" Monsento asks. "Are we supposed to follow him?"

"No. He's arranging for Zeaflin to be transferred to the visitation room. He'll come back," Vila replies. Then he points to a wooden bench sitting along the wall of the atrium adjacent to where we are standing. "Shall we sit while we wait?"

I gaze down the hall after the ghost guard. We passed many doors on our way to the atrium. Was one of them the visitation room? I watch the guard vanish through a door farther down the hall from the conference room we exited earlier. *So we didn't pass the visitation room*, I think. Suddenly, I sense eyes boring into me. I look back at our group and notice Vila is staring at me sternly. He must be waiting for me to join Toby, Billy, and Monsento, already seated on the bench. Under Vila's cold gaze, I quickly walk over and sit down in the empty spot next to Toby. Vila strides over after me but, with little space left on the bench, he opts to remain standing.

It isn't long before the guard returns. He ignores us all sitting on the bench and instead addresses Vila. "The defendant is ready for your visit," he says.

Vila shakes his head. "Only the living man will visit."

Monsento flinches and rises slowly from his seat, suddenly looking very nervous. He must have thought Vila would be joining him, but apparently not. Instead, Vila steps past Monsento to take his now-vacant space on the bench. Once seated, Vila crosses his legs, places his hat on his lap and leans back. After giving a wave of his hand to Monsento to indicate he should carry on, Vila closes his eyes.

Chapter 20

Vila gives me a dismissive wave and appears to have decided to take a nap, so I look to the guard for direction. "Room 134," the ghost says, then turns away to return to his post at courtroom five.

After a final glance behind me at the kids, all sitting glumly on the hard bench in the atrium with a very relaxed Vila, I take a deep breath and head back down the long narrow hall we'd only just exited. I'm not sure what I'll say--not sure what I *can* say--to Zeaflin. I wish the kids could come with me, or at least Vila; that'd take some of the pressure off me, or at least provide a distraction. But Vila shows no interest in visiting his old colleague, so I suppose it's better he remains behind to keep watch on the kids. Or to catch forty winks, whichever the case may be.

I pull up in front of room 134 and try the knob. It turns easily so I push the door open and peer inside. My eyes land directly on the face of another gray-glowing ghost guard. He is standing beside a door labeled "Visitation Room 134" in what is a closet-sized ante-room. The guard looks at me with mild interest before he reaches over and opens the door behind him. Surprised by the polite gesture from an UnderWorld law officer, I give him a thank you nod before I take a step inside the visitor's room. The door closes quickly behind me.

In the corner of this room, which thankfully is much bigger than the previous one, is another ghost guard. He is dressed same as the other guards—that is, in matching gray shirt and slacks with an official-looking badge tacked on the left shirt pocket. But this guard is a little different in that he is armed with a baton hooked on his belt, likely for use on unruly living visitors such as myself. The baton-toting guard gives me a bored look and leans against the wall nonchalantly, obviously trying to appear cool. I scan the room and notice Zeaflin, sitting on the other side of a glass partition in the back. He is wearing what I guess is prison garb here in the UnderWorld; a dark gray tunic over black slacks. After a quick glance at the guard in the corner, who is now picking at his fingernails, I walk over to sit across from Zeaflin on the hardwood chair so kindly provided for my comfort. Zeaflin looks haggard. I push away thoughts about what might have caused him to look so weary. He tries to give me a cheerful smile but the corners of his lips don't cooperate and the smile comes out lopsided.

"You know that I'm always glad to see you, Mr. Monsento, but you honestly shouldn't be here. You don't belong in this realm and you may begin to fade," Zeaflin says, allowing his uncooperative smile to drop into a concerned frown.

"I could stand to lose some weight," I respond, examining him closely. He has wrinkles around his eyes I'm fairly certain weren't there before. "You doing okay? Need anything?" I ask.

A trace of a smile tugs at the corner of one of Zeaflin's deep red lips. "A cake with a file, perhaps?" he suggests. I turn to look at the guard in the corner. He's still picking at his nails so I guess he isn't listening.

"Sure thing, I'll get on that right away. Any specific flavor? Devil's food, maybe?"

Zeaflin's smile reaches his eyes this time. "To be honest, I'm more partial to angel food cake," he confides.

"Hey! We don't allow those nasty kinds of words in here!" the guard interjects angrily, startling me into almost falling off my chair.

I turn around to glare at him. "What? Cake?"

The guard shakes a gray glowing finger at me. "You know very well what I mean. Tell your friend there to keep it clean or he's going back to his cell early." I give the guard a shrug and turn back to Zeaflin.

"I think it's those sorts of preferences that got you into this trouble," I tell him in a low voice. "You may want to keep those sorts of things to yourself."

"Is that a fact?" he responds, his amused smile morphing into his familiar sharp-toothed grin.

"More of an opinion than a fact," I respond, happy to see Zeaflin's good humor return. I lean closer to the glass and lower my voice further. "Anyway, we're going to do everything we can to help you get a lighter sentence. Abby said she'll testify that you're still creepy and weird, and I can second that if you'd like. We're still working on Toby's testimony but I suggested Billy testify how cowardly you were in our first case whenever Vila was due to arrive. He can even toss in the time you hid in the kitchen with the kids, leaving me alone to deal with Vila, for extra points."

Zeaflin looks puzzled at first, then he catches on and smiles but this time the smile is sad. "I don't think that will convince them I am still impure. Are you certain there isn't something a bit more dreadful you can say about me?" he asks.

"Well, there was that one time in the cemetery when you offered me your cane for protection from the crazed graveyard ghosts so they'd think I was you and attack me instead. Is that dreadful enough for you?" I reply, trying to give him a disgusted look but feeling more sad than angry.

Zeaflin frowns. "I'm sorry but it was necessary. I don't believe I'd have made it to Elizabeth otherwise. And I did agree to provide hazard pay, did I not?"

I open my mouth, close it, then sigh. "Yeah, you did. And I suppose I was a sucker to accept that cane. I should have known better than to believe an UnderWorld spirit would be concerned for my safety over his own," I reply. Zeaflin winces, making me regret the remark. "Anyway, you're right," I concede hastily. "You needed to get to Elizabeth. But we don't have to share *that* tidbit on the stand. The defense attorney was thrilled you used me as a decoy and I bet the judge will be too." Then I hesitate. Maybe I should warn him about Toby and Billy's plan to declare Toby's dinner invitation was all just a dare. Zeaflin is staring at me in silence with a furrowed brow, mulling over my last remarks, so I take a deep breath and lean closer to the small speaker holes drilled in the glass partition so the guard won't overhear.

"Look, Zeaflin, Toby and Billy plan to testify that the dinner invitation to Toby's house was a dare--that Billy dared Toby to do it." I lower my voice to almost a whisper. "It's not true. Toby really did want you to come to his house for dinner."

Zeaflin's eyes widen and he shakes his head vehemently. "No, Mr. Monsento, no! Toby mustn't lie during testimony! None of you should! You promise you'll tell the children this?"

"Time's up!" the guard snarls from behind me. "It's time for the prisoner to report for the sentencing hearing."

Zeaflin slowly rises from his seat behind the glass; I do likewise. Glancing behind me at the guard, Zeaflin repeats his request. "You *will* tell the children this, won't you, Arthur?"

Even though I don't intend to do that because it'd only make matters worse, I swallow down the lump in my throat and nod. Zeaflin nods back. "Goodbye, then. Thank you for a most delightful visit. Say hello to the detectives for me, won't you?" he says.

It's now or never. I clear my throat to find my voice. "Will do, Lucius."

Zeaflin is half-turned from me when it dawns on him that I just called him Lucius. He turns back with a bewildered look on his face. "Lucius," I repeat. "That was your living name: Lucius Tailor." Zeaflin stares off into space.

"Didn't I just say visiting time is over?" the guard barks out from behind me. Zeaflin snaps to and looks over my shoulder to give the guard a nod. Then he turns away and silently walks toward a door in the back of the prisoner's section of the room. Just before he exits, he looks back at me and softly says, "Thank you, Arthur. See you soon."

A pang of guilt suddenly twists in my gut because the next time we see each other, Zeaflin's going to be stabbed with a phurba. It's for his own good, but I still feel like I'm betraying him. I stand in place and watch Zeaflin walk away until they close the prisoner's door behind him. After that, I stumble out into the hallway to make my way back to Vila and the kids.

I sit quietly on the bench and keep a worried eye down the hall until I see Monsento coming back from his visit with Zeaflin. He is walking slowly with his shoulders slumped and his head hung low. My heart jumps to my throat and I try not to imagine what could have happened during his visit with Zeaflin that would make him look so downhearted. Toby and Billy are busy chatting so it takes them a minute to notice Monsento is heading our direction. As soon as they do, they both jump up and rush over to meet him halfway.

"How's Mr. Zeaflin?" I hear Billy ask, as they join Monsento's walk down the hall toward the atrium and the bench where Vila and I are still seated.

"Fair to middling," Monsento replies, his focus on Vila, who is still leaning back on the bench with his eyes closed. *Is Vila sleeping? Can the undead sleep?* I wonder, studying his tranquil form for signs of slumber.

"Did you tell him his name?" Toby asks. Monsento nods.

"What'd he say?" Billy asks.

Monsento sighs and sinks down on the bench next to me. "He said thanks."

"That's it? Just thanks?" Billy responds with a look of astonishment.

"Just thanks and that he'll see us at the hearing," Monsento says.

The door to courtroom eight opens and a gray ghost that must be our bailiff leans out. "It's time," he calls over to us. Vila's eyes immediately pop open and he stands up abruptly from the bench. He looks alert so maybe he was awake after all and merely disinterested in how Zeaflin is coping with imprisonment. Vila sweeps his arm to indicate the four of us should proceed to the courtroom before him, so Billy takes the lead and we all head inside.

———— ◆ ————

Seated at a table in the front of the courtroom is a ghost in a blue pinstripe suit and what I assume (hope!) is another ghost, wearing a hooded cloak. Since the ghost in the suit is shuffling through some papers on the table in front of him and is dressed like a lawyer, he is probably the head prosecutor, making the hooded ghost his assistant. At the defense table sit Ravat and Zeaflin, both facing the front of the courtroom. I'm nervous Zeaflin is going to turn around and read the guilt of betrayal in my eyes, but he remains in place, staring down at his hands folded neatly on the table in front of him. There is also a ghost audience here, about twenty strong, seated in the far back of the room. They look very much like ordinary people, other than emitting a faint gray glow that appears to be endemic to UnderWorld spirits. The ghost audience turn their heads to watch us walk down the aisle to the front of the courtroom, all of them expressionless and creepily silent.

There is an empty bench behind the defense table and my heart starts to pound when the bailiff motions for us to sit on it. That means I'll be sitting close to Zeaflin and it will be easier to impale him before anyone can stop me. I'm taking a quick step toward the bench when the prosecutor suddenly calls out to the bailiff, "Did you search the living for contraband?" The bailiff shakes his head. The prosecutor narrows his eyes. "Would you?" he demands.

With an angry glare in the prosecutor's direction, the bailiff instructs Monsento and the boys to raise their arms for him so he can perform a quick pat-down. Finding them clean, he looks over at me. My heart starts hammering so hard that I wouldn't be surprised if the whole courtroom could hear it. I try to catch Vila's eye, in hope that he'll intervene if the bailiff does start to frisk me but Vila isn't even looking my way. Instead, he is looking up toward the ceiling with tightly pursed lips, intentionally ignoring the scene in front of him. Trying not to panic, I look back at the bailiff. He is still staring at me so, with a deep breath, I lift my arms up tentatively. The bailiff glances back at the prosecutor, who has gone back to shuffling the papers on his table and is no longer paying us any attention. Then he looks back at me and, with a quick wave of his hand, gestures for me to drop my arms. After giving the inattentive prosecutor a surly scowl, the bailiff turns away and walks to the front of the courtroom to stand watch over the upcoming proceedings. I let out a small inward sigh of relief. If the bailiff had decided to search me, I would have had no other choice but to stab him with the phurba. And that would have alerted Zeaflin--not to mention the entire courtroom--of our plan to purify him and spoiled everything.

Billy has already taken the seat on the bench directly behind Zeaflin so I slip in beside him to take the seat behind Ravat. Toby slides in next, then Monsento. As if ashamed to be seen with us, Vila opts to sit at the far end of the bench, leaving a large gap between him and the rest of us. In front of our bench is a low wall about three feet high, built to separate the audience from the official members of the court. The wall has a gap for entry to the front of the courtroom but that's now being guarded by the bailiff, so I'm going to have to leap the wall to get at Zeaflin. That, or wait until they call me to the witness stand. And since Vila has arranged for me to testify last, if I *do* wait until I'm called to the stand, I will have to endure the long, torturous delay of at least three other testimonies beforehand and I'll be sure to lose my nerve. Or my mind.

"All rise for the honorable Judge Hovrel!" the bailiff bellows out. We all stand as one, living and dead, and watch the judge enter the room from a door behind the judge's box. I was afraid he'd be a demon like the judge in the dream I had, back when the Hammersly case was just beginning, but this judge is just a gray-glowing, over-weight, middle-aged ghost in black robes.

Judge Hovrel steps into his box and turns to face the courtroom. I glance around the room. Everyone is standing with their attention focused on the judge so this might be the perfect opportunity to stab Zeaflin. Ravat is immediately in front of me but Zeaflin is standing just off to the right of Ravat and is a very tempting target. I reach inside my pocket and stroke the phurba with my fingers, feeling the cool smoothness of the silver. *Should I try to stab Zeaflin now, while he's standing?* I look down at Ravat and Zeaflin's chairs. *But what if I trip over one of the vacant chairs when I lunge forward?* While I'm debating whether I should get the stabbing over with here and now, the opportunity is lost.

"You may all be seated," the judge instructs and takes his seat inside the judge box. With a whir of living and ghost garments, the audience and my intended victim sit down so, with a disappointed sigh, I pull my hand out of my pocket and reluctantly join them. The judge gives a curt nod to the prosecutor, who rises from his seat to call his first witness. Zeaflin's sentencing hearing begins.

———— ◆ ————

"The prosecution calls Tobias Moore to the stand," Mr. Prosecutor announces. Toby leans over and gives Vila a horrified look. Poor kid--it figures they'd pick him to go first. Vila gives a slight head jerk to indicate that Toby should get moving, so the kid slowly rises and heads toward the open gap in the half-wall that leads to the front of the courtroom. I glance over at Abby, wondering if she will try to stab Zeaflin before Toby testifies but she sits perfectly still with her hands on her lap. I guess she isn't ready yet.

Toby shuffles to the front of the courtroom, avoiding eye contact with Zeaflin and Ravat as he passes the defense table to complete his lead-footed way to the witness stand. Once there, Toby steps inside the witness box and sits, staring down at the podium in front of him, his complexion so pale one could easily mistake him for one of the undead. I can't help but wonder what they'll ask the kid to swear on, a Bible likely being out of the question. But instead of a swearing-in, Mr. Prosecutor approaches the witness stand. It would appear that "telling the truth, the whole truth, and nothing but the truth" is optional--or possibly even undesirable-- here in the UnderWorld.

"Tobias Moore, please tell the court how you know the defendant, Zeaflin," the prosecutor requests.

Toby looks up from his hands briefly to glance at Zeaflin, who is sitting straight-backed with his long-nailed hands folded on the defense table. Then Toby looks back down at his hands. "He's a client for our detective agency," he mumbles.

The judge leans over. "You'll need to speak loudly, boy." Toby repeats his answer louder and Judge Hovrel nods approvingly.

"Ah, yes. A *client*. Pray tell, Tobias Moore, is it standard practice to invite your agency's clients to your dinner table?" Mr. Prosecutor inquires, wasting no time in jumping straight to Toby's Achilles' heel.

Toby's eyes widen and he looks at Ravat. From my angle, I can see Ravat is moving his lips and I think he's mouthing the words "dinner dare, dinner dare" over and over, but Toby keeps shaking him off like a pitcher shakes off a catcher's signs. Mr. Prosecutor takes notice and spins around to catch Ravat in the middle of another silent "dinner dare".

"Objection! The defense is coaching the witness!" the prosecutor exclaims. The judge looks at Ravat, who gives him a very fake look of innocence.

"Sustained. The defense will please refrain from coaching the witnesses," the judge instructs with a weary sigh, glancing down at a watch on his wrist.

"Is it standard practice to invite ghosts and the undead to your home for dinner?" the prosecutor nudges. Toby shakes his head.

The judge leans over. "Louder boy."

"No!" Toby says sharply.

"But you invited the defendant, didn't you?" Mr. Prosecutor states. I look over at Ravat, wondering why he doesn't object. Not that I'm a legal expert, but isn't the prosecutor leading the witness?

"Yes," Toby replies weakly. The judge looks down at his watch again and makes a "hurry it up" gesture. He seems to be anxious to get home to the little wife.

"Could you provide the court with the reason for this exception?" the prosecutor asks. Toby blushes and looks at Zeaflin. He appears to be fighting an internal struggle.

Billy jumps up from his seat next to Abby. "Because I dared him to do it!" he cries out. Toby's blush mottles and he slaps his hand on the podium in front of him. *Oh no, here we go!*

"That's not true!" Toby shouts. "I asked him because I like him and I wanted him to meet my mom!"

The ghost audience lets out a collective gasp. The prosecutor turns away from Toby, wearing a smug smile. "Because he likes him and he wanted him to meet his mom," he repeats for dramatic effect. Then he waves his hand at Ravat. "Your witness," he declares, crossing back to his seat at the prosecution table.

I look at Ravat. He is staring down at the table in front of him with his hand on his head. "The defense has no questions for this witness, Your Honor," he groans.

"You may step down, boy," the judge tells Toby, who slips out of the witness box and slinks toward the half-wall, staring at the floor. He looks up as he draws close to Zeaflin, his cheeks still mottled red and white. "I'm sorry, Mr. Zeaflin. I couldn't lie," Toby says in a barely audible voice.

"That's all right, Toby. I didn't want you to," Zeaflin responds, reaching out to lightly touch Toby's arm.

"Don't touch the witnesses!" the bailiff barks, striding quickly to the defense table. Zeaflin draws his hand back in surprise as the bailiff grasps Toby by the shoulder and propels him to a seat on the bench next to Vila.

Chapter 21

"I would like to call Arthur Monsento next," the prosecutor announces, still wearing his smug smile. After the fiasco with Toby, I hope Abby can work up the nerve to stab Zeaflin before I say something stupid too. With a nervous glance at the girl, I stand up and head over to enter the witness box.

Swell. The witness seat is a hardwood bench, just like the one I just vacated in the audience area. Of course, the UnderWorld wouldn't want the witnesses to be comfortable during testimony, now would they? Zeaflin has gone back to sitting straight-backed with his hands folded one over the other. He should be an easy target if Abby aims high. None of us are sure what's going to happen after she stabs Zeaflin, but we have little choice at this point. We simply cannot allow the UnderWorld to put him in Malebolge, where he'll most likely turn into some sort of demon.

The prosecutor rises from his table and walks toward me, stopping just to the left of the witness stand. Apparently, I'm not going to be sworn in either. The prosecutor eyes me curiously, a trace of a smile on his thin red lips. "Mr. Monsento, please state your profession for the court," he requests. Simple enough question.

"I'm a medium," I reply.

"And could you define what services you perform as a medium?" he asks.

"Mostly, I summon spirits. Sometimes I conjure them and sometimes I read tarot cards."

"And which of these services have you performed for the defendant?" the prosecutor asks, with a sweep of his hand toward Zeaflin.

I hesitate, looking over at Abby. She's sliding across the bench to trade places with Billy and get closer to Zeaflin. No one in the audience seems to be paying her any attention. This is good.

"Mr. Monsento?" The prosecutor draws my attention back to him.

"All of them," I reply curtly.

The prosecutor nods. "Could you tell the court why you perform these services for Zeaflin?"

"Easy. He pays well," I reply with a shrug.

The prosecutor leans forward. "No other reason?" he probes. I glance at Zeaflin. He is looking down, apparently studying his hands, still folded on the table in front of him.

"None come to mind," I respond. Mr. Prosecutor frowns, displeased with my answer.

"All right. Then perhaps you can share with the court how you like your coffee instead. With cream? A little sugar, perhaps?" the prosecutor asks. The strange change in direction pulls Zeaflin's attention away from his hands. I lock eyes with him briefly and then look at the prosecutor, who is leaning casually on the witness podium.

"Objection!" Ravat suddenly cries out. "Relevance?"

"The court will see, in a moment, the relevance of this question," the prosecutor responds.

The judge looks at his watch again. "All right. But let's get there sometime today. We only have this courtroom booked for an hour," he says irritably.

"Arthur Monsento?" Mr. Prosecutor prompts.

"Black," I respond, knowing exactly where this conversation is heading.

"And how about the defendant?"

I do my best not to look directly at Abby so as not to draw attention to her. Instead, I focus on Zeaflin. He is still sitting stiff-backed in his chair, staring at me, his expression placid. In the background, I detect an Abby-shaped form seated at the end of the spectator bench just behind him. I draw my eyes back to the prosecutor.

"I couldn't say for certain, but I'd say probably black," I reply gruffly.

"And how do you know of this caffeinated beverage preference of Zeaflin's? Do you and the defendant imbibe in it together?" the prosecutor asks, his smile becoming a leer.

I squirm a little on my uncomfortable witness seat, wishing Abby would hurry up and perform the deed. "Sometimes," I say.

"So the two of you drink coffee together where? A diner? A park bench?"

I look at the judge. I don't think he's paying attention anymore. He's just staring at his watch, watching the seconds tick by, probably willing the clock to reach 11 am so he can give his pre-determined sentence to Zeaflin and head for home.

"My kitchen," I respond, looking back at the prosecutor. A bubble of laughter slips from the prosecutor's lips and ripples through the audience chamber. *What's so funny about that?*

"Ah, yes. So the two of you would sit at your kitchen table, sipping coffee, reading fortunes from tarot cards like two gossiping chambermaids. Did you do this often?" the prosecutor asks, turning away to face the courtroom and his tittering audience.

He's going to notice Abby is sidling over to close in on Zeaflin! I need to do something! I slam my hand down on the podium in front of me, taking great satisfaction in the prosecutor's startled body jerk back in my direction. "Objection! He's disparaging the witness!" I shout.

The judge bangs his gavel. "Get a hold of yourself, man, or I'll hold you in contempt of court," he warns, giving me a deep scowl from above.

"I do *not* gossip like a chambermaid," I retort with mock outrage, trying to buy some more time. "Okay, *maybe* Zeaflin gossips like a chambermaid but I gossip more like a teenage girl."

The judge bangs his gavel twice. "I won't warn you again, Arthur Monsento," he growls, looking down at his watch again. "We don't have time for this. It's almost ten-thirty and we still have a few more witnesses to wade through before the 11 am sentencing."

I look at Zeaflin. He appears nonplussed, giving me an almost imperceptible head shake that is probably some sort of body language for *"what do you think you're doing?"* so I give him an almost imperceptible shrug in return. Behind him, taking advantage of the distraction I've provided, Abby decides to make her move.

———— ◆ ————

Everyone is focused on Monsento and the judge, including Zeaflin, so now is the time. I reach into my skirt pocket and grasp the hilt of the phurba tightly. All I need to do now is jump off the bench and lunge forward quickly, before the bailiff can stop me. The half-wall between Zeaflin and me is going to block my blade low so I will need to aim high--between the shoulder blades, I guess.

Zeaflin is giving Monsento a faint head shake of bewilderment over his sudden loss of control on the witness stand. I'm about to make him even more puzzled. With a silent prayer that this doesn't haunt me for life, I yank the phurba from my pocket and throw myself over the wall in front of me. Through a haze, I can hear the ghost audience gasp as I thrust the phurba deep into the space between Zeaflin's two scapulae. My body knocks him out of his chair and we both fall to the floor of the courtroom. Ravat pushes his chair away from the defendant table with a loud screech and backs away from the two of us in horror.

The chaos in the courtroom becomes white noise as I tumble off Zeaflin's back and fall into a crouch beside him, staring at the phurba sticking out of the middle of his back. Zeaflin half-turns his body, taking care not to lie back on the blade, to look at me. "What did you do, Abby?" he groans.

"I'm sorry," I whisper hoarsely. "Please ascend; please don't fight the purification this time." I watch him closely for any change to light drops, but he isn't changing. He's just lying there staring up at me, trying pathetically to reach the phurba to pull it out. Taking pity, I reach over, gently remove the phurba from Zeaflin's back and set it down on the floor next to him. Then I roll Zeaflin over and look directly into his eyes. I lean in close, trying to block out the noise of the judge banging his gavel and the ghost audience's murmuring, to focus solely on convincing Zeaflin to ascend.

"Please don't fight the purification, Zeaflin," I repeat. He's staring up at me blankly so I grab the front of his prison tunic and ball the fabric up in my fists and give him a shake. "Do you hear me? Please, I need you to do this. It's not that bad in the OtherWorld; it's certainly better than jail," I tell him, perhaps a bit more sharply than I should. Still nothing. Tears of frustration pop into my eyes and I lean closer to Zeaflin, so close I could almost kiss him, and in my frustration, I give him another shake, this time a little rougher. "Please ascend, please ascend, please ascend," I beg as a mantra. Still nothing but a blank stare. "Please," I moan. "Please don't stay here and go to prison. Please go to the OtherWorld. If you go, I'll let you be my guardian angel. I need one, I really do," I sob, the tears of frustration changing to tears of pain. *What's wrong with him? Why won't he listen to me?*

The teardrops run in torrents down my face. I close my eyes tightly to try to stop the flow and fight against the rising sense of panic that we're running out of time and moan, "Won't you please, please do this for me?" I open my eyes to look at Zeaflin and my heart starts pounding wildly. There are several sparkles, right there on his face! *Is he turning to light drops and ascending?* Then I realize it's just my tears. They are rolling down Zeaflin's face, leaving streaks that make it look like he's the one crying. Zeaflin reaches up to wipe away a few of the drops running down my cheeks and gives me a weak smile. And then I see it: the soft, warm glow of a candle in a cold, dark room. The smile of Annie's angel.

"It's all right, Abby. You don't have to cry," Zeaflin says gently and then he starts to become blurry. I swipe at my eyes but it's not the tears this time. Zeaflin is finally accepting the purification and is turning into droplets of light.

Reality around me starts to seep back in. "I said, get her off the defendant right now!" I hear the judge order harshly.

"I can't! She has a phurba. She could *stab* me with it," I hear the bailiff respond. I tear my eyes off Zeaflin and look down at my hand. *When did I pick up the phurba?*

I look back at Zeaflin but he's no longer there. All that is left of him are the small droplets of light now floating upward from the floor one by one, sparkling like tiny diamonds. They rise to the courtroom ceiling and pop with little flashes of bright blue light, giving us all a miniature firework show.

I sit back on my haunches and start to laugh. I keep laughing until Monsento comes forward and places his hand on my shoulder. "You okay, kid?" he asks, helping me up off the floor and carefully extracting the phurba from my hand. I nod. And then I grab hold of him and start crying again. Monsento places an awkward arm around me and stands silently while I cry against his chest.

———————— ◆ ————————

Abby is letting out the pent-up stress she must have been feeling all day, so I stand quietly and let her cry it out. Billy and Toby are on their feet, watching us, their expressions a mix of worry and relief. Mr. Prosecutor's expression is also a mix but his is very different from the boys'. Confusion and outrage fight for control of his face as the prosecutor begins banging his fist over and over on the witness stand in frustration.

Vila rises from his seat. "May I approach the bench?" he asks the judge loudly, trying to be heard over the bangs of the prosecutor. Vila doesn't wait for an answer. Instead, he strides past the bailiff, pulls a parchment from his suit pocket and hands it to the judge, announcing with pompous flourish, "While the girl's actions here are unsanctioned by the OtherWorld, this document proves she is an

OtherWorld Ambassador and thus has diplomatic immunity from her offense."

Mr. Prosecutor stops banging his fist and his jaw drops in incredulity. The ghost audience murmurs fill the courtroom as the judge pulls out a pair of reading glasses to look over the document. As he reads, his hands start to tremble and his face turns red. Struggling to control his temper and failing tremendously, the judge looks up from the paper at Vila, his face contorted with fury. "Vila, you get that girl and that phurba out of here immediately! How dare you allow her to defile my courtroom and make a mockery of this hearing!" he rages.

The prosecutor has regained his composure and is now glaring coldly at Vila. "Rest assured, my office will be filing a grievance with Ambrogio about this matter. The living girl couldn't have obtained a phurba without your assistance, and the Department of Living Affairs had no right to assist in the extraction of a duly convicted criminal in our realm. There will be repercussions for your and this supposed 'ambassador's' renegade behavior. The two of you may even be taking Zeaflin's place in our prison here," he snarls.

"Indeed? File away, then. I'm certain Ambrogio will give your grievance all the consideration it deserves," Vila responds, unperturbed. He motions for Billy and Toby to join him by the judge's bench, then he steers them toward me and Abby.

"We need to make a circle so we can leave now, Abigail, so let's calm ourselves and attend to it, shall we?" Vila requests. Abby pulls herself away from my chest and wipes her eyes. I look down at the slobber on my best suit and sigh.

"You okay, Abs?" Billy asks. She gives him a wan smile and reaches out to grasp his and Toby's hands.

"Yeah, I'm okay. It's all going to be okay now, right, Mr. Monsento?" she responds, looking up at me with sparkling eyes.

"I said get her out of here!" the judge wails.

"Sorry kid, no time for chit-chat," I say and grab Billy and Vila's hands. Toby grabs Vila's other hand and we dissipate to realm shift back to the land of the living.

———— ◆ ————

Vila realm shifts us straight into Monsento's salon. On the return trip, I don't feel as light-headed as I did on the way out, so maybe the adrenaline is keeping me alert this time. But that's not true for Monsento; he looks even greener than he was when we entered the UnderWorld. Billy grabs an arm to lead him to the easy chair in front of the television while Toby rushes to the kitchen to fetch a glass of water.

I look over at Vila. He is standing next to me, passively watching the fuss over Monsento. "The prosecutor said he plans to complain to Ambrogio. Should we be worried?" I ask. Not that I believe Ambrogio would allow us to be punished after he arranged this entire affair, but it would be nice to hear Vila confirm there is nothing to be concerned about. The prosecutor and judge were very angry.

"Surely you know the answer to that already, so let's not spend time asking silly questions," he responds, keeping his gaze on

Monsento. I bite my lower lip. Vila is one cold undead man; I wonder sometimes why any of us even try to strike up a conversation with him.

Vila abruptly leaves my side and marches over to Monsento, now seated in his easy chair, sipping the glass of water Toby brought. He holds his hand out, palm up. "Ambrogio's phurba, if you will, Mr. Monsento."

Monsento places the glass of water down on a table next to his chair and reaches into his suit coat pocket to extract the phurba. "You'll let us know about Zeaflin, right?" he requests as he passes the phurba to Vila.

Vila lets out a frustrated sigh. "Let you know *what*, Mr. Monsento? Zeaflin has ascended; he is now in the OtherWorld. As Ambrogio made clear during your visit to the OtherWorld last summer, when Zeaflin is purified, he will not retire to Halcyon. Instead, he will probably be assigned a position in one of the departments of the StopOver." Vila shakes his head in disgust and adds, "A position likely more senior than he deserves."

"Will he come visit us?" Toby asks.

Vila frowns at Toby. "No doubt he will, with or *without* the appropriate permits. However, I imagine he'll be busy learning the trade of whatever position Ambrogio assigns to him, so don't be surprised if you do not see him for some time. Zeaflin will find the OtherWorld less accommodating to his 'devil-may-care' attitude. We have official protocols for agents in our realm that must be followed, and he will be trained accordingly."

I cringe inwardly. The one thing that bothered Zeaflin the most about the OtherWorld, its rigid rules, appear not to have relaxed one bit with Ambrogio's pending transfer of rule to his heir, Elizabeth. I feel bad that I returned Zeaflin to the bureaucratic nightmare of the OtherWorld by stabbing him. But surely even *that* is preferable to an UnderWorld prison, isn't it?

Vila tucks Ambrogio's phurba into his coat pocket. "The OtherWorld is pleased that Zeaflin has returned and is grateful to you for your assistance in this matter," he says in a cool, stiff voice that reveals his discomfort over having to deliver that message. Then Vila vanishes in a puff of blue smoke.

I take another sip of water to help calm my protesting stomach before trying to get up from the easy chair. Traveling back and forth between the UnderWorld and here has been particularly grueling; I don't remember feeling so awful when I traveled to the OtherWorld. I stand up slowly, steady myself with a hand on the arm of the easy chair and fight against the nausea. All three kids are watching me with concerned faces so I muster up a smile and some encouraging words, something Vila was unwilling to provide.

"Well done, kids. Looks like we've completed the case of the great guardian angel rescue. It's *Miller* time," I say, motioning toward the kitchen.

Billy's eyes light up. "You're going to let us drink beer?" he asks breathlessly. Abby frowns at me.

"No, I'm going to let you drink some warm milk. I think we could all use some; I know I could, anyway," I reply. Now Billy is the one frowning at me.

"Can we add some chocolate to the milk, Mr. Monsento?" Toby asks. I shrug.

"If you want, sure. You got some on you?" Toby shakes his head. "Then warm milk it is. Why don't you two boys get on it?" I suggest.

Honoring me with an angry huff of annoyance, Billy heads off for the kitchen. After a pause, Toby joins him. I glance at Abby, still standing by the séance table where Vila dropped us off. She is looking at the stains on my suit coat. "I can pay for the dry cleaning," she offers.

"That's okay. It was dirty when I put it on," I lie. I look her over. Her eyes are still red from crying. "You all right there, kid?"

Abby sighs and walks over to join me in the living room. "Yes, I'm okay. Do you think Zeaflin will be angry with me for stabbing him?" she asks.

"He didn't seem angry from where I was standing. Did he seem angry to you?"

Abby shakes her head. "No. But he might be later on, after the OtherWorld starts bossing him around," she says with another sigh.

"You did the right thing, kid," I reassure her.

Abby nods. "I know. Still, I hope Zeaflin thinks so too."

"What'd you say to him to get him to accept the purification?" I ask, feeling curious.

"I told him he could be my guardian angel. I think that's when he agreed to ascend."

"You sure you want Zeaflin to be your guardian angel? He has a poor track record," I point out. "You know, with that Martin kid and the lake."

Abby gives me a scowl. "That's not nice, Mr. Monsento," she scolds. I shrug. Maybe not so nice, but it is true. Though I'd have to admit, as guardians go, Zeaflin is still preferable to Vila.

"You know who my guardian angel was when I was a kid?" I say with a laugh.

Abby's eyes widen. "Zeaflin?"

I shake my head. "Vila." Abby gives me a look like she thinks I'm pulling her leg. "Seriously," I say.

Abby giggles. "That's crazy, Mr. Monsento." Billy steps into the salon, carrying two steaming mugs. "What's crazy?" he asks.

"Vila was Mr. Monsento's guardian angel when he was a kid," Abby replies.

Billy's jaw drops and he lets out a low whistle. "Really? Wow, Mr. Monsento! How'd you find out?"

"Vila told me. With him looking out for me, it's a wonder I wasn't even more messed up as a kid. No surprise they dissolved *that* agency if most of the angels were like Vila," I say with a roll of my eyes.

Abby gives me a bewildered look. "They dissolved the guardian angel agency?"

"Yeah, but they apparently didn't call it that. Vila said they called it the Department of Living Aegis," I respond.

Abby frowns. "Why did they dissolve it?"

"I have no idea, kid. Maybe because of the snafu with Zeaflin and the Hammersly family," I reply.

"So Zeaflin can't be my guardian angel then? Even if I want him to be?" Abby asks, clearly distressed.

"Hey, look who suddenly became a fan of Mr. Zeaflin," Billy teases.

"Who's a fan of Mr. Zeaflin?" Toby asks, stepping out of the kitchen carrying the second set of hot milk for our foursome. He sets them down on the coffee table in front of my couch. Billy points at Abby, who gives him a quick head shake.

"Hardly. He's still creepy," she declares, but we all can tell she no longer believes that's true.

I take a seat on the sofa and pick up a mug of milk. The kids each take their mugs and I hold up my milk for us all to clink our cups while I make a toast. "To the Fantastic Phantasmic Detectives and their fine work in the Zeaflin and Hammersly case."

"And to their medium, without whom they'd have no agency," Billy adds.

"*And* no comic relief," Abby interjects with a smirk.

I tip my mug slightly in her direction. "I'll drink to that."

———◆———

After two weeks pass by with no word from or about Zeaflin, I finally agree that we should conjure up Mary to find out if she has any news. Sadly, the most Mary can tell us is that Zeaflin is sequestered in the OtherWorld infirmary and can receive no visitors, other than Ambrogio and Elizabeth. And since those two are difficult to approach for information, being the busy royalty they are, we sit here in limbo with no updates on Zeaflin's condition.

Time passes slowly. I do my best to keep the kids upbeat, particularly Abby, who still worries Zeaflin will be angry with her for stabbing him with a phurba and convincing him to ascend. But given that my talent for comic relief wanes with each passing day of no news about Zeaflin, the best I am able to provide is a distraction by assigning the kids household chores to keep them busy. And while that may not do much to cheer them up, on the plus side my car is spotless and the garden looks great!

After weeks of moping around my house, the kids finally agree to an outing with Billy's sisters to visit the amusement park near Morrisville. In a zany moment of insanity, Billy asks me if I'd like to come with them and, while witnessing me screaming like a little girl on a roller coaster might have brought some levity to our somber crowd, I'm sure my back couldn't handle the rides. Not to mention my nerves probably couldn't handle Billy's sisters; I haven't had to deal with teenage girls since I was a teenage boy, but I remember what they're like. Therefore, I graciously decline the nerve-rattling, back-crunching invitation and instead plan for a busy day of sleeping in and watching Sunday afternoon television. They usually play old movies on Sundays and it's been weeks since I've had some time to myself for such trivialities.

The kids decide to head home around 6 pm for dinner and to rest up for the big day in Morrisville tomorrow. It sounds like Billy's sisters are planning for an early start, giving me yet another reason to decline joining them. I see the young detectives out the door and head for the kitchen to scare up some dinner. Only finding a can of mushroom soup and a box of pretzels in the pantry, I decide to head off to the local eatery and treat myself to a nice steak. Then maybe I'll take a walk around the block before I hit the sheets for a good night's sleep.

Chapter 22

I have a dream this night. For a change, it doesn't seem to be a nightmare because I am at the beach and the sun is shining brightly. I am sitting on a towel on the sand, wearing my favorite pink sundress that I rarely wear (because Billy teases me for being "such a girl" whenever I do) and a big, floppy straw hat. My sandals are sitting next to me and I have my feet dug deep in the warm, soft sand. There is a gentle breeze carrying the smell of salt from the crashing surf to my nose so I close my eyes and breathe deep to suck the scent deep into my lungs.

"You chose a pretty setting for our meeting today," a familiar voice says.

I open my eyes and peer up at Zeaflin, standing next to me, gazing out to sea. While his voice hasn't changed, his appearance certainly has. Where his long black hair was always slicked back with some sort of gel, in my dream he's wearing it natural so the sea breeze can ruffle it around. His deep red lips look less red--they are almost a normal pink--and he is dressed in khaki pants with a loose-fitting white shirt instead of his usual suit and tie. His eyes haven't changed though; they are still the same deep amber color.

"You've changed," I tell him.

Zeaflin sits down on the sand next to me, his eyes still focused on the ocean. "I thought my usual attire might be a trifle formal for the seaside," he replies.

I shake my head. "Not just your clothes. *You've* changed too." I look down at his hands. His long fingernails are now neatly trimmed.

Zeaflin looks at me and gives me an impish smile. "Is that a fact?" he asks. I laugh at his playful jab at one of Monsento's common retorts.

Zeaflin picks up a seashell from the sand between us and turns it over in his hands to study it. It's your standard lilac-tinted scallop shell but he seems to be delighted by it, because his smile widens enough for me to see his sharp incisors are gone too. I take a deep breath and begin my apologies.

"I'm sorry I stabbed you."

"Are you?" Zeaflin responds, still examining the seashell. I hesitate, thrown off by the bluntness of the question. *Am I?*

"Well, I'm sorry I *had* to stab you but I'm not sorry you ascended." *There, I've said it!* I think defiantly. Then I pause. "Are you?" I ask timidly. Zeaflin tucks the seashell into his shirt pocket and looks back out to sea.

"There has definitely been a period of awkward adjustment. I am unaccustomed to adhering closely to rules, and the OtherWorld is unfamiliar with realm walkers who do not directly follow orders. Because of this complication, Ambrogio has yet to assign me to a department in the OtherWorld. I fear he will place me in the same department as Vila and I will be required to report to him." Zeaflin laughs. "Can you imagine that?"

I smile. "But that would mean you'd be in the Department of Living Affairs and you could visit us anytime you wish, right?"

Zeaflin shakes his head and looks back at me. "I'd still require a permit from Vila or Ambrogio. Of course, I am fairly proficient at forging their signatures." He grins. "I suspect you'll see more of me."

"I'd like that," I say.

Zeaflin's grin fades to a wistful smile. "Things will be different." His eyes look sad.

"Sometimes different is good," I tell him.

Zeaflin looks back at the ocean thoughtfully. "Is it?" he asks himself.

I touch his arm tentatively. "Yes, Zeaflin, this time I think it is."

———— ◆ ————

The sound of my alarm clock rattle breaks up my dream. I lie in bed, wondering, *Was that only a dream I made up in my head or did Zeaflin actually visit me at my dream beach?* Then I remember that Zeaflin left "gifts" when he visited Annette in her dreams.

Maybe he left me something! I sit up abruptly and scan the room, but I see nothing out of place. Odds are, my mind made up that dream because I've been so worried about Zeaflin being angry with me.

With a sigh, I slip out of bed to ready myself for a day of roller coasters, corn dogs and Ferris wheels--tame stuff after visiting the UnderWorld. But before I hop into the shower, I open my desk drawer and pull out the moonstone Zeaflin planted last year for me to find. It's still cracked in half (not that I expected it would spontaneously reassemble) so I only pull out the half with Billy's, Toby's, and my blood inside. Zeaflin said we'd see ghosts as long as our blood remains inside the stone. I hold up the rock and peer at it with one eye closed. The blood drops are still in the center so even though Zeaflin isn't an UnderWorld realm walker anymore, I guess we can still see ghosts and keep our detective business open.

Billy and his two older sisters, Suzy and Luanne, are in the kitchen chatting with Mom when I come down the stairs. Suzy passed her driver's test last month so she's the driver for our trip to the amusement park, almost twenty miles away. Luanne is facing my direction and notices my approach first. She gives me a disapproving frown. "You really ought to consider changing your hairstyle, Abby," she says. "Pony tails are for little girls. You're like, what? Almost thirteen?"

Mom walks over and places an arm around my shoulders. "It's true that Abby turned thirteen in March, but she's still my little girl."

A blush rises to my cheeks as Billy snorts out a laugh. I tug away from Mom's arm, embarrassed. "We should get going," I mumble.

"Yeah, we still need to stop by Toby's house to pick him up," Billy says. Suzy and Luanne say goodbye to Mom and head out the door. Billy stays behind to wait for me while I grab my jacket and we walk alongside each other down the front path of my house.

We're almost to Suzy's car when Billy suddenly pipes out, "I like the way you wear your hair," and tugs on my ponytail playfully. I freeze in place and turn to look at him, my heart pounding, trying to determine whether he's teasing me or not. But Billy just breezes on past and hops in the back of the car, leaving the door open for me to slide in beside him.

I look back at my house. Mom is still standing at the door and must have heard Billy's remark because she's wearing a troubled frown. I give her a wave goodbye. Mom smiles and waves back. I slip into the back seat of the car and look out the side window to watch my mom, standing on the porch, her hand held high in goodbye, until we pull away and she fades into the distance.

———————— ◆ ————————

I hop out of the shower and don a pair of sweat pants and a baggy T-shirt in preparation for lazing in my easy chair and watching the Sunday afternoon movie. Today's movie is *Gone with the Wind*. Not exactly one of my favorites, but it's either that or sports, and I'm not too hip on sports. After the movie for today is announced, the channel switches to a commercial break so I take the opportunity to run to the kitchen to pour a glass of lemonade and slap together a sandwich.

As I get closer to the kitchen door panel, I notice a bright white light is shining out of the crack under the door. That's a bit odd. My kitchen window faces east and it's 3 pm, so the sun should be shining overhead. I'm sure I didn't leave the ceiling light on but even if I did, it wouldn't shine out from under the door like that. I approach the kitchen cautiously and slowly draw the panel back. The bright light floods through the threshold and into my eyes. I squint at the seated figure at my kitchen table.

"Ambrogio?" I ask. It's him, all right. He looks up from one of my coffee mugs sitting on the table in front of him, notices I'm squinting and tones down his radiance to a faint glimmer. Then he gives me a broad smile. "You are looking well, Arthur," he says and motions for me to sit down in the chair across from him. There is a mug in front of that chair also.

"I hope you don't mind but I took the liberty of making us some tea while you were occupied in your back bedroom," Ambrogio continues.

"I was taking a shower," I tell him, unsure why I feel the need to explain.

Ambrogio nods in understanding and holds out a box toward me. I look down at it. It's a box of *Nilla Wafers*. "Cookie?" he offers.

I shake my head and sink slowly into the chair in front of the extra tea mug, never taking my eyes off the peculiar OtherWorld ruler. He is wearing what I saw him in last: a snow-white gown and flip-flops. His silver hair still hangs to his shoulders and he still has the long beard that closely matches his gown. I'm guessing there are no barbers in the OtherWorld…or maybe Ambrogio enjoys looking like Santa Claus in a toga.

Ambrogio dips one of the cookies daintily into his tea before popping it into his mouth. He closes his eyes while he chews the cookie, evidently savoring the sweet goodness of the wafer. After he swallows the cookie, Ambrogio takes a sip of his tea, opens his eyes and looks at me. "I can't find a baker in the OtherWorld that can bake these cookies. They always overdo the butter and vanilla flavor," he tells me with a sad sigh.

I stare at him, unsure what to say. *Did he honestly travel down here just to talk about cookies and drink my tea?*

Ambrogio notices my confused expression. "But you are not interested in discussing baked goods, are you, Arthur?" he says. "No, you are likely more interested in hearing how Zeaflin is faring. He is faring well."

"Mary said he's in a hospital," I reply.

Ambrogio nods. "Yes, he was in a care unit, but he is out now. The initiation rituals to convert Zeaflin to an UnderWorld realm walker had corrupted his essence and there were a few rough patches to get through before he could join the other spirits of the OtherWorld."

"Is he okay now?" I ask, trying to push away images of Zeaflin strapped to a hospital bed, going through evil withdrawal like some sort of recovering junkie.

Ambrogio smiles. "Yes, thanks to you and the children. I would like to thank you personally for your assistance in extracting Zeaflin."

"You should probably be thanking Abby. She was the one who stabbed him and convinced him to ascend," I say.

"Of course. I will do so when she arrives," Ambrogio responds.

"Could be a long wait. She's at the amusement park today, so I doubt she'll come this way until tomorrow."

Ambrogio shakes his head lightly. "Actually, she's due to visit you very soon. Toby ate too many corn dogs and too much cotton candy before joining Billy on a ride I believe they call a '*Tilt-A-Whirl*'. Unfortunately, that cut the outing a bit short. Abby will visit you soon, once she's made her discovery."

"Is that a fact? And just what discovery would that be?" I ask, returning his head shake with one of my own. The OtherWorld ruler does seem to take great pleasure in being enigmatic.

Ambrogio says nothing. Instead he stands up from the table, grabs a mug from my cabinet and pours out another cup of tea from my teapot. He places the mug in front of the chair next to mine and settles back down into his chair. No sooner has Ambrogio sat down than my front door opens and Abby's voice rings out across my salon and into the kitchen. "Mr. Monsento? Are you here?"

Ambrogio gives me a broad grin. Geez, conversing with the "all-seeing" can be very annoying sometimes!

———————— ◆ ————————

Monsento calls out to me from his kitchen so I hurry over to find him. I'm in a panic and I have no idea what to do so I rushed over here as fast as possible. I hope Monsento can explain why the blood in the moonstone has disappeared. Zeaflin said Billy, Toby, and I will see ghosts as long as our blood remains in the stone he gave us, but now the blood drop is gone! Could that mean something bad happened to Zeaflin?

I step into Monsento's kitchen and nearly have a heart attack! The OtherWorld ruler is sitting with Monsento, drinking what smells like *Earl Grey* tea and eating out of a box of *Nilla Wafers*. The moonstone drops from my paralyzed hands and onto the floor tiles with a thud.

Ambrogio glances down at the stone. "You are upset over Zeaflin's Seeing Stone and you are here for an explanation as to why the blood is no longer inside the stone," he declares.

I look at Monsento in a daze. He is staring at the stone at my feet, equally stupefied. "Won't you sit down, Abigail? I can explain," Ambrogio says, gesturing toward an empty chair with a cup of tea in front of it. I stumble over and sit down.

"I felt it would be wrong to leave your blood in Zeaflin's Seeing Stone. You were not born with the talent to see spirits, nor did you volunteer to see them; it was imposed upon you using trickery, and I believe you should be given a choice," Ambrogio states while he reaches into his robe and pulls out a plum-sized opalescent stone with rose-colored swirls. He pushes the stone toward me and gestures for me to pick it up, so I grab the stone and turn it over in my hand to examine it. There is a tapered hole lined with silver that looks like a tiny funnel on the underside. I look up at Ambrogio questioningly.

"One of my Seeing Stones," he explains. "Unlike Zeaflin's creations, which have a built-in sharp edge, mine requires you prick your finger to add the drop of blood. If you and the two boys still desire to see spirits, you may add your blood to this stone."

I look at Monsento. "What about Mr. Monsento?"

Ambrogio smiles. "Arthur's talent is natural; he requires no Seeing Stone," he replies.

I examine Ambrogio's stone, taking the time to think this over. Now that I have a choice, I'm not sure I still want to see ghosts. Billy and Toby probably will, but I'm not sure I should offer this to them; maybe I should keep it to myself. Ambrogio covers my hand with his. It feels warm and soft. "Each should choose for themselves," he tells me. I nod my understanding and Ambrogio draws his hand back.

"Is everything all right with the UnderWorld?" Monsento asks. "Mr. Prosecutor and the judge were pretty upset over the courtroom phurba debacle. I imagine the UnderWorld ruler was too."

Ambrogio leans back in his chair and sighs. "Oh, he certainly was. But Razuul has a soft spot for the Elixir of Life, a delightful cocktail made with the water from one of the rivers that run through Halcyon. I brought him a flask and promised him an unlimited supply if he'd forgive the horrible transgression committed by Vila and my Living Affairs Ambassador, Abigail." Ambrogio looks at me and winks. "With the stipulation, of course, that he pardon both Nathan and Zeaflin and allow them to remain as OtherWorld residents."

"That must be some amazing cocktail to get him to agree to all that," Monsento comments.

"It is indeed," Ambrogio agrees. "I must be going now but I would like to thank you for your help with Zeaflin, Abby. He has recovered from the purification and will soon be assigned to a department in the OtherWorld. I fear he'll still be a challenge for any department I select but I'll figure it out somehow." Before Monsento or I can respond, Ambrogio blinks out with a bright flash of light.

"What are you going to do, kid?" Monsento asks. "Are you going to add your blood to that stone?" I stare at the tiny funnel in the rock in my hand.

"I don't know. I've never had a choice before. If I don't and the boys do, it'd change things a lot, wouldn't it?" I draw my eyes up to see Monsento nodding in agreement.

"It would. But you could still be part of their detective agency, maybe as a secretary or accountant. The agency could use someone to keep the books. I know I'd sure appreciate it, because none of you kids ever keep track of expenses or ask for any money up front," he responds with a neutral expression, so I can't tell if he's joking or not.

I get up from the table. "I should be going now. I told Mom I'd be home by 4 pm to help her make dinner and it's almost four now." I tuck Ambrogio's stone into the pocket of my jacket and walk over to pick up Zeaflin's stone from the floor where I'd dropped it. I tuck that stone into the pocket on the opposite side of my coat and wait by the kitchen door panel until Monsento stands up. He rises slowly and walks me to the front door in moody silence. Before I step outside, Monsento places a hand on my shoulder.

"I'm behind whatever you decide to do," he tells me.

I give him a weak smile. "I know you are. But will the boys be?"

Chapter 23

I have a restless night of tossing and turning, first making the decision to add my blood to the stone and then coming up with a new argument not to. I go back and forth for several hours, until sleep finally arrives and gives my troubled mind some rest. Fortunately, no dreams creep in and I wake to sunlight streaming into my bedroom window.

After a hearty breakfast of corn flakes and buttered toast with jam, I help Mom with the dishes and head over to the Fantastic Phantasmic headquarters to find Billy and Toby so I can tell them about Zeaflin and Ambrogio's stones. Weary of arguing with myself, I decide to leave the final decision to the boys. I'll add my blood to the new Seeing Stone if the boys add theirs. I've met demons, spirit dog witches, undead realm walkers and UnderWorld lawyers, so what else could I run into if I stay in the ghost detective business?

Werewolves and vampires? If there is one thing I do know, it's that life will be much duller if I go back to being an ordinary girl who can't see ghosts.

Toby's bike is leaning up against the tree of the treehouse in Billy's backyard when I arrive. I finger Ambrogio's stone in my pocket thoughtfully before I climb up the makeshift ladder of small planks nailed in the side of the tree and enter the treehouse. There I find Billy and Toby, seated at the table playing checkers. The spirit communication machine sits silent on the table next to them.

"No new cases, huh guys?" I ask, before I realize the device might not be working because we can't see ghosts right now.

Toby looks up from the checkerboard. "No, not yet," he replies.

"It's been over a month now. Maybe we should have Mr. Monsento conjure Mary and ask her to run some advertising in the StopOver," Billy suggests with a sigh. I take a seat at the table and, with a deep breath, commit to showing the boys Ambrogio's Seeing Stone.

"What's that, Abby?" Billy asks, reaching forward to pick up the stone. "Wow! This is a cool rock; where'd you get it?"

"Ambrogio," I reply, watching the surprise cross both boys' faces.

"Is Mr. Zeaflin okay? Did you get a chance to visit with him?" Toby asks quickly. He must think I visited the OtherWorld last night.

"Ambrogio said he's okay, Toby. He was in Monsento's house yesterday afternoon when I went to visit there. Zeaflin wasn't with him though," I reply. I pull out our old Seeing Stone. "Our blood is gone,"

I say and push the stone toward Toby. Toby lifts the rock up and both he and Billy examine the now-flawless piece of moonstone.

"How'd that happen?" Billy asks with a deep frown.

"Ambrogio, I think. He wants us to decide if we want to still see ghosts. If we do, then we can add our blood to his stone through that little funnel," I explain, pointing to the silver-lined hole in Ambrogio's rock.

"I do," Billy says eagerly. But Toby looks hesitant.

"Do you, Abby?" Toby asks.

"If you guys want to keep up the agency, I'll add my blood with yours. If you don't, I won't," I reply. Billy looks at Toby expectantly. Toby bites his lower lip and looks at the stone in Billy's hand. "We don't have to decide right now," I hastily add, not wanting to pressure Toby into agreeing to something this important.

But Toby decides right away. "Let's do it," he says. "We can always ask Ambrogio to take our blood back out if we ever decide we'd like to go back to being boring, ordinary kids."

Billy jumps up in his excitement and pulls out his pocket knife. *Oh, no! He's not cutting my hand with a knife!* "I brought a pin, Billy," I quickly inform him.

With a shrug, Billy tucks his knife back into his pants pocket and sits back down. He pushes the stone into the middle of the table between us and I pull out the safety pin I'd clipped earlier to the bottom of my T-shirt, just in case we decided to add our blood to the stone today. Billy holds out his hand to go first so I pass him the pin. With a wince, Billy pokes his index finger and squeezes out a few drops of blood into the tiny silver funnel. We watch closely as his blood travels down the funnel and pools in the center of Ambrogio's stone. Toby goes second, then holds the pin out for me to use.

Screwing up my face in anticipation of the pain, I prick my finger and milk out a few drops over the funnel. My blood merges with Billy and Toby's blood in the center of the stone, then the blood suddenly begins to move around. The three of us stare at the stone in awe as the blood drops assemble themselves into what looks to be a tiny red rose.

"Wow! That's totally cool!" Billy exclaims. The spirit communication device immediately starts clicking and the ticker tape feeds out a message from Mary. Toby reaches out and tears off the tape to look it over.

"Recently deceased client wants you to locate her missing ghost brother, Joseph Green. Last known whereabouts: haunting their family house at 18 Oakdale Ln. in Terrington. Sister fears an exorcism by the new living owners has expelled Joseph. Please investigate," Toby reads.

"Great! Let's go see if Mr. Monsento will drive us out there tomorrow so we can start the investigation right away," Billy says.

"You know, Mr. Monsento isn't going to be thrilled over having to drive all the way out to Terrington. That town is over forty miles from here," I tell him. "Not to mention if this ghost was exorcised, we'll have no idea where he was sent. He could have been sent anywhere, maybe even in-between realms." Billy shrugs.

"Maybe the client can tell us where her brother is buried and we can obtain a personal item and summon him here instead?" Toby suggests. I glare at him. Why does digging up a grave always enter the conversation in every one of our cases?

"If this ghost is in-between, we can't summon him, Toby. Remember? That's why we couldn't summon Nathan. In that case, a personal item won't be of any use," I respond with an irritated shake of my head.

"But we don't know that he's in-between, Abby. He could still be in the living realm," Billy says.

"True. But do you seriously think that Monsento will agree to dig up a grave? It's not easy to do and it's certain to have a much stiffer penalty than vandalizing a tombstone," I reply. Both boys look thoughtful.

"What if we start with asking the people who live there now if they even arranged an exorcism? All this says," Toby holds up the ticker tape, "is that the client fears there's been an exorcism. That means she doesn't know for sure."

I draw in a sharp breath at the thought of asking such a nutty question to the new home owners. "If they didn't arrange an exorcism, they'll think us crazy for asking," I respond.

"We can have Mr. Monsento ask. He's a medium, so if they didn't perform an exorcism, he can volunteer to do it for them, right? And that would give us an excuse to search the house for Joseph because maybe he's still there and just hiding in the attic or something. But if the new owners did hire someone to exorcise their house, we can find out who and ask that person where they sent the ghost," Billy outlines. I stare at Billy, completely flabbergasted. There is so much wrong with his plan, I don't know where to begin.

"For one thing, Billy, mediums don't perform exorcisms; priests do. Secondly, it's unlikely the priest will know where the ghost went after he exorcised him," I counter.

Billy huffs. "*Fine!* Mr. Monsento can dress up like a priest then, just in case they didn't hire someone yet. And if a real priest has already exorcised Joseph, Mr. Monsento, a fellow man of the cloth, can ask the priest if he has any idea where he might have sent the ghost," he replies. I look at Billy in amazement. Does he honestly believe Monsento will agree to dress up and pretend he's a priest? Billy is grinning at me like he's just solved a Rubik's cube. I look over at Toby. He is giving Billy a hearty nod of agreement. All right, then. It might be fun to watch these two try to convince Monsento to agree to all of this.

"Okay, Billy. That sounds like a good plan. Let's head over to Mr. Monsento's house and tell him about this new case then," I say, doing my best to suppress a smirk.

———— ♦ ————

I finally decide to replace my small doorknocker with a larger one to cover up Zeaflin's symbols rather than trying to sand them off; I remember how well the sanding worked the first time. I'd keep the carvings around for old time's sake but I'm sure my landlord will not be as nostalgic about them as I am. I'll hide the symbols as best I can with this lovely brass lionhead and call it "home improvement."

I drag out the power driver, grab a few wood screws and head for the front porch. After extracting my old Colonial-style doorknocker, located just above the carved symbols, I toss it onto the porch chair cushion and reach for the new one. I'm just lining the lionhead up over Zeaflin's artwork when the three detectives come up my front path.

"Hey, Mr. Monsento," Billy calls out. "You get a new doorknocker?"

Toby stops short and narrows his eyes. "Are you covering up Mr. Zeaflin's symbols?" he asks petulantly.

"Look, kid, I can't leave these carvings here for my landlord to see, so yeah, I'm covering up Zeaflin's handiwork," I respond. Geez! I know Toby's partial to Zeaflin but it's not *his* door all marred up.

Fortunately, Abby speaks up. "The symbols will still be there, Toby. They're just going to be under the doorknocker."

Toby mulls it over and steps forward to take the lionhead from my hand. "I'll hold it for you, Mr. Monsento, while you put in the screws," he offers. Apparently, he's decided it's better to let me cover up Zeaflin's marks than to replace the door again and get rid of them entirely.

After the new knocker is installed, I lead the way to my kitchen so I can offer the detectives some lemony libations. Once we all settle down at the table, Toby asks the same question he asks every day now. "Have you heard from Mr. Zeaflin or Mr. Vila yet?" And I answer the same way I do every day, with a shake my head.

"Not yet, kid. Guess they're still too busy filing paperwork or stamping documents to pay us a visit," I reply.

"To be honest, I've been busy spell-checking Vila's old reports from his early days in the Department of Living Affairs. As for Vila, I can't say for certain what he's been up to the past few weeks while I was recovering in the infirmary," Zeaflin says from behind me, causing me to knock over my lemonade glass. The yellow liquid runs across the table and makes a beeline for Toby's lap. I jump up to grab the dish cloth next to the kitchen tap before spinning around to give Zeaflin an angry glare.

"Stop doing that!" I snap. Sure, I'm happy to see him but he has got to stop sneaking up on me like that!

Zeaflin gives me a bemused look. "Spell-checking reports? Sadly, I must, or Vila will become quite cross," he explains. I stare at him. *Is something in his eye or did he just wink?*

"Mr. Zeaflin! We missed you!" Billy exclaims.

"Speak for yourself, kid," I grumble.

Toby jumps up and rushes over to Zeaflin's side. "You look different, Mr. Zeaflin," he observes.

I examine Zeaflin while I sop up the lemonade from the table and Toby's vacated chair. The kid is right. Zeaflin is different. He is dressed in his usual black suit and crisp white shirt, but his tie is now gray instead of red. His black hair is not slicked back but *au naturel,* topped with a gray fedora that matches his tie. His lips are still blood red, albeit maybe a little less so. I look down at his hands. The fingernails are long but not as pointy as I remember.

"Filed your fingernails, Zeaflin?" I ask.

Zeaflin looks at his hands, then shakes his head. "No, Mr. Monsento. Why do you ask?"

"They're blunter," I respond.

"They are?" Zeaflin looks at his hands again with a frown.

"You're not angry that I sent you to the OtherWorld, are you?" Abby suddenly blurts out, drawing a startled look from Zeaflin. He recovers quickly and gives a very red-faced Abby a smile.

"Angry? Of course, not," he replies, then reconsiders. "I am perhaps *regretful* at my assignment as assistant to Vila, but it will provide me an opportunity to visit the living realm from time to time, and I might then have occasion to visit with you."

"Swell," I say grumpily, suppressing the silly grin threatening to cross my face at that possibility. I remind myself this new and improved Zeaflin will probably still enter my house uninvited and unannounced and scare the bejesus out of me.

"Do you think Mr. Vila will allow you to come to my house for dinner?" Toby asks shyly. "I mean, if you want to, that is," he hastily adds. Zeaflin purses his lips and looks at me questioningly.

"What? You want my permission? It's your call," I say. I put a stop to the dinner date the last time Toby brought it up; I'm not running interference on that play again.

Zeaflin gives me a puzzled smile before he looks back at Toby and places a hand on his shoulder. "No, Toby, Vila would never authorize my dining with you and your mother." Toby looks down at his shoes before Zeaflin adds with a grin, "But I think I know where he keeps the permit forms required for realm walker interaction with ordinary living beings, and I've just about perfected Ambrogio's signature." Zeaflin's once-jagged teeth almost look like normal people teeth, but the canines are still too long and too sharp. His grin now reminds me more of a vampire than a crocodile, but I can't say that's much of an improvement.

I glance over at Abby, expecting her to object like she did the last time Zeaflin and Toby tried to set up a dinner date, but she sits quietly. I guess knowing that Zeaflin used to be an "angel" calms her worries over how Toby's mother may react to him dining at her kitchen table. Still, unless Zeaflin reverts to a more "normal-looking" undead guy before the event, I can't see how Toby's mother won't be horrified when he shows up at her door. Maybe we should all be there to provide a buffer...*and* to keep things cool if Zeaflin and Toby's mom do "hit it off." I clear my throat.

"Why don't we all join Zeaflin at Toby's house and make it a real dinner party? I'll bring the wine," I offer.

Toby gives me a dirty look but Zeaflin nods approvingly. "An excellent idea, Mr. Monsento!" he exclaims.

"Our kitchen table is too small to fit everyone," Toby objects, now glaring at me with dagger-filled eyes. Zeaflin's smile fades.

"Is that a fact?" I say to Toby. "Then tell your mother I have a folding table she can use instead. I'll bring it over once the date is set." I turn away from the searing heat of Toby's fury to address Zeaflin. "And I suggest you introduce yourself as Lucius, Zeaflin. It's a more normal sounding name."

Zeaflin looks thoughtful, then nods. "Of course, Lucius it shall be. When I locate the appropriate form for visiting a naïve living being, I will contact you all and we can set a date then," Zeaflin responds. Then he reaches into his shirt pocket and extracts what looks to be a scallop shell. He places it on the table in front of Abby. "I believe this belongs to you, Abigail. I'd like to thank you for allowing me to borrow it for a short while. I found its simple beauty very comforting after I was informed of my assignment as aide to Vila."

Abby stares at the shell, deep in thought, before picking it up. She holds it out toward Zeaflin. "You can keep it," she tells him. "It's the least I can do after stabbing you." Zeaflin smiles broadly and reaches out to extract the shell from Abby's palm using two of his long fingernails.

"Why, thank you, Abby! I shall cherish this in memory of our time at the seashore together!" he declares. The boys and I exchange a look. When did Abby and Zeaflin visit the seashore together? *How* could they visit the seashore together? It's at least 500 miles from here. Did he carry her there by dissipation? Zeaflin interrupts my thoughts.

"I'm afraid I must be going before Vila notices I am gone. I expect this will be the first place he'll check if he cannot find me in the OtherWorld." After kindly giving me *that* horrible prediction of a visit from Vila whenever his office assistant goes missing, Zeaflin tips his hat and vanishes in a puff of gray smoke.

"When did Mr. Zeaflin take you to the beach, Abs?" Billy asks Abby.

Abby looks at the fading gray smoke wisps and smiles. "He didn't. I took him," she replies. Then she looks at me. "You know what I'd like?" I shake my head, still trying to puzzle out how Abby took Zeaflin to the beach. "A strawberry soda, that's what I'd like," she declares. "My treat."

"That's all right, kid, I'll treat. I sold Marzee's pin, so I'm flush," I respond. I place the dish cloth into the kitchen sink and usher the kids out the back door. As we pass by the front of my house on our way to the ice cream parlor, I glance at the new doorknocker covering Zeaflin's symbols and realize I am glad the symbols are there but I'm not sure why I'm glad. Even though he's not a guardian angel anymore, it's reassuring in some odd way.

"Say, Mr. Monsento, I almost forgot. We have a new case," Billy says, just before we reach our destination. I give Abby a quick glance.

"You all added your blood to Ambrogio's stone, then? You're keeping the agency going?" I ask, feeling a little surprised that Abby decided to keep up with it.

"We sure are, Mr. Monsento!" Billy exclaims.

"And you're going to just *love* our new case," Abby says. *Why is she smiling like that? Something's fishy here...*

"Okay, so what's this new case about?" I ask warily. Abby's cryptic smile grows wider.

"Exorcisms in Terrington. Have you brushed up on your Bible lately, Father Monsento?" she responds with a giggle and skips ahead of the boys and me merrily, her ponytail wagging back and forth behind her.

Debra L. Dugger has worked in the biotechnology business for over 18 years and, as a departure from penning dry science reports, decided to try her hand at weaving bizarre stories about the afterlife.

Chicago-born and a loyal Cub fan, Debra currently resides in the San Francisco Bay Area. When she's not working on goofy paranormal tales, she spends her time assisting her wood-carving husband with his art shows, using her poor art skills to create ugly metal jewelry, and torturing herself with unhealthy, highly addictive time-management computer games.